American Moses

STEPHEN WITT

Author, Publisher and Book Information

For upcoming titles on Never Sink Books, discounted book club and wholesale rates to purchase American Moses, and/or to contact Stephen Witt and read his blog log onto www.neversinkbooks.com and click the appropriate link.

ISBN: 0-615-22799-6
ISBN0-13: 9780615227993
Library of Congress Control Number: 2008909203

Visit www.amazon.com, www.createspace.com/1000247873, or neversinkbooks.com to order additional copies.

ACKNOWLEDGEMENTS

The author would like to acknowledge and give thanks to the Creator of all things. Also a mighty thank you to Never Sink Books editor D. Amanda James, who along with a keen eye for detail and love of literature, shares a strong affinity for the subject matter. Others I would like to thank are the editorial staff at Courier Life Publications (now CNG and News Corp), with a special shout out to Gary Buiso and Myia for their readings of drafts and input. A thank you for reading drafts and/or emotional and spiritual support goes to Amyre Loomis, Dena Chen, Johnny Coughlin, Mark Ersckoff, my mother and the good people of East 3rd Street. Thanks also to the entire Russotti family, and in particular Tom, for his friendship, input, advice and ability to listen to me ad nauseum about this book. Finally, a heartfelt thanks to the many friends, family and associates who heard me banter on about this novel for a embarrassingly long time.

To D.E.W. - For all that you've given me,
with love and forgiveness

Fortunate is the man who has not walked
in the counsel of the wicked,
and in the way of the sinful
he has not stood,
and in the seat of the scornful he has not sat.

-Psalms

PROLOGUE

The man who would later become known as the American Moses was a far cry from his biblical namesake. There was no drama of being tossed into the Nile River at birth, nor opulence of being retrieved and raised in Pharaoh's golden court. In fact, the closest Southie Lewis ever came to royalty was eating regularly at Burger King.

He was born in Chicago and raised in Skokie, a near-north suburb filled with Jewish-, Irish-, Polish-, German- and Italian-Americans. On good days, he was average in school. On bad days he skipped classes and rode the El-train downtown Chicago where he horsed around at Marshall Fields department store and along the green Chicago River. His parents married young, and between his father's infidelity, his mother's unyielding nature and the couple's inability to make any real money, the relationship soured. Their final breakup, just before Southie's high school graduation, served as a passageway for his escape. After which, he began traveling.

For several years, Southie wandered around America working as a dishwasher in Seattle, logging in Colorado, fishing in the Florida Keys and baking in Boston. Then he circled the globe doing hotel work in London, grape picking in France, kitchen help in Tel Aviv and a crewman across the Indian and Pacific Oceans. In his wanderings, he also enjoyed the company and pleasure of women, recalling most fondly a green-eyed lady in Aspen, a blonde beauty in Sweden, a mysterious Serbian gypsy in Israel and certain women of the night at undisclosed locations.

But leave these tales for another night, because the following account tells how Southie Lewis later became known as the American Moses. For that, the story begins not too long ago in Brooklyn.

CHAPTER 1

Of all the dead-end jobs this one scrubbed the bottom of the barrel, Southie Lewis thought while parking his car. Coffee in hand, he strode past the Kings County Morgue meat wagon and an unmarked New York City Police car, and into a cream white door, cracked open with a small red brick. Inside, Tony Napo, his wiry and balding supervisor, paced the narrow, yellow-tiled intake area between four body bags and two NYPD detectives.

"Be right with you fellows," said Southie, slipping across the room and through the clear plastic-strip doorway to the locker area.

"Late again," said Napo, following him.

Southie ignored his boss and opened his locker.

"What? You can't hear me now? I said you're late."

"Things got bottlenecked at the Lincoln tunnel," said Southie, putting on his green hospital gown.

"That's not my problem."

"Come on Tony, cut me a break."

"We've got four stiffs out there, nobody to do intake, and you want me to cut you a break? It ain't my fault you moved to the country. Now you want special favors."

"Believe me I wouldn't ask you for a gargle of water if I were dying of thirst."

"Good, because I wouldn't give you any. And next time you're late I'm docking your pay."

"I said I'm sorry," said Southie.

"No you didn't."

"Didn't what?"

"Say you're sorry."

"Okay, I'm sorry," said Southie, closing the locker with a slight clang and facing his boss. "Can we move on now? We have intake. Remember?"

He chugged down the rest of his coffee, and threw it in a nearby garbage basket. Then he brushed past Napo to intake, took the chart off the closest gurney and unzipped the body bag. It was a male, black, 19, dead on arrival, from Bushwick. The corpse looked light-skinned and young. Muscles lean and taught, with a small bullet hole in the chest. The eyes remained open, fixed in a panicked state, but now glazed over in the blank stare of death. A child not more than a few years older than his own daughter, Southie thought.

"You going to stare at that stiff all day or are you gonna catalogue it," said one of the cops from across the room.

"Funny, I pictured for a moment it was you on this gurney," replied Southie without looking up

The cop looked at Southie coldly.

"Napo, you got a real primadonna here. He comes in a frickin hour late and then he's a wise guy."

Napo, who was standing by the locker entrance, took a stick of gum from his pocket and crammed it in his mouth. Then he walked to a smaller overflowing garbage pail near the entrance door and threw the wrapper on top of it, but it bounced off a bloody rag, a candy wrapper and a Pepsi can before landing on the floor. Even with the back door cracked open, the place stunk like hundreds of rotting dead mice stuck between the walls. Ignoring the litter, Napo walked over to victim number two, picked up the chart, and unzipped the body bag.

"What you got there, Napo?" said the first cop. "Another scumbag?"

"One less thug in the world always makes my day," replied his partner.

Southie rested the clipboard on the victim's chest and looked up. "Can't you guys check your prejudice at the door?"

"Oh, look! Mr. Late Man talks," said the cop. "I got two words for you, numb nuts. Alarm clock. Get a frickin alarm clock."

The cop's partner began laughing. "Yeah, get a frickin alarm clock."

"Why don't all three of you shut up so we can get some work done," said Napo, quieting everyone down.

The morgue grew quiet after that until intake was finished. Then Napo signed the cops' paperwork and sent them on their way.

"We going to put these stiffs on ice or what?" he asked Southie after they left.

Southie grabbed the head end of the gurney and they wheeled the corpse down the narrow, yellow-tiled hall and through another doorway of plastic slats. The odor of rotting bodies and bleach became thicker and nauseating as they made their way past the autopsy room to the back morgue. Here, one of thirty-two numbered metal compartments, many smeared with blood, awaited a new tenant.

"You got a real attitude problem. You know that," said Napo as they approached compartment number 16.

"Attitude problem? I come in two minutes late and..."

"Two minutes? Try forty-five minutes. Then you compound everything by mouthing off at those cops. That was really stupid."

"Stupid are those prick cops judging every black kid that comes in here like St. Peter or something."

Napo gave a quick shove of the gurney toward Southie, pissing him off.

"Come on," he said. "You're just sensitive because you married a black woman."

"Because I married a block woman? That has nothing to do with anything!"

"Then stop being so sensitive. Black kids are killing each other every day. It's the nature of the race."

"Sounds like you're just jealous of me, that's all," he said.

"Jealous?"

"Yeah, jealous!" This time Southie jerked the gurney back toward Napo.

"Jealous? What can you have to make me jealous?"

"That I have a beautiful black wife, two children and a home in the country."

"Don't be a fucking moron..."

"And you're still unmarried and living in the basement under your parents' home in Bensonhurst."

"I don't care where the fuck you live. Just make it to work on time. Got that? And if you don't like it, just give me two weeks!"

Napo again shoved the gurney toward Southie, but this time as he let up, Southie pushed back hard, pinning his boss up against one of the metal compartments.

"What the fuck you doing? Stop it!" said Napo.

"Two weeks, huh?" Southie let go of the gurney and began walking out of the morgue.

"Where you going? We've got stiffs to catalogue!"

"Catalogue them yourself. I'm out of here!"

"You can't just walk out on me like that."

"Watch me," said Southie, leading him back to the locker room.

"You don't like the job, fine. Just give me two weeks!"

"I don't have two weeks," said Southie, putting on his street clothes. "My family in the country needs me more!"

"You leave me like this, Lewis, and I swear you'll never work another morgue as long as you live."

Southie zipped up his jacket and closed the locker with hardly a sound. Then he turned to his ex-boss, smiling.

"You know something, Napo? I feel sorry for you. I really do."

⌘   ⌘   ⌘

Southie spent the rest of the day in the city having a few beers to cool off and then a couple of coffees to sober up. When he came out of the Lincoln Tunnel for the long drive home night had already fallen. Neon lights from shops now stretched along Route 3 like florescent torches along the sides of the highway. They began to disappear after he turned north onto Route 23, and into the desolate New Jersey countryside. His eyesight, never the best to begin with, had trouble adjusting. Headlights from motorists coming in the other direction blinded him and then they would pass, giving way to country blackness again. Strip malls emerged along the sides of the road, here and there, along with gas stations, diners, roadside shops and bars.

The dotted, yellow road line separating oncoming traffic mesmerized him as he followed its' contour. Trees appeared just off the road and surrounding hills loomed as dark shadows beneath a moonless sky. The car radio lost reception, and to stay alert, Southie opened the drivers' side window and let the cold-night air blast into his face. After some minutes, the car became icy, so he closed the window again. He began to drift in and out of sleep. Spirits of the long day swirled around his head, passing through his nostrils and choking him of oxygen. They whispered, "You are worn and tired. Give in. Join us. We are here waiting."

Suddenly, Southie was jarred awake as his car hit the jagged ridges along the shoulder of the road. The vehicle veered from the highway and onto a field. He opened his eyes and thought, 'Put your foot on the brakes,' but nothing happened. "Put your foot on the damn brakes!" he said out loud. This time, his feet instinctively answered.

The car came to a stop in an open field. He took a deep breath, and after some moments, got out of his car and stood in the cold, night air. A giant oak tree was ten feet directly in front of him. He rubbed his face and looked into the star-speckled sky, then saw headlights in the distance driving north towards him. His eyes followed the car as it passed both him and a neon-lit Dunkin Donuts shop in the distance.

Several minutes later, he stumbled into the near empty shop and past the Indian immigrant counterperson and a scraggily old man in overalls on one of the middle stools. Southie, still in a sleepy daze, made a beeline straight to the bathroom in back. Here he splashed cold water on his face, and looked into the mirror, smiling at his own haggard image.

"Glad to see you're still alive, old boy," he said out loud, splashing more cold water on his face.

After reentering the coffee shop, Southie took a seat toward the bathroom end of the counter and ordered a medium coffee and chocolate frosted doughnut with sprinkles. While waiting for his order, he picked some crust from the corner of his eye.

"Going off the road must've scared the living shit out of you."

Southie looked up to see the old man perched on the stool beside him. Perhaps it was the fatigue, but he felt sure he sat further down the counter, but now he studied the man. Deep wrinkles were etched into his cheeks and crows feet slid on his skin away from his brown eyes.

"Yes sir, Route 23 gets pitch black once night falls," continued the old man. "The spirits have claimed many a commuter fighting to get home."

"You're speaking to me?"

"Waiting for you to be exact. It was you that nearly slammed into that tree, wasn't it?"

Southie took a gulp of coffee. "Look mister. I just stopped for a cup of coffee on my way home."

"God picks all kinds, I guess," the old man said, ignoring him.

A sudden thought popped into Southie's head. Perhaps he hit that tree and was...

"You ain't dead," said the old man, reading his mind. "Life's going to get pretty interesting for you, though. Guaranteed."

"Who are you anyway and what are you doing here?"

"The Creator sent me. The presence whispers in my ear to meet a soul. Usually it's to greet spirits killed in crashes along this stretch of highway. This is the first time I've met a living soul."

"So what are you here to tell me?" asked Southie.

"That you didn't die because there's a plan for you. A road show. Some kind of adventure."

Southie closed his eyes for a fleeting second. When he opened them the old man had vanished. Although the short conversation seemed real enough, he was too tired to know for sure, and by the time he got up for the last leg of the journey, he forgot it ever happened.

Thirty minutes later, when he arrived home, everybody was asleep. Zippy had the house tidy and left a covered plate of food for him on the stove. After eating, he showered and came to bed, kissing his wife softly on the back of her neck. She turned over and faced him.

"I missed you," she said sleepily.

"I have some news."

"What's that?"

"I quit my job."

Zippy pulled her husband close and he smelled the cocoanut fragrance in her natural hair.

Then, she whispered in his ear. "Good. Now I'll have more of you to myself."

CHAPTER 2

Port Decker's American roots went back before the Revolutionary War, and during the Civil War, the town became a major staging area for the northern army. Here, battle-hardened veterans nursed wounds, while green recruits formed company battalions before marching across the Delaware River into Pennsylvania and Gettysburg. Confederate prisoners of war passed through too, shipped north to camps via the railroad that ran along the river.

Following the war, the railroad spawned a large repair yard and turntable. With it came a stream of uneducated Germans, Irish, Scottish and Italians immigrants. Factories popped up and bluestone was mined in the nearby hills for New York City sidewalks. Musicians found gigs at the numerous local bars, while prostitutes worked the brothels upstairs. Port Decker was designated small-city status, and quickly gained the reputation of being blue collar and rough around the edges.

Blacks, of course, were also part of Port Decker's history. They arrived with the earliest Dutch settlers as slaves. Their descendents lived on a three-block stretch of Knox Street that dead-ended with the African Methodist Church. It was an old wooden building that once held the funeral for the last black man ever lynched in the state of New York. A local chapter of the Klux Klan kept them in their place burning crosses in the nearby hills. Shut out from city jobs, the blacks worked in local factories, their names popping up here or there as star high school athletes or on the police blotter.

After World War II, the city enjoyed a golden period where rail yard workers and veterans, flush with money, received bank mortgages and business loans on handshakes. A J. C. Penny's discount store anchored a thriving Front Street full of hardware, shoe, furniture, toy and linen shops. The annual Soap Box Derby drew kids countywide and Friday nights was reserved for the high school football game. Afterward, everybody piled into local soda shops, filled up on apple pie and ice cream, and washed down with hot coffee.

But by the time Southie and his family arrived, Port Decker was reduced to a semi ghost town serving as only the last stop from New York City on the Metro North line. Weeds grew over the repair yard and a graffiti-strewn caboose was all that remained on the turntable. A Fiberglass shelter and automatic ticket machine was all that was left of the once grand train station and empty storefronts littered Front Street. Even the Penny's building had a 'For Rent' sign in its naked window. The once thriving population shriveled and most of what was left were poor whites living below the poverty level in dilapidated, century old wooden houses or in nearby trailer parks. Teenage pregnancy was rampant, and illegal drug use flourished.

After some time, Southie found steady work distributing the daily newspaper to coin-operated stands and small stores for three-hundred and twenty-five dollars a week. The paper came in at four-thirty in the morning from Middletown, and was dropped at a warehouse. His route ran through Port Decker and across the river, eleven miles into Pennsylvania past the Wal-Mart, Home Depot and other big box stores where everybody in the area shopped, and many worked. Zippy brought in some money as well, drawing charcoal and pastel portraits of people, children and pets at the local flea market, occasionally nabbing an oil portrait. The family also received government food stamps and medical assistance. Between it all, they scraped by month-to-month.

⌘   ⌘   ⌘

Like the rest of Port Decker, the town's only synagogue saw better days. Though it was well maintained with a neat lawn, and pointed A-frame sanctuary, the once fairly large Jewish population was down to a trickle, but Southie being a Jew, wanted to put some God into his family. So every once in a while he took them to the Friday night Sabbath services. Here, on a good night, the congregation numbered no more than twenty people. Even though Zippy was Christian and steadfastly refused to convert, she genuinely loved her husband's people, and enjoyed the Sabbath services. She especially loved the reading of Psalms, some of which she memorized as a small child in Jamaica.

While it seemed a small congregation, Southie learned differently several months later on Yom Kippur, the most holy day on the Jewish calendar. He went to the service by himself, and planned on parking several blocks away as Jews are not supposed to drive or eat on the holiday, and then walk to the synagogue. However, as he drove through town on Main Street, he passed a large party with several motorcycles and cars in the gravel driveway, and about thirty-five people hanging out in front of a large wood-frame house. Music blared from the open living room window, and draped from a second-story window was an enormous Nazi flag, its swastika emblazoned in black against a red background.

At first, Southie couldn't believe what he saw so he drove around the block once to make sure. Then he raced home to get Zippy, and with the kids left at home, the two of them flew back to the synagogue to tell the other Jews. Inside, more than a hundred people turned up in the sanctuary for the all-day service, but after Southie and Zippy made a commotion in the lobby, Rabbi Boyd, the synagogue's spiritual leader, along with a few temple members, came to the lobby to see what all the fuss was about.

"Let's march down there with baseball bats and let them know never again!" said Southie.

"I'll call the television news,'" said Zippy. "Is there a phone in the office?"

"The flag? It is on private property?" Rabbi Boyd asked.

"What difference does it make?" Southie shot back.

"That as despicable this act may be, people can do what they want on private property."

Southie's throat was parched and his face felt hot. "Bullshit," he said. "We've got to do something."

"It is Yom Kipper. We must finish the service first," said Rabbi Boyd, resolutely.

"There won't be a service to finish if you let people like that go flying flags on Main Street," Zippy replied.

The rabbi looked down his nose at Zippy. "The ram's horn will sound in about an hour signifying the end of the holiday. Then we will go down there and assess the situation," he said, and quickly walked back into the sanctuary.

For the next hour, Southie and Zippy remained in the lobby until the ram's horn sounded. Then the Rabbi reluctantly agreed to go with several other men, and they followed in their cars behind Southie's beat-up Oldsmobile.

The police arrived at the party before them, and were talking to several skinheads, who apparently had thrown the party. Southie and Zippy leapt from the car to confront them, but the police stopped them. Meanwhile, Rabbi Boyd rolled down the window from the driver's seat of his car.

"I'm sorry to disturb you, officer. But this flag draped from that window is not acceptable to our community."

"We have a right to hang any flag we want from the window. It's private property and a free country," said one of the men. He had a shaved head with a large gut, tattoos and a nose ring.

"And we have a right to peacefully demonstrate across the street with baseball bats," responded Southie.

"And no jail cell in the world can bring you back if somebody decided to cap your ass," Zippy chimed in. "Cause this black woman is not like these peaceful Jews."

"Officer, they're threatening us," said the man with a shaved head.

The cop turned to Southie and Zippy. "You two better pipe down," he said, and then turned to the skinhead. "And you, Ned. Take the God damn flag down!"

Ned turned and nodded toward the window from where the flag was draped. Several people then rolled it up.

"There. Situation diffused," said Rabbi Boyd, breathing a sigh of relief. "We should all go home and be thankful to God for our wonderful homes and beautiful community."

CHAPTER 3

Isaac Rosen just finished the graveyard shift unloading a Wal-Mart tractor-trailor truck and then stacking fifty-pound sacks of Old Roy's dog food in the pet department when he smelled smoke while driving home. He first caught the scent while crossing the underpass just past the Delaware River Bridge, and it became stronger after he turned left on Main Street. Then, at the stoplight in front of the Port Decker Diner, he saw a plume of white smoke rising into the cool autumn night air. Further down the road, he saw it coming from behind the synagogue.

He quickly pulled to the curb and spotted two suspicious figures emerge from the nighttime shadows and hop the back fence of the synagogue. For a second, he considered chasing the bastards, but changed his mind after seeing flames shoot out the side exit door. Instead, he called the police on his cell phone and then ran to put out the blaze. But it was too late, and even after the all-volunteer fire department arrived, everyone's hands were full in just keeping the fire from spreading to the surrounding wood-frame houses.

Word spread almost as quickly.

Sarah Levy, a single mom, heard about it on the kitchen radio between sorting bills and reading psalms. A buxom woman with a straight back and strands of gray streaked in her brown hair, she formally taught at the synagogue's Hebrew school, and knew the services sometimes better than the part-time rabbi.

Sol and Myrtle Katz, the retired couple and former shoe shop merchants, learned of the incident over coffee at Elmer's diner the following morning. More attuned to Judaism's cultural side, as opposed to the religious side, they rarely missed a social function at the synagogue, while attending services only for the more important holidays, and the occasional Friday night Sabbath.

The Hasid family, Aaron Gotbaum and his wife, Faygie, caught wind of the event shortly after Aaron came home from morning prayers in Monticello some twenty miles away. Yakov, the eldest of their seven children, read about it after sneaking time on the family's rundown computer. The Gotbaums' were from the Chabad sect of Hasidim and fairly new arrivals in town. While not members of the synagogue, they had introduced themselves to a few of its congregants.

By noon, Port Decker's entire Jewish population learned of the blaze, and as a hundred people or so assembled in the synagogue parking lot gaping at the smoldering ashes, a blue Lincoln Town Car pulled up and skidded to a stop. The mayor, a large heavy-set man, smelling of K-Mart cologne, got out and solemnly eyed the congregation. Then he addressed Rabbi Boyd.

"I promise you here and now," he proclaimed in a booming voice. "We will not rest until the culprits of this heinous act are caught and brought to justice."

Considerably shorter, but no less pudgy than the mayor, the rabbi's eyes welled with tears. "You've always been our friend," he said, embracing the mayor.

After the town's top dignitary left, Rabbi Boyd took a wrinkled white hanky from his breast suit pocket and blew his nose. Then he cleared his throat and addressed the congregants.

"We will rebuild," he declared. "Port Decker is a wonderful community and we are loved here."

"No wonder Hitler was able to load ya'll into cattle cars," came a woman's voice from the back of the congregation.

Everybody turned to see Zippy, the only black woman in the group, standing next to Southie. Beside the couple were their two biracial children. Coree, a teenager, dressed in tight jeans and blouse, accentuating the blossoming of a young woman's shape, and Billy, eleven years old, medium of height and skinny as a railroad tie.

Rabbi Boyd approached Zippy with hunched shoulders and put an assuring arm around her. "I know you're upset, but..."

"Butts are for asses," Zippy said, pulling away. "God only saves those that save themselves."

"Zippy's right," said Southie, stepping in front of his wife. "Fuck Port Decker."

Some congregants gasped. Others perked up their ears.

Rabbi Boyd pinched the chin part of his goatee. "And this is the way to talk?" he said for all to hear. "To fight a hateful act with hateful words?"

"I'm just speaking facts. People in this town don't like us. Well we don't have to like them. Right Zippy?" Southie said.

"This is one ignorant town," said Zippy from behind him.

"A regular shithole," said Southie.

The congregation turned quiet for a minute except for the Gotbaum children, who were running in small circles around their parents' legs in a game of tag.

"So you have an idea?" asked Aaron Gotbaum at last, adjusting his Borsalino black hat to the top of his head.

"Why not leave Port Decker," replied Southie.

Rabbi Boyd straitened his dark suit jacket, pursed his lips together and stared at Southie.

"Run away. That's what you propose?"

"I call it starting over. Away from this Port Decker riffraff."

"And where exactly do you propose we go?"

Southie eyed the part-time religious leader wearily. This man who was quick to point out how Southie's children weren't Jewish, because he didn't marry a Jewish woman; as if he or the rest of the congregation didn't already know that.

"Las Vegas! I've been checking it out on the Internet. It's the fastest growing metropolis in America. Opportunity on every corner."

A sly smile crept across Rabbi Boyd's lips. "Las Vegas, huh? And who will lead us out of Port Decker to this new Promised Land of yours?"

"I will."

"With all due respect, you have trouble providing for your own family," said Rabbi Boyd, loudly. "Just look at that jalopy of yours."

The congregation eyeballed Southie's Oldsmobile station wagon in the synagogue parking lot. Flakes of rust covered the roof, sides and tail, and the brown driver's side door didn't match the rest of the car's dirty blue color.

"I assure you they don't make cars like 88 Custom Cruisers anymore," replied Southie proudly. "She may look like a rust bucket, but her engine purrs like a kitty, even with over two-hundred thousand miles on her."

A few congregants snickered. Others scratched their heads and rubbed their chins.

"What fools would listen to this man?" said Rabbi Boyd, his voice growing shrill. "We'll rebuild. These are God fearing folks here."

Beneath the smoldering ashes of what was once the synagogue an ember crackled, emitting a puff of smoke that quickly disappeared into the frosty morning air. Then a strong and sure voice rang out from amongst the congregation.

"Count me in," said Isaac Rosen, dirty with soot from a night of helping to fight the fire. He was a burly man in his early thirties, and wore a yarmulke pinned atop his curly red hair.

"But Isaac, you saw the culprits who did this," protested Rabbi Boyd.

"All I know is Southie and Zippy were the only people to stand up for us when they hung that Nazi banner not more than two weeks ago."

"And we'll go too," said Sarah Levy stepping forward and clutching the hand of her lean and handsome 17-year-old son, David. "Port Decker is no place for us."

Sol, the barrel-chested senior citizen, walked over to Southie and gave his cheek a good hard pinch.

"Maybe you don't have a pot to piss in, but you've got moxie kid. I like that," he said. "Me and Myrtle will sign up for this little trip of yours."

"Stop pestering the man," said Myrtle, chiming in. "My Sol, he's such a pesterer."

"It was a pinch, Myrtle, not a pester. What, you don't know the difference between a pinch and a pester?"

Southie rubbed his cheek and rolled his eyes toward Zippy. "Anyone else?" he asked with a shrug.

A few fire marshals poked through the embers and a plume of smoke rose again from some ashes.

"We'll come also," said Aaron Gotbaum stepping forward. He was a giant of man, six-foot-two, and husky, with a thick black beard. White fringes signifying all of God's commandments hung outside his white dress shirt, providing a contrast against his black pants.

"But Aaron, leave? What will we do?" moaned his wife, Faygie. She had a baby on her hip and wore a long denim skirt with a scarf covering her hair. Behind her, their other children milled about in their game of 'You're it.'

"Listen to me Faygie. We drive twenty miles just for kosher food. What's a few thousand more?"

Southie looked around. No one else made a move.

"Then it's settled," said Isaac, looking at Southie. "When do we leave?"

Southie thought a minute.

"Next Friday at seven in the morning sharp. Pack your cars with essentials and take care of as much personal business as you can. We'll meet right here in this parking lot."

⌘   ⌘   ⌘

"We're not going anywhere," said Zippy to her husband as soon as they drove off.

"But the synagogue was torched…"

"Well they've lynched black people here. You don't see my people running out of town."

"Your people can't even get a job sweeping the street here. This place is like the south before civil rights."

"Maybe, but this is America. It's not Hitler's Germany."

"Exactly. This is America. Anything's possible and Las Vegas is booming with opportunity."

"What about the house? We have money invested in it," said Zippy

"We're already months behind on the mortgage. Let's just write it off. Besides, Zippy, we can go to Las Vegas and start a business just like you're always saying."

"What about my friends?" chimed in Coree from the back seat. "I can't leave them."

"You'll find friends in Las Vegas."

"You're actually happy the synagogue burnt down, aren't you? That's you. Always ready to run at a second's notice."

"That's ridiculous, Zippy," said Southie. "Besides, these people are expecting me to lead them to Las Vegas."

"They went to fool school, just like my husband."

"Well I can't help it if Rabbi Boyd has the backbone of a worn radiator hose."

"At least he's willing to rebuild and fight for his community."

"Damn it, Zippy. Will you listen to me just this once?"

Zippy sucked air between her teeth making a hissing sound. "Whenever I do things go wrong."

"Nothing will go wrong. You'll see."

CHAPTER 4

A lump formed in Zippy's throat as she unlatched the lace trim curtains she had made from the bedroom window and studied their backyard. The property and house appeared as she always dreamed. A little more than a half acre just outside Port Decker at the base of the Green Mountain with a stream gurgling down the lush hill that bordered the back of their property. The wild greenery reminded her of childhood visits to her grandmother, Mammy, in the hills of Jamaica. Mammy was a shapely, hard-working woman with smooth, dark skin and heart-shaped lips. There, she also met up with her Uncle Allen, big and strong as a horse, who would curse under his breath at the treatment given to his poor, half-starved and timid niece from Kingston. Whip in hand, he would force her to drink a concoction of Guinness stout, raw eggs, sweet cream and nutmeg to fatten up her thin, scraggly body. Then Mammy put her to work. There was fetching water from down the hill and carrying it back on her head, feeding the chickens, and digging up roots and yams, and selling them at the market.

And Zippy cultivated her own property, just like Mammy. The thorny, wild raspberry bushes were harvested for fruit rather than cleared, and all sorts of roots and wild plants were examined. Some were discarded. Others found use as wild teas and remedies. While Southie cleared a small patch for a vegetable garden, Zippy would walk the property, sprinkling seeds here and there. One summer, a watermelon patch spread its vines just outside their bedroom window, taking up a large portion of their backyard, and the next spring that same brown earth brought forth violet, yellow and white wildflowers from seeds she bought on sale at Wal-Mart.

Zippy also loved her pets just like Mammy. Cats kept mice away. Dogs had to be kind to family members and mean to outsiders. If they showed loyalty then they were loved. If they took off once too often they were discarded. Her favorites were the hens. How she loved the way they would come running towards her in the morning when she fed them, calling "Coo, coo, coo." Zippy also loved what she called God's creatures; be they four-legged, feathered, swimming or crawling. Turtles, frogs and fish from the stream were captured and kept as pets. Wild baby birds that fell from nests were swept up before the cats got them. Some were nursed back to health, others died in her care. A baby robin with a crippled leg was once brought back to health and roamed free in their house for a fall and winter, before flying out the back door that Coree carelessly left open, and for which she received a good beating.

Now as Zippy folded the curtains and packed them into a cardboard box, thoughts of the other part of her childhood forced their way into her mind. The shared house in Kingston, where her mother dropped her off when she was six years old before vanishing off in a taxi. There, beatings with the electric chord came from the elders steady and hard as pounding rain, even after she passed out. To this day, she didn't know what she ever did to deserve them. Then there was the older lady next door who forced Zippy's mouth on her pussy, and nights when it was her turn to sleep in daddy's bed. He would fondle her and put his fleshy penis up to her face. She would turn, pretending to be asleep. It was her mother who rescued her from this life, sending a ticket for her to come to America when she was fourteen. That first night in Brooklyn, she told her mother of what happened with her father, and her mother beat her with a stick, telling her it never happened, and if it did, it was because she seduced her father. That was the last time she ever mentioned what happened in Jamaica to her mother.

As for Southie, he was a good man, although sometimes lagging in confidence of his own abilities and faith. She taught him most everything he knew, even how to fuck. When they first met he fucked like a typical white boy - a jam, a jam a jamma. Now though, he moved in time with her, slowly and rhythmically, and kissing soulfully. One thing she didn't have to teach him was hard work. That came naturally and helped in their getting the house. At the time they lived in an apartment in Brooklyn, and he worked at the morgue. Then, one day she read a magazine article about acquiring a house with no down payment. When she told him about it, he proclaimed that buying a house with no down payment was impossible. Zippy reminded him that faith grows wings and is powered through action. Within weeks, she packed lunches and the family would drive upstate in a beat-up old Ford until they found their dream house - one with no down payment.

Zippy taped the box shut and looked around the half-empty room for what to pack next. The house meant the world to her, but she made up her mind to go with her husband. It wasn't an easy decision and she strongly considered staying, but that would require finding another man. Not that she couldn't catch one, but she was getting older, and had Coree and Billy to think about. Southie was a known entity, who made her laugh. Besides, he was trained in lovemaking and still dreamed big.

She also had no love lost for Port Decker, starting with the all-white neighbors in the subdivision where they lived. To them, this wilderness was part of some great suburban sprawl. They worked endlessly chopping down trees and clearing their own half-acre lots, replacing it with vast, well-manicured lawns and gardens, which became the expression of their lives while holidays added an exclamation point. At Christmas, decorative lights came out, at Thanksgiving cardboard cutouts of turkeys appeared in their windows; and for Halloween, mock gravestones, ghosts, and witches appeared scarily on their front lawns.

When they first bought the house, Zippy tried to make friends with the neighbors. She would go knocking on their doors bearing freshly laid eggs or other small gifts, but behind their polite "thank you," she found an undercurrent of hostility. They were, after all, a self-sufficient people, in need of nothing this black woman offered. They had their own cars, lawnmowers, snowmobiles and barbeques. They even owned their own basketball hoops and small pools, where Coree and Billy weren't invited to play. Needless to say, the gift giving stopped. The neighbors proved a fairly uneducated lot, whose standard of living differed from those poorer folks in Port Decker proper because they worked high-paying union jobs as correction officers in a slew of area prisons. The only blacks they knew were inmates, convicted of small and large crimes committed in New York City.

The neighbors, though, were mistaken in thinking Zippy would go quietly away in the night. For she owned a house just like them, and possessed a strange spirit; one moment filled with laughter and a child's delight, and the next moment, troubled and brimming with wrath. A spirit melded with a strong dose of cast-iron Jamaican discipline, and intuition. And when it came to outsiders scorning her children, Zippy could rival a mother bear.

The confrontations started in earnest on the morning trips to the school bus stop. While other mothers kissed their children good-by at the front door, Zippy insisted she walk her kids the quarter mile down Black Rock Trail to the Old Horn Road where the yellow school bus stopped. Often it resembled a parade with Zippy leading in her pink yard coat and a leashed dog, and Coree following a step or two behind, dressed in homemade clothes and pushing Billy in a stroller. Bringing up the rear was one or two of Zippy's favorite cats, which were always somehow friendly with the dog. This in itself was amazing, considering the beast was a ferocious, snarling canine that would sometimes lunge at other children along the parade route. Meanwhile Zippy – the grand marshal of it all, would sing loudly in the morning air:

> Wide lawns narrow minds
> Ignorant people so unkind
> Yet I will sing strong and loud
> I am here black and proud

It didn't take long for the neatly-packaged neighbors to realize something of an eccentric lived in the neighborhood, and as tensions rose, Zippy would pull Southie aside after he'd come home from work in Brooklyn exhausted.

"I don't like these neighbors," she said.

"You wanted the house in the country and now we must learn to get along," Southie replied.

"That is easy for you to say. You are not black. How would you like to come home one night and see a cross burning on our front yard? Or worse, maybe the whole house burning down with your family inside it?"

Southie told Zippy he was sure such a thing could never happen, but deep inside he knew it could. After all, this was America, and such things still happened from time to time. It was shortly after this conversation, that he left his job in Brooklyn.

CHAPTER 5

It all worked out perfectly for Southie. The government, which held the mortgage, let them out of it on account of the synagogue being razed, and deemed a hate crime. They had about sixteen hundred dollars in cash, which Southie saved in a strongbox for the property taxes, A hundred and fifty came off the top from that for storage of their furniture and non-essential household items. He also borrowed a thousand dollars from his credit card, leaving him with about twelve hundred dollars left in credit. Enough, he figured, for a few months' rent once they got to Las Vegas.

Zippy, on the other hand, relented to leave only after a fair amount of coaxing and convincing. The clincher was his agreeing to take along three of her animals. This included Buttercup, their rottweiler mix, which was loyal and loving towards family, but mean as a two-fisted drunk to outsiders; Mouser, the orange tabby; and Miss Red, her favorite hen.

With the money and domestic situation straightened out, Southie went about readying his beloved 88 Custom Cruiser for the trip. It was a three-seater with the ability of both the middle seat and back seat to fold down, providing ample space to pack things, and the burgundy interior, although worn, retained its soft plush leather. More importantly, the engine never gave him trouble, and the car would start through the harshest winters and steamiest summers. He purchased it for a song at six hundred dollars off a backyard mechanic, and even though Zippy affectionately named it, 'Rust Bucket' because of its beat-up old body, he loved it more than any car they ever owned. It had a strong V-8 engine and he religiously followed the backyard mechanic's advice, which was to change the oil with only a thicker 20-50 brand. So during the week, he personally and lovingly changed the oil, and replaced both the oil and air filters. Then he drove to the Sears in Middletown and bought two new tires, throwing away the oldest two, both of which had steal tread showing from its sides. He also made sure the break pads had some life left on them, and checked the battery to ensure it still had some juice left.

Friday rolled around, and at dawn, the family pulled away from their house at the base of the Green Mountain for the last time. There was Southie in his early forties, an inch under six-foot, physically fit and with thick, dark hair sprinkled with gray; Zippy, also in her forties, well-kept and curvy without a trace of gray; Coree wearing low-cut jeans and a tight blouse exposing her midriff, and Billy, absorbed in a Spiderman comic book.

They arrived at the synagogue parking lot as daylight broke into a misty morning and Southie peered through the fog at the charred rubble, which days earlier had been a synagogue. Zippy, meanwhile, poured a cup coffee for him from a silver thermos she packed and kept at her feet in the front seat.

"Nobody's coming. I can just tell," he said.

"Don't be so impatient," said Zippy.

Two minutes later, Isaac pulled up driving a blue Ford Taurus, which in turn hauled a small U-Haul pop-up tent. His car was also fairly loaded down with supplies and belongings.

"Ready as Freddy," he said, thanking Zippy for the cup of coffee she poured him. "Got some camping equipment just in case we need them on the trip."

Some minutes later, Sarah and David arrived with their red Dodge Voyager stuffed with belongings, save for the two relatively empty middle seats. Then came Sol and Myrtle driving a late-model blue Cadillac with an empty back seat and several suitcases in their trunk. Finally, Aaron and Faygie arrived in a white Ford Econoline van loaded down with supplies and their seven children ranging from Yakov, 11, down to the infant, Itzy, in diapers and a t-shirt.

Southie pulled out the Rand McNally road atlas before the assembled group.

"Here is the plan," he said. "We are going to take I-84 west where we will catch 81 south…"

"What? You got something against Interstate 80?" said Sol loudly with a raspy voice, pulling out his own map.

"Marco Polo you're not," said Myrtle, elbowing her husband in the ribs and looking at Southie. "He thinks he's Marco Polo. My Sol can't explore his way out the bathroom, and he's telling you how to get to Vegas."

"Leave me alone already, Myrtle, will you," said Sol, putting his map away.

A white Lexus pulled into the parking lot, stopped with a screech, and Rabbi Boyd got out.

"Thank God you're still here," he said excitedly. "They caught the people who burned the synagogue down. It was two teenagers."

"Two teenagers?" Sol asked.

"Yes. The mayor just called me. He said they are too young to be tried as adults, but they confessed. You don't have to leave now. Things are beginning to get better already."

Everybody began to mull the news over until a blue Buick Skylark packed with belongings also pulled into the parking lot, and an old man with a long gray beard, thick arching eyebrows and piercing, deep-set blue eyes, got out.

"I'm ready to leave," he said.

Southie recognized the old man, who everybody called "the Rebbe," from the couple of times he took his family to Friday night Sabbath services. He was a fairly quiet man, who always sat by himself near the front of the tabernacle. Even Rabbi Boyd respected "the Rebbe" for his Talmudic knowledge. In fact, rumor swirled around the synagogue that he was a Kabbalist, a Jewish mystic.

"You too want to leave, Rebbe?" said Rabbi Boyd. "But they found the kids who burned the synagogue down."

"I may be old, but I'm not blind," said the Rebbe looking at Rabbi Boyd, and then turning toward Southie. "My place now is on the road with them."

"Then it's settled," said Southie. "We will follow the speed limit. If somebody needs to stop to fill up their gas tank or use the restroom, let them honk their horn twice and we'll stop at the next rest area."

Everybody piled into their cars. They drove down Front Street, and through Port Decker's once thriving downtown district, which was now a hodge-podge of empty storefronts with 'For Rent' signs in the windows mingled with a few antique shops, a 99 cent store, a Chinese restaurant and two bars. Then they circled around the train stop to New York City, and beneath the underpass to the bridge across the Delaware River into Pennsylvania. Here, just past the Wal-Mart, was the entrance ramp going west onto Interstate 84.

CHAPTER 6

The rust bucket chugged up one hill and down another as it drove west toward Scranton. Squashed deer, bear, squirrels, ground hogs and skunk lined the shoulder of the road, along with sporadic peeled rubber from blown tires. Southie stayed the sixty-five mile per hour speed limit, occasionally looking through the rearview mirror making sure the caravan followed. Meanwhile, speeding sixteen-wheeler trucks roared by in the left lane with a whoosh, as did the faster moving cars. The day turned into a bright sunny morning. Half-naked deciduous trees danced in the autumn breeze between evergreens spaced out on the brown-dirt between the rocky hillsides.

After twenty minutes on the highway, Southie cracked the driver's side window letting the air hiss into the car. The dotted white interstate lines seemed to intersect into one as his station wagon whizzed along and his mind drifted to the ten years spent in Port Decker. Billy was in diapers when they first bought the house and Coree still in grammar school. Back then he held lofty dreams of being a writer, but the struggle to keep up on the bills took its toll. Then there were the comments from locals about his being in an interracial marriage. It wasn't at all like the city, where everybody minded their own business. In Port Decker everybody knew everybody, except when someone burns a synagogue down and then it seemed nobody knew anything. Good riddance to bad rubbish, Southie thought now about Port Decker, and with each passing mile, it was as if some imaginary chains were being unshackled from around his waist and feet. He felt young and free again; not the boy-freedom of his youth when he wandered recklessly, but the responsible man-freedom of being on the road with his family in tow. And for this, he thanked Zippy.

He met her some eighteen years earlier while living in New York City. At the time, he washed dishes at a jazz café in Greenwich Village. After his shift ended, he would wander the West Village watching street musicians and talking to the vendors before retiring for the night to his rooming house. She was a sidewalk portrait artist on Sixth Avenue, and one night after being paid, he stopped to get his portrait drawn. She sketched his face, and after paying her twenty dollars, he stayed to chat while she drew tourists. She had brought green grapes with her to work as a snack and shared some with him. Later, when the night turned windy with a smattering of rain, he helped her pack up. Then they strolled arm-in-arm for several hours among the storefronts of the deserted Village streets. Toward daylight, they rode the subway to her small apartment in Brooklyn where they made love through the morning.

Zippy was then and remained a strikingly beautiful woman with rich, cocoa brown skin, high cheekbones, expressive almond-shaped eyes, and a nose that flattened at the bridge, but came out shapely at the nostrils. When they met her hair was short, but now it came down past her shoulders in natural twists and braids. She had filled out a little since they first met, but with all the weight evenly distributed making her even more curvy and soft. She also knew how to dress, combining cottony colored dresses that accentuated her curves and allowing for a seductive amount of cleavage. Additionally, he was attracted to her natural smell, a feminine, musky scent that aroused him physically and mixed well with any perfume she wore.

More than anything, though, Southie loved watching Zippy paint after receiving portrait commissions. He would follow her around, carrying her easel as she found bright light in either the yard or by the living room window. Then he would sit with her as she painted people, pets and homes, natural as sunshine. Each color, line and stroke painted on the canvas arousing him spiritually and sexually. Now, as he drove, he slid his left hand from the steering wheel to the inside of her thigh and she turned from the window.

"Keep your eyes on the road, mister," she said smiling, but then moved her hand onto his groin and he felt himself get hard.

"You know I just want to tell you how much I love you, baby," he said softly.

"You kick that word love around like a soccer ball. Love is an action, not a person, place or thing.

"Well, I wouldn't mind a little action right about now."

Zippy smiled and rubbed his throbbing penis through his pants. "Humph," she whispered, "you have a problem."

"Yeah, and I know just the woman to fix it."

"Mom, will you tell Billy to give me my paper back. He won't give me any," said Coree, interrupting her parent's conversation from the middle seat behind them.

"They're my papers," said Billy. "Mom gave them to me."

Zippy turned around and looked hard at Coree's tight blouse and low-cut jeans.

"How many times do I have to tell you to stop dressing like that."

"But mom, Billy stole the paper I was drawing on."

"I don't care what he did. Get something else from the suitcase behind you and put it on. Now!"

Coree crossed her arms. She was a younger version of her mother, almost as dark as her and slimmer.

"Don't you get belligerent or I'll slap you till kingdom come," said Zippy.

"Come on Zippy, she's a teenager," said Southie.

Zippy slid her hand from Southie's lap. "I don't know what kind of daughter you want to raise," she said, her emotions beginning to rise. "But when I was a teenager, I didn't show off my tits like two tourist attractions."

Through the rearview window, Southie saw fear and embarrassment rise in his daughter's face, and he knew better to anger his wife any further.

"Everyone just chill out," he said. "Zippy, turn on the radio and find us some music? And Coree, you're dressing like a whore. Put on some damn clothes!"

"Don't order me like I'm your daughter. I'm your wife."

"Alright, Zippy. Can you pretty please turn on the damn radio and find us some music?"

Southie winked at Zippy and smiled.

"Don't be giving me that face, mister. I'm not your daughter," said Zippy, turning on the radio.

The caravan of cars made their way through Scranton, where it caught Interstate 81 South, driving through Wilkes-Barre. Then past Hershey, the chocolate-manufacturing capital of America, before entering the Stoney Mountains. The six-lane interstate now wound around the hilly landscape dressed in autumn trees, lifting their orange, yellow and red leaves up and down the valleys like sexy skirts blowing in the breeze.

⌘ ⌘ ⌘

Sarah Levy, eye on the interstate and hand on the steering wheel, pondered the past and what the future held as the caravan rolled southwest through Harrisburg, and into the Blue Mountains. But mostly she thought about her son, David, now riding shotgun next to her and lost listening to his iPod. He was such a good boy when he was younger, and very religious, even wearing a yarmulke to public school. All that changed with his teenage years, though. Now he was moody, and she could hardly ever get him to attend the synagogue except for high holidays. He even said recently he wasn't sure if God existed. His grades remained fairly good, but they hardly spoke anymore and when they did it often ended in a disagreement. She glanced at him now in the passenger seat, eyes closed and listening to his iPod with earplugs buried into his brain.

"Hey, punk," she said, tapping him on the shoulder.

He took out the earplugs. "Yeah."

"Whatcha listening to?"

"There's this new punk band, Fast And Furious. They're Irish."

"Your father loved Irish music. I remember one song he used to sing to me," she said and began to sing.

In Dublin fair city
Where the girls are all pretty
I first set my eyes on sweet Molly Malone
She wheeled her wheelbarrow
Through streets broad and narrow
Crying cockles and muscles alive alive oh

"That was cool, mom," said David after she finished. "Was my dad a good singer?"

"Very good. And he could tell quite a story, especially after he drank."

"Where do you think he is now?"

"Hard to say."

"Well, I'm going to find him some day."

"That's fine. As soon as you finish school..."

"Stop telling me what to do."

"I'm not telling you what to do, David. It's your..."

"Yes, you are."

"I am not. You're free to do whatever you want, but you've got to be mindful of your grades and college."

"I didn't say I wasn't going to college. I just said I'm going to find my father."

"And I'm not saying you shouldn't."

"You're impossible, mom," he said, beginning to reinsert the earplugs.

"Wait a minute, punk," she said, touching him on the shoulder with her free hand. "I really didn't mean it like that. I understand you wanting to find your father."

"Mom, why did you fall in love with my dad?"

Sarah thought a few seconds. Outside, the caravan moved southwest around Harrisburg, and then through a long, dark tunnel blasted through the Tuscarora Mountains, before coming out and over the Tussy Mountains.

"I often think I married your father out of rebellion," she said. "My parents – your grandparents - were very religious. Maybe I married your father to hurt them."

"Do you think Southie married Zippy out of rebellion."

Sarah thought about the interracial couple a minute before answering. "Southie's parents probably were not thrilled at his marrying a black woman."

"How do you know that?"

"I just think that mixed marriages are hard. I'm sure there was an element of rebellion in Southie marrying her."

"Well you had a mixed marriage with my father. He wasn't Jewish."

"Yes, but I was young..."

"You had me through him."

Sarah smiled. "That was the best thing I ever did."

"Well I know if my father's out there, he would be proud of me."

"I'm proud of you, punk."

"You just don't understand."

"Understand what?"

"Just never mind."

David put his earphones back on and again closed his eyes. He resembled his father, she thought, the same lanky, toned body, square face and turquoise eyes. She wondered now if perhaps he shared his father's wandering spirit and eye for women.

⌘ ⌘ ⌘

In the early afternoon, the caravan pulled off the Interstate and into the Country Skillet Truck Stop. After refueling, they parked in a large stopping area replete with sixteen wheeler trucks woven intermittently, like a patchwork quilt featuring the many sizes and shapes of road vehicles. Although bright, the sun appeared distant, barely putting warmth into the chilly autumn air. While Southie and Zippy walked Buttercup to the edge of the parking lot, Coree and Billy ran ahead past the islands of gas pumps into the truck stop. Soon, the adults joined their children.

Inside, they found a complex with all the amenities of home. There were private showers, a grocery/gift shop, a doughnut shop, a small movie theatre with two-dozen seats, a laundry room, a television room, a video arcade, and even a small Christian chapel. Then there was the Country Skillet Restaurant, a busy diner type set-up with stools at the counter and plenty of tables, some of which were filled with truckers. Many were enjoying a buffet featuring all you can eat pot roast and mashed potatoes swimming in brown gravy, soggy hot vegetables, a salad bar and full dessert bar.

As Coree and Billy played in the video arcade, Southie, Zippy, Sol, Myrtle and Isaac had coffee at the doughnut shop counter. Meanwhile, Aaron's family, Sarah, her son David and the Rebbe finished stretching their legs and readied their vehicles in the parking lot.

"Aaron, do you think Southie knows to stop for Shabbat tonight?" asked Faygie, pulling at her husband's sleeve. She was diapering the baby as their other children ran wildly in circles around their van. "We can't be traveling on the Sabbath."

"I know," said Aaron, and he walked over to the Rebbe, who was studying Talmud in his car.

"Do you think Southie knows to stop for Shabbat?"

The Rebbe looked up, rubbed his nose and with a slightly raised voice, called towards Sarah's car. "David, come here a minute."

The young man moved swiftly toward the Rebbe with a youthful gait. He had clear skin for a teenager with the beginnings of a beard, and a cleft in his chin punctuating his square face.

"Go to the truck stop and inquire from Southie where he plans to stop for the Sabbath. Tell him there are some in this caravan who will not travel on this day."

David bounded through the parking lot, past the gas pumps and into the truck stop. He found Southie studying a large road map of Pennsylvania bolted to the wall behind a thick sheet of Plexiglas.

"Everybody wants to know when we will stop for the Sabbath," he said.

"The Sabbath? I thought maybe we'd drive straight through to Las Vegas."

"But Aaron's family and the Rebbe – they all keep the Sabbath."

"And what about you?" asked Southie.

David paused a few seconds. "I'm not even as religious as my mom."

Southie studied the young man as he considered the half request, half demand.

"Tell them we'll make the Pennsylvania border and then we'll stop for the Sabbath."

CHAPTER 7

Two hours later as the sun began to set, Southie pulled the caravan off the highway and into the gravel parking lot of the Golden Eagle Truck Stop overlooking Interstate 70. It was located just over the Pennsylvania state line on a sliver of West Virginia before the Ohio border.

"Well, here we are," he announced after all the congregants got out of their vehicles. "Let's celebrate the Sabbath."

Everybody looked around. They were on the edge of a hill near a clump of trees. Some fifty feet down the hill was the sight and sound of whooshing traffic passing east and west along the interstate and into the coming night.

"What kind of organization are you running here, Mr. Across-The-Country Guide?" asked Sol.

"Hey – you all wanted to stop for the Sabbath."

"So a hotel is too much to ask for?"

"I reckoned we could sleep in our cars on the way to Las Vegas. That way we'll have more money to get settled once we get there."

Sol banged his forehead with his palms and then lifted his arms skyward.

"He figures he can save us money by sleeping in our cars. For this we leave Port Decker? Oy Vey, what was I thinking?"

"Now Solly. You know about your blood pressure," said Myrtle, nudging her husband, but he again banged his forehead.

"I must have been in a trance. I tell you, I was hypnotized!"

Southie looked around at the rest of the congregation, who all seemed to agree with Sol, except the Rebbe, whose wrinkled face showed the trace of a smile.

"I agree with Southie," he said. "Why not celebrate the Sabbath bride beneath one of the Creator's first creations – the stars. It was only later that God created hotels."

"Yes," jumped in Isaac, addressing Sol. "Why don't you and Myrtle use my pop-up tent tonight? I'll unhitch it and set it up. It's quite comfortable with a large bed and I'm sure Southie will stay at some hotels along the way. Right Southie?"

"Yeah. Sure. We'll stay at some hotels. I didn't think it would be such a big deal."

And so as the sun went down in the West Virginia sky, the congregants ushered in their first Sabbath on the road.

> Come my beloved to greet the bride
> The Sabbath presence, let us welcome!
> For it is the source of blessing!
> From the beginning from antiquity she was
> honored
> Last in deed, but first in thought.
> Come my beloved to greet the bride
> The Sabbath presence, let us welcome!

After singing a few Psalms, Faygie took from a bag, several Sabbath breads wrapped in tin foil, and the Rebbe said the prayer over it.

"I'm sorry, I don't have enough food for everybody," she said.

"Not to worry," said Sarah reaching into a bag of her own. "I brought plenty of sardines."

"Sardines?" said Southie, making a face.

"I like sardines," chimed in Zippy, looking at her husband. "You can't always eat expensive meats, mister."

Southie turned toward Coree and Billy with a face, making them smile.

So they had their Sabbath meal gathered around Aaron and Faygie's white van, feasting on bony sardines, bread, grape juice and hot tea from a thermos. The meal broke up with songs of praise and prayers, then Coree took Billy inside the truck stop to the bathrooms, while Zippy made sleeping quarters out of the car. Meanwhile, Southie walked Buttercup to the clump of trees, and through it, saw the passing headlights of cars and trucks moving like shooting stars along the interstate. Above him, clouds raced swiftly, muddying up the night sky. Walking back to the car, Southie heard the low murmur of sixteen-wheeler generators penetrate the still night air as truckers settled in their rigs for the night. Across the parking lot the lights of the truck stop beckoned.

By the time Southie came back to the car, Zippy flattened the middle and rear seats, and covered them with blankets. On the ground beneath the back fender, Mouser and Miss Red were in their respective cages next to some luggage and supplies. Zippy took the leash from Southie and tied Buttercup to the back fender near a dish of water and a makeshift doggie bed made of a raggedy plaid blanket. Meanwhile, Billy came running up to them with tears in his eyes.

"What's wrong? Where's your sister," Zippy asked the child.

"Inside… talking with some boy."

Zippy's eyes flashed with anger.

"Now Zippy, just because she is talking to some boy doesn't mean she's sleeping with him," said Southie.

"You better go get her before I do."

"I will. Just calm down."

Southie walked quickly across the darkened parking lot to retrieve his daughter. Inside, he found her talking to a young man working behind the counter.

"Your mother wants you now," he said.

Coree turned around to see her father, and then looked around for her brother.

"Where's Billy?"

"He came to the car crying."

"That little tattle-tale. Wait till I get a hold…"

"Of who?" said Zippy storming through the truck stop door.

"Billy," said Coree. She felt her heart race and she began to tremble. "He wanted candy and when I said, no, he went crying to you."

Zippy gnashed her teeth and lowered her voice.

"You were supposed to be watching your brother. Now where is this boy you've been talking to?"

At this, the counterman sheepishly looked at Zippy. He was a gangly kid, no more than eighteen with a few pimples, the beginning of facial hair and an oval face.

"Didn't mean nothing Ma'am. Just chit-chatting with yo' daughter, that's all."

"Well let me tell you something about my daughter. She's known as the town tramp in the place we come from."

Coree's face twisted and her jaw dropped open.

"Don't you look at me that way. You better get back to the car before I slap your face off in front of your little boyfriend here."

Coree looked for a second as if she would cry, but instead obeyed her mother's orders by storming out of the truck stop.

Southie glared at his wife. "You didn't have to embarrass her like that," he said.

"Don't get between me and my daughter."

Southie pursed his lips together.

"Coree's my daughter, too, and she has feelings," he said, and left to comfort his daughter.

"Why does mom always have to blow up my spot?" Coree said to her father through tears as they walked past the gas pumps and toward their car together.

"She just worries about you, Coree. And you were supposed to be watching your brother."

"I was watching him. He just wanted candy and when I wouldn't buy him any he ran to tell on me."

"And who was that boy you were talking to?"

"Just a boy. It wasn't like I was going to do anything with him. You do believe me daddy, don't you?"

Southie stopped walking in the parking lot and looked into his daughter's dark, pleading eyes. It seemed only yesterday that she was a little girl, who used to run to greet him when he got home from work.

"Of course I believe you. I was a teenager once too you know."

They arrived back to the car, and Zippy joined them a few minutes later, still fuming.

"Why did you follow your daughter out?"

"Damn it, Zippy! You're too heavy handed with her. Coree's a teenager."

"Heavy handed? She was supposed to be watching Billy."

Southie looked at his ten-year-old son, cowering in his corner of the middle seat and bracing for a loud argument.

"Give it a break, Zippy. Coree had things under control. She was just talking to the boy."

"Yeah, mom, I was just talking to the…"

Zippy turned around, and without warning slapped her child across the face.

"I brought you into this world. I sure as hell can take you out of it."

Coree grabbed her cheek and burst into tears.

"Okay, you made your point," shouted Southie, " and she was punished for it, but I don't think the punishment fits the crime."

"Since when did you become Coree's attorney?"

"She is our daughter!"

"That's right and I'm your wife."

"Stop it! Stop it!" Billy screamed, covering his ears.

Southie rubbed his face. "I can't believe this," he said, opening the car door.

"Where are you going!" Zippy demanded to know.

"Out."

Southie slammed the car door and cut back across the parking lot, now filled with truckers hunkered down for the night, and back into the truck stop. Inside, he grabbed an empty stool at the restaurant counter where a shapely waitress with tired eyes served him coffee. As he warmed his hands on the mouth of the cup, Isaac came from the bathroom, and sat next to him, ordering a cup of coffee.

Southie looked at Isaac's yarmulke. "I thought you're not supposed to handle money on Sabbath."

"Everybody believes in God in their own way. What about you?"

Southie knocked the countertop.

"Had a fight with the old lady."

"Your wife is a blessing, no?"

"When she's going good, yeah. But when the Richter scale goes the other way, watch out. The ground opens up and everybody gets swallowed."

"At least you have a woman to keep you warm. Love was never my strong suit."

The waitress came over and refilled their coffee. She had hazel eyes and the paint on her nails was worn off in patches.

"Say, I got an idea," Southie said after she moved back down the counter to serve some road weary truckers. "What say you and me go get a drink?"

"A drink?"

"Sure. A toast to Sabbath. Besides, you can't get in the pop-up tent and I sure as hell don't feel like dealing with Zippy and the kids. We can take your car."

"But how do you even know there's a bar around here?"

Southie caught the eye of the waitress and motioned her back over.

"Say darling," he said. "You wouldn't know a place around here where some fellers could find some liquid refreshment?"

"You mean a bar," the waitress said, smiling.

"Yeah. A place to take in some of that famous West Virginia nightlife that I've always heard about."

The waitress took a napkin from a holder on the counter along with the pen held behind her ear.

"Well just down the two-lane there's a roadhouse that you boys might like," she said and began drawing a map.

CHAPTER 8

The Winning Circle Tavern featured a beat-up old stock car perched on its roof and inside smelled of stale beer and worn wood. The bar had about twenty stools, most of them empty, and behind it, a large man with a handlebar mustache and flannel shirt served an old-timer a shot and beer. Three women, two of whom had considerable girth, giggled and drank further down where the bar bent at ninety-degrees toward the bathrooms. In the back area, two men - also in flannel shirts, shot pool on a small-sized red-felt table. Against the front window was a small wooden stage with a speaker and PA system on it. Meanwhile, Alan Jackson's *Chasing That Neon Rainbow* blared from the jukebox.

"What can I get you boys?" said the bartender, wiping the old bar with a rag and throwing two coasters down on top of it.

"Southie took a twenty from his wallet and put it on the bar. "A Jack and ginger for me. What'll you have Isaac? First round's on me."

"A beer – Budweiser will be fine – thanks."

After they were served, Southie moved the straw aside from his drink and took a gulp.

"That was mighty nice of you giving that pop-up tent to Sol and Myrtle," said Southie. "Until you did that, I thought Sol would throw a fit because we weren't staying in a motel."

"We have a long trip ahead of us. We may as well all get along."

"How long were you living in Port Decker?"

"Practically my whole life," said Isaac. "My parents moved there from the Bronx when I was a baby. I was an only child. After my dad died, I took care of my mom. After she passed, I sold the house, but stayed in Port Decker."

"What about your job at Wal-Mart?"

Isaac took a swallow of beer.

"Wal-Mart, humph. They start you off at minimum wage and raise you to poverty level."

"Why work there then?"

"Everybody's got to have a job."

A carload of young people came into the bar. They were in their young twenties. Two wore military fatigues. Others wore jeans and work shirts. A few sported blue, button-down factory shirts.

Shortly thereafter, four musicians strolled in and began to set up on the small stage near the window. There was a guitarist, mandolin player, fiddler and banjo player. Southie heard them tune up over the jukebox, which played Patsy Cline's *Crazy*. Then the guitarist caught the bartender's eye, making a motion with his finger of slitting his throat. The bartender nodded and turned off the jukebox from behind the bar and the band kicked into a raucous country two-step.

I walked into a bar
On a cold rainy night
Feeling real low
I ordered a beer
Saw no one I knew
And sat down at a table

Courtney sweet beauty
Won't you please come home with me
Courtney sweet beauty
Won't you please please please
Come home with me

The song ignited the bar into whoops and hollers, and Southie and Isaac watched in silence as the bar began to fill up even more. After the band broke into *Arkansas Traveler,* one of the girls sitting at the end of the bar came over to Isaac. She looked in her thirties, and although on the heavy side, had a cute round face with straight, brown hair and green eyes.

"Excuse me for asking," she said, with a mischievous smile, and glancing over at her friends, who giggled back at her. "But me and my girlfriends were wondering what that beanie is on your head?"

"It's a *yarmulke*," said Isaac. "A head covering that Jews wear."

"Is your friend a Jew too?"

"Yup."

"Well, I don't see him wearing no head covering."

"Not all Jews wear them," Isaac said.

The woman looked back toward her friends. "They's Jews," she hollered and then turned back toward Isaac. "Name's Francine," she said, extending her hand.

"I'm Isaac," he said, shaking her hand.

"If you don't mind me saying, that's a sexy beard you have, Isaac," Francine said.

"Thank you." Isaac stroked his beard.

"I used to have a beard, too," chimed in the bartender. "Till my girlfriend made me shave it off. Said it scratched her thighs when we did the dirty."

"Get outta here, Elmer," Francine said with a smirk before turning back to Isaac. "Tell me something. I see Jews are allowed to drink. Can they dance, too?"

Isaac hesitated, but Southie nudged him.

"Go for it. I'm a married man."

Francine led Isaac to the small dance floor just as the band was breaking into the *Salty Dog Blues*.

Standing on the corner
With the low down blues
A great big hole
In the bottom of my shoes
Honey let me be your salty dog
Let me be your salty dog
Or I won't be your man at all
Honey let me be your salty dog

The whisky warmed Southie's belly and he began mulling over the home front situation. Zippy had long raised Coree with brutal force. While she called it a 'spare the rod, spoil the child' approach, he knew deep inside his belly it was abuse. For instance, when Coree was a child she played with the knobs on the stove, which led Zippy to heat a spoon to red hot on the stove and then burn Coree's palm with it. "This will teach her not to touch the stove," she told Southie. Other times she would whip Coree with a belt until she was marked with welts for not cleaning her room, and then she would make her sleep on the kitchen floor. These incidents upset Southie, but he did little to stop them from happening. This was partly because he lacked the courage to stand up to his wife, and partly because being an interracial couple, he feared that if authorities were called, they would be all to happy to take his children and break up the marriage. So mostly, he would yell a little and then leave the house and go to a bar until things blew over, especially when his daughter was younger.

Then Coree entered middle school and began spreading foundation and lipstick thickly on her face, which she had bought with her small allowance. Zippy decided it was too much and promptly took the makeup away. Coree, now getting too big to beat, began stealing it back. One thing led to another and before Southie could say "duck," makeup was being heaved around the house, marking up the walls and hallway carpet. Then, two days later, Zippy made a surprise trip to Coree's school and found her daughter wearing a friend's makeup. She wound up calling her daughter a prostitute in front of the whole class, and the principal called Southie to come get Zippy.

Ever since then, Southie tried to keep the peace between the two, but it came less often than not. Coree's grades started to fall and she began hanging out with friends away from home, and Southie spent many a night worrying about her.

Southie finished his drink and motioned the barkeep over for another. Cigarette smoke choked the tavern air and you couldn't make a straight line to the bathroom for all the people. It was a wild crowd, and Isaac and Francine were in the middle of it, flaying away on the dance floor like the chickens in their Port Decker yard.

Everybody has their own Sabbath, reckoned Southie, and these West Virginians, unlike most of the congregation he was traveling with, carried their burden well. If it were up to him, they would have been half way through Ohio by now. But what could he do? Isaac at least seemed to have it right wearing his Yarmulke, a little in the religion and a little out. He glanced at him now on the dance floor having a right good time with Francine, and his ill feelings toward Zippy softened.

Zippy loved to dance and nothing in the world matched the pleasure of dancing with her. Usually, they danced at home where Zippy put her happy self into the music, full of sexual innuendo and perfect rhythm, moving effortlessly to the music be it up-tempo country numbers, soul music or grinding dancehall reggae. Zippy may have her crazy side but what person doesn't, he asked himself.

The band announced they were doing one more song before going on a break, and as they did, Southie had a brainstorm. So he got off his stool and made a beeline across the dance floor, approaching the band as they finished their set.

"Excuse me, boys, " he said, drunkenly. "My friend and I, here, are traveling through West Virginia and..."

"This ain't West Virginia," the banjo player said. "It's a scrap of dirt between Pennsylvania and Ohio."

"Shut up, Floyd. Just cause you from Ohio ain't mean you so educated," the guitarist responded.

"Well at least I ain't from West Virginia."

The guitarist turned toward Southie and Isaac.

"Where you fellers from?"

"New York. We're just passing through."

"Well let me give you all a crash course on this here state. Know what the state bird of West Virginia is?"

"No, what?"

"A horsefly."

Isaac turned to Southie smiling slightly.

"A horsefly... Git the fuck outta here, Floyd," said the guitarist.

"A horsefly..." said Isaac, breaking up with laughter.

"You calling us West Virginians ignorant?"

"No. Not at all," said Southie, stifling his own laughter. "In fact I'd like to offer you boys a gig."

"A gig," said the banjo player.

"See, my friend here and me are staying down the road at the Golden Eagle Truck Stop. There's a whole group of us. We're there for the Sabbath which our people liken to a wedding..."

"Southie..." Isaac warned.

"Why not?" said Southie, cutting his friend off.

"These here are some Jews, Floyd" Francine chimed in. "Thar's a whole group of 'em and they's traveling to Las Vegas to start over or something."

"A gig, huh?" asked Floyd.

"At the Golden Eagle Truck Stop parking lot tomorrow afternoon. Just one set," said Southie.

"Well, it's a possibility. The rest of the band has to work tomorrow, but maybe me and Clarence here can make it. What do ya say, Clarence?" said Floyd.

Clarence scratched the stubble on his face,

"I reckon it's a possibility. What's it pay?"

"What do you want?"

Clarence looked at Floyd and Floyd looked at Clarence.

"Twenty dollars and a couple passes of the hat ought to do it," Clarence said.

"You boys got a deal."

CHAPTER 9

Southie woke at daybreak in the back seat of Isaac's car, shivering like a puppy from the morning cold. Still he managed to scrunch up beneath his leather jacket and doze off until Aaron tapped on the window at about eight.

"Isaac – you awake? We're starting our Sabbath service by Sarah's car," he said.

Isaac sat up in the drivers' seat and rubbed his eyes. "Be there in a minute."

"You up?" he asked Southie, turning around to see him in the back seat.

"Halfway," Southie said with his jacket over his head. "Unless you heard me snoring."

"Why don't you come to Sabbath services?"

"No thanks. You make your peace with God. I've got to make mine with Zippy,"

After Isaac left, Southie sat up and shook the cold off. The congregants were all parked next to each other in a semi-circle. Many of the truckers were already up, and had lined up at the edge of the Golden Eagle Truck Stop waiting to turn onto the interstate for a day of driving.

Southie looked at Rust Bucket a few cars away. Coree and Billy were taking care of Miss Red and Mouser. He then spotted Zippy walking Buttercup in the clump of trees overlooking the interstate. Jumping from the car, he threw on his jacket, turned the collar up for extra warmth, and made toward the trees. As he approached, Buttercup, who was slightly blind, growled.

"It's me, girl," said Southie, scratching the dog's head, and the beast wagged its stumpy tail.

"Cold as hell in Isaac's car last night," he said, facing Zippy.

"I saw you and Isaac drive off last night."

"The waitress in the truck stop told us about a bar."

"My father was a drunk," said Zippy, turning away from him. "I never liked drunks."

"Come on Zippy. Between the drama with the kids and these people making me stop for the Sabbath, I just had to blow off some steam."

Zippy became quiet for a second to measure her words.

"Do you know why I slapped Coree last night?"

"Because she wasn't looking after Billy."

"It was because of the way you took up for her. A husband shouldn't be defending his daughter like that before his wife."

Zippy paused for Southie to respond, but he didn't say anything.

"Listen to me, Southie," she said. "I love Coree as much as you, but she mustn't be coddled. She needs to learn there are consequences for her actions and I certainly didn't raise our daughter to become a loose woman. In Jamaica, you walk one way or the other. And once a woman spreads her legs, she better go live with the man she spread them for."

"But this is America, not Jamaica."

"Exactly. Coree can be anything she wants here, but not without discipline. I tell her that all the time."

Southie rubbed the stubble of beard on his face.

"It just really hurts whenever the family quarrels," he said.

"I bet there were a lot of pretty girls," she said.

"Where?"

"At the bar."

"I didn't notice any."

"Why not?"

"Because all I could think of was you."

Southie grabbed Zippy's hand and gave it a little squeeze.

"I'll bet," Zippy said, softening. Her almond-shaped eyes shined smooth, like precious black rubies against soft white cotton. The smell of coconut oil lingered in her hair.

"You're the only woman I want. Ever."

He tried to pull her toward him, but she pulled away with a flirty smile.

"You're still in the doghouse, Mister."

"Come then. Let's get the kids and grab some breakfast."

Behind plates of eggs, toast, bacon, potatoes and coffee, the family got along fabulously. Coree and Billy whispered together while Southie and Zippy talked and openly flirted. Then the entire family had a rip roaring good time recounting a dog they once had that actually walked on two legs. The mutt's name was Scruffy. They saved it from sure death at a pound in rural New Jersey. It was a loyal and loving animal that had a habit of hopping around on two legs like a bunny rabbit, whenever you pulled even slightly on its leash. Everybody was bowled over thinking about old Scruffy, and one by one the entire family got up to do their impression of how the animal would do this unusual dance. Then they each recounted with sadness how Scruffy suffered severe convulsions from time to time, and died following one on the kitchen floor.

After breakfast, the family walked around the truck stop, took care of their animals and wound up at the complex's mini-movie theatre to see "Men In Black."

Meanwhile, after morning prayers, Sol and Myrtle spent a good part of the day in the coffee shop, and gift shop. Isaac watched a few college football games in the television room and David engrossed himself in the magazine aisle pouring over sports and music magazines. Sarah stayed with Faygie in the parking lot gathered around the van while her children played around it. Later, the Rebbe, Aaron and Sarah talked a little religion, and David soon joined them from the truck stop. Then they went over the week's bible passage beginning with God telling Abraham:

> Go for yourself from your land, from your relatives, and
> from your father's house to the land that I will show you.
> And I will make of you a great nation; I will bless you
> and make your name great, and you shall be a blessing.
> I will bless those who bless you, and him who curses you,
> I will curse; and all the families of the earth shall bless
> themselves by you.

After the movie, Southie and his family went back to their car, tending the animals again and packing things away. As Southie leaned against his car studying the map, an old Ford Pickup came barreling into the parking area. It had one headlight taped in place and the rear fender was hanging from a wire. Slapped on the bumper was a sticker reading, 'I'd rather pick bluegrass than my nose.'

"How ya'll all doing," said Clarence, jumping out the passenger side. "Where do you want us to set up?"

Southie snapped his fingers, remembering his idea from the night before.

"I guess right about here would be good."

Clarence and Floyd began to unload their instruments from the pickup truck bed. Meanwhile, Zippy, who was feeding Miss Red, looked up to see the musicians.

"Who are these people?"

"There was a band last night and I wanted to dance with you. So I hired two of the pickers."

Southie grabbed Zippy, and although she frowned like she didn't approve of such public displays of affection, she allowed him a quick kiss. Her lips were soft and large, and slightly moist.

"I can't believe you," she whispered in his ear.

Southie broke off the embrace and shouted in his best carnival bark. "Hey folks. Gather round. I got the best Sabbath surprise ever for us. Some good old West Virginia bluegrass picking."

Isaac came over quickly and pulled on Southie's sleeve. "I'm not sure this is such a good idea," he whispered.

"Nonsense. You heard the Rebbe – the Sabbath is a bride," answered Southie. "I got the wedding band."

The entire flock of congregants looked at Southie as if he lost his mind. The silence was broken, however, by Clarence tuning his banjo and Floyd his guitar. Meanwhile, Buttercup let out a few barks and Miss Red began clucking.

"Ready, Floyd," Clarence said.

"Ready Clarence."

"Ah one, ah two... Ah one, two, three four."

Down the road there from me
Is an old hollow tree
Where ya' lay down a dollar or two
Then ya' turn ya' back
And when ya' came back
There'a jug of that good ol mountain dew

They call it that good old mountain dew
And them that refuse it are few
I'll shut up my mug
If ya' just fill my jug
Of that good old Mountain Dew

Zippy began stamping her feet and clapping time, and Coree followed suit. The rest of the congregation appeared stunned, except for Aaron and Faygie's children who watched intently at Clarence's spidery fingers moving nimbly along the banjo neck while Floyd kept steady rhythm on guitar.

"I don't know about the rest of you, but I'm going to dance a bit with my wife," Southie shouted above the music.

He winked at bright-eyed Billy and grabbed Zippy, doing a do-si-do in the parking lot. Coree grabbed her little brother and followed suit. Several truckers came over and joined in to dance. Others stomped their feet, clapped their hands and laughed.

Rolling in my sweet baby's arms
Rolling in my sweet baby's arms
Laying 'round the shack
Till the mail train comes back
Rolling in My sweet baby's arms

From near their car, Sarah's son, David, surveyed the entire scene with wide-eyed interest.

"What is so pleasant to your eye, punk," said Sarah, poking her son in the back with a finger.

"Nothing mom," he replied, stifling his look of admiration, but not turning around to face his mother.

Sarah, seeing she could not stop her son's enthusiasm, went to the others.

"I don't like this," she said. "He is teaching the children the wrong thing. With Jews like Southie our religion would dissolve like a pinch of salt in a pot of water."

"See what we get when we follow them," said Faygie in agreement. "We go blindly into America like this. I say we go back tomorrow. Realize we made a mistake and give Port Decker another chance."

"Go back to what, Faygie?" said Aaron. "Appeasing Port Decker? This is our lot now. We're here to spread Jewish light."

"But think of our children," said Faygie, motioning with her eyes at the party of musicians, truckers and Southie's family dancing wildly. "This is a *shonda* – a scandal to do on Sabbath."

"Southie's deeds may be lacking, but his intentions are good," said the Rebbe, observing the small concert and tapping his foot unnoticeably. "When the Sabbath ends, I'll talk to him."

After about an hour of music, Southie, seeing the congregation's lack of participation, told Floyd and Clarence to close it down. He then gave them each twenty-five dollars and the truckers kicked in generously when the hat was passed. Soon after they left, the sun went down and the congregation did prayers ending the Sabbath. After that, the Rebbe took Southie aside.

"The congregation was not happy with you," he said.

"I don't see what the big deal is. I thought the Sabbath is supposed to be like a wedding."

"Not exactly, the Sabbath is a presence that should be greeted like one greets a bride."

"Well, I just supplied the wedding band."

"Both your parents. They are Jewish?" the Rebbe asked.

"As Jewish as anybody here. I went to Hebrew school after regular school until my bar mitzvah."

"But your name, Southie? It's not Jewish."

"My real name is Samuel, but people have been calling me Southie for as long as I can remember because I'm left-handed. We're called southpaws in baseball."

The Rebbe smiled slightly. "You are familiar with Einstein's thinking about space and time – yes?"

"A little."

"It's also the theory behind the Sabbath. See, God created the universe from empty space in the time span of six days. On the seventh day he created the sanctity between time and space. The Sabbath pays homage to the differences between the secular space that the universe fills and the time in which it was created."

Southie mulled over the Rebbe's words.

"I get sanctity from the road," he said. "When I'm driving I feel God's presence more than ever."

"Ours is a religion full of miracles," replied the Rebbe. "There are many on the road."

"You mean like the sun rising every morning?"

"That miracle, yes, but special other miracles, too."

"Like what?"

"Like the Golem, for instance. The special half-human, half-angel that comes and helps Jews in times of need."

"The Golem!" Southie laughed. "I remember my grandmother used to tell me about the Golem. I always thought that was an old Jewish folktale."

"Some folktales are real, you know."

"Then maybe you should talk to Zippy. She believes in that kind of hocus pocus, too."

The Rebbe narrowed his eyes. "Maybe Zippy is on to something. Miracles are always within reach."

CHAPTER 10

The congregants woke as dawn broke through the hilly and tree-lined eastern sky. Zippy and the kids shivered as they packed away the blankets and took care of the animals while Southie made a run to the truck stop for coffee and hot chocolate. At the self-serve hot drink station, he ran into Sol.

"If it isn't Mr. Shabbat. That was quite the concert you promoted yesterday." Sol wore thick sweatpants and a warm plaid hunter's jacket. "What's up your sleeve now? Stopping for pork chops?"

"Come on, Sol. Every one said the Sabbath was like ushering in the bride so I figured I'd bring the wedding..."

"Just pulling your chain, kid, no need to explain," said Sol, stirring his coffee. "I like a good string band myself. So when do we leave?"

Southie smiled. "Soon as I pay for this coffee and you help me get everybody together."

Back outside, puffs of condensation from Southie's breath danced with the steam rising from the hot drinks as he carried them to the station wagon. The air was thick with moisture and blue-gray clouds raced low across the sky as truckers formed a line at the highway entrance. Even at this early hour, the great American interstate whistled its Yankee Doodle Dandy song with giant whoosh sounds every time a series of trucks passed.

Just after seven, the caravan pulled out from the Golden Eagle Truck Stop, descending through the hills with the last autumn leaves clinging hopelessly to near naked trees. Then they drove through Wheeling, West Virginia, a town where wooden church steeples lurched skyward above old redbrick factories and row houses. After crossing the wild Ohio River on a green steel bridge, a 'Welcome to the Buckeye State of Ohio' billboard greeted them.

Toward mid-morning the hills became smaller, rolling out like carnival kiddie rides into America's Midwest. Farmlands became flat with fields of withered, brown cornstalks finding a troubled, cold winter sleep. Patches of naked trees separated the fields, and residential trailer parks popped up, as did large manufacturing plants and drab white-brick distribution warehouses. Paved parking lots bordered these work places and each had loading docks for the sixteen-wheelers to back into and pick-up their wares for places unknown.

The exits off the interstate were marked by retail districts filled with big-box chain stores, or truck stop oasis, where those earning a living on the road could pull off for a hot meal and shower. The American Plains stretched westward endlessly.

Meanwhile, the clouds skipped quickly and low across the sky, blotting out the sun with huge puffs of white and casting a gray hue over the land. From time to time, Southie peered through his rearview mirror, doing a visual roll call to make sure the rest of the caravan was keeping up. Then he fumbled with the radio dial until coming to a country station, and soon after, the Columbus skyline appeared on the horizon with its metallic skyscrapers reaching into the increasingly darkened sky.

As they drove westward it began to drizzle, which quickly turned to heavier rain, pelting the car tops with loud thuds, challenging windshield wipers to keep up. Blackened storm clouds enveloped the Columbus skyscrapers as the interstate followed a route around the city, and lightening flashed across the wide, open sky. Seconds later, thunder cracked with an exploding sound like bombs bursting and echoing off the plains around them.

"Oh God, we're going to die," screamed Billy, terrified.

"Yeah... We're all going to get electrocuted and burn alive," said Coree in her best creepy voice.

"Can we get electrocuted?" Billy shrieked loudly.

"Yeah, get ready to die," she replied with a cackling laugh.

"Stop scaring your brother. No one is going to die," said Southie, but as he spoke, the wind took hold of the station wagon making it sway. He gripped the steering wheel tighter.

The rain turned into a steady drizzle and the clouds moved higher in the sky. Past the city of Springfield it began to mix with snow, splattering on the windshield like white insects.

"Perhaps we should stop," Zippy said.

"We're fine," said Southie determined to press on.

The snowflakes turned thicker and wetter, mixing in with the gray-white sky and covering the earth with snow. Meanwhile, the interstate turned slick and icy from the fallen rain beneath the snow. Traffic slowed to a crawl, and trucks and cars pulled off the roadway and onto the shoulder of the Interstate, flashing their emergency lights. Southie turned on his headlights and moved his body closer toward the steering wheel for better visibility.

"Stop being so stubborn. We should stop, Southie," Zippy said again.

"It'll break. We just have to drive through it," said Southie.

The storm now turned into a full-blown blizzard of white and even with the headlights on, Southie couldn't see more than two car lengths ahead. Zippy began singing "Amazing Grace" to calm everybody in the family down, and after three verses, Southie couldn't take it any longer.

"All right, we'll stop," he said, seeing an exit sign through the blanket of snow.

Although he was only going about thirty miles per hour, he now slowed to twenty. Through the rearview mirror, he saw the others follow suit. As the wagon train of cars curled around the sloped exit, Southie felt his car tires skid out and he pumped his brakes twice, managing to regain control of the vehicle.

"Good thing I bought those new tires," he thought aloud.

Just off the exit was an embankment running down onto a snow-covered plain between the exit and the highway. He slowed to a crawl and peaked into his rearview mirror, watching Sarah deftly maneuver her vehicle through the ice slick. Then as if in slow motion, he saw Aaron and Faygie's van spin on the ice slick and slide across the snowy exit, down the embankment and into the ravine. Southie carefully pulled off onto the shoulder of the curved exit area and put on his emergency blinkers.

"What is it?" asked Zippy.

"Aaron's family went off the road," he said.

Zippy looked over her shoulder and saw the Econoline down the embankment; its emergency flashers blinking red like Christmas lights through the snow.

"Wait here. I'll see if everybody is alright," said Southie, zipping up his black leather jacket and opening the door.

Outside, the air was still, save for the tap tapping of thick dense snowflakes against several inches of snow already on the ground. Off the interstate was a clump of trees, and Southie heard the occasional loud crack of waterlogged and frozen limbs snapping from the weight of snow and ice. Behind him on the shoulder of the road, he saw the blinking flashers from the rest of the caravan, and he walked in the station wagon's tire tracks towards them, until coming to Sarah's car and she rolled down the window.

"Everybody all right?" he asked.

Sarah nodded and Southie suggested that her son, David go back and tell the others to wait in their cars while he checked on Aaron, Faygie and their children. Then he began to make his way down the embankment to where Aaron's van slid off the exit. However, he didn't walk more than three steps down the four-foot slope, before he slipped and rode down the embankment on his backside; snow running up his leather jacket and shirt, settling on his chest and belly. At the bottom, he got up with a shiver and shuffled his feet through several inches of snow to the van. Aaron rolled down the window.

"The car wouldn't listen to the steering wheel," he said with a shrug.

"We tried this, but it isn't working," added Faygie, holding up a cell phone.

Behind them, in various stages of turmoil ranging from fighting to crying, were their seven children.

"Will you shhh! I'm trying to talk," said Aaron.

Southie looked through the blizzard and could barely make out the interstate, only about a quarter mile off the exit and all but shut down.

A large splintered limb snapped off the only tree in the field and lay on the ground nearby.

"Okay," he said. "Time to abandon ship. We'll find someone to tow the van once the weather breaks. For now, turn off the emergencies to save the battery, pack a few things and bundle the kids up. We'll divide them up with the others up there and make our way to the nearest hotel."

Aaron and Faygie quickly dressed their children warmly and packed three small suitcases. Carefully the family got out of their car into the silent blizzard. Southie and Aaron carried two of the younger children piggyback style, while the four eldest held hands. Faygie held the infant, Itzy, tied in a cloth baby carrier strapped to her chest, and she also carried a suitcase.

They made their way up the embankment, where Sarah and David took in the older children and the rest of the family squeezed in with Sol and Myrtle in their Cadillac. The snow settled into Southie's shoes and as he inched back to the wagon his toes burned from the cold.

"Everything alright?" Zippy asked after he slid back into the driver's seat.

"Colder than a freezer in hell out there," he said, rubbing his hands together.

Southie started the car and put the heater on full blast. It was dusk when the van slid off the road and the night showed up quickly. The caravan made their way slowly up the ramp and turned right on Route 44 toward a sign pointing the way for gas, food and lodging. Just past that was another sign reading, 'Dayton, Ohio Welcomes You – Home of the Wright Brothers: Birth Place of Aviation.'

CHAPTER 11

A sliver of gray light beamed from between thick drawn curtains waking Southie in their Motel 6 room. He sat up in bed, rubbed crust from his eyes and took inventory of his family. Beside him Zippy still slept, and the kids, with Mouser curled between them, shared the other bed. Meanwhile, Buttercup snored on the floor next to the nightstand while Miss Red lay on a clump of hay in her cage next to the closet, separating the sink and shower from the toilet area. He quietly got out of bed and poked his head between the curtains for a look.

Outside the storm stopped, leaving in its wake a thick blanket of snow covering the motel parking lot. Some cars were half-buried in drifts. Others, like his rust bucket, escaped the wind-blown fluff and snow only slightly covered the tires. From their second-floor room window, Southie could see plow and salt trucks already working at clearing the two-lane outside the motel. He quietly dressed and kissed Zippy, who opened an eye.

"Where you going?" she asked.

"Have to take care of some business. Get some sleep."

Southie bundled up into his leather jacket to brace against the cold as he walked along the outside veranda and down a flight of stairs to the office, where the day clerk had just come in from shoveling snow.

"Good morning, sir. Coffee?" said the clerk, pouring coffee from a small brew maker.

"Sure. Thanks."

"Quite a storm out there last night. The weatherman said we got over ten inches. Supposed to warm up the next few days though. Sugar?"

"Just a little milk, thanks," said Southie. "Sure glad we found this place. A bunch of us are traveling together from New York…"

"I know. My brother told me. He's the night clerk. Any of you from Brooklyn?" asked the clerk, handing Southie a cup of coffee. He had a dark complexion and friendly business-like manner.

"Lived in Flatbush a few years," said Southie.

"No kidding. My family's from Canarsie originally."

"Name's Southie. How long you been out of Brooklyn?"

"Six years. The name's Mohammed," said the clerk and offered his hand.

"Say Mohammed. Perhaps you can help me," said Southie. "See, one of the families we're traveling with lost control of their van in the storm and it's in a ditch off the interstate. You wouldn't happen to know somebody looking to make a few extra bucks towing it out?"

Mohammed sipped his coffee and thought a minute.

"Dick McAllister," he said at last. "He's the only one who made us feel welcome when we first moved to Dayton."

"Do you know how I can get in touch with him?"

"He owns a cell and computer store about a mile just down the road from here in the strip mall. It's called Dick's Modern World."

Southie took a gulp of coffee. "Did your brother tell you that we are Jews," he said.

"So what? You're Jews. We're Muslims. We're all Americans here."

Southie studied Mohammed as he finished his coffee. He was dressed for the winter, wearing a plaid flannel green shirt – the kind you'd see in Wal-Mart and an orange Cleveland Browns knit hat perched on his head. In the corner by the door was a wet snow shovel with a wooden handle.

"Well thank you. Thank you very much for your kindness."

⌘   ⌘   ⌘

Aaron Gotbaum finished his morning prayers as dawn's gray light filtered through the half-drawn curtains. This time of morning was always his most peaceful, especially with his family sleeping all around him. There was Faygie in their bed with Itzy cradled in her arms, and then the three next youngest, Natie, Mendy and Dena sharing the other bed, while Hinda, Benji and Yakov camped out on the floor. It was quite a crew, his family, and things sometimes got out of hand when everyone was awake. Now, though, he pondered both this trip he was on and his life.

Unlike Faygie, he did not come from a Hassid background. In fact, growing up in Atlanta, Georgia, Aaron always felt more American than Jewish. Being big, his father put him in Pop Warner youth football, and he wound up playing the offensive line all through high school. His parents forced him into Hebrew classes after public school, but he quit soon after his bar mitzvah. Then, after high school he moved to Brooklyn, where he had an aunt, and attended City College on 136th Street. When not in school, Aaron spent a lot of time on 42nd Street, splitting the hours between watching movies in Times Square and hanging out at the main library. As for life, he still didn't know what he wanted to do. All that changed one day when he was approached by several Chabad youth in the subway tunnel beneath 42nd Street, and asked if he was Jewish. After he told them he was, they led him upstairs into a truck to put on *Tefillin.* It had been years since Aaron had put on *Tefillin,* the leather straps to wrap around the head and arm, and each holding boxes containing written prayers.

While not feeling particularly religious, Aaron went along with the Chabad boys mainly to humor them. With all the Christians, Scientologists and Hari Krishna preaching on the street, he figured the least he could do was show some solidarity with members of his own tribe. To his surprise, however, putting on the *Tefillin* lit something inside him like a pilot light.

Several weeks later, he ventured to Eastern Parkway in Crown Heights Brooklyn, where the Chabad sect of Hasidim called home. Within six months, he moved to the neighborhood and into the home of Rabbi Mendy Shrenzel, where he fell in love with and married Faygie, the Rabbi's third of six daughters. Then the children began coming, and Aaron began feeling stifled under his father-in-law's roof. Finally, one day he went to him for advice.

"I feel locked into this community, which I love," Aaron told his father-in-law, "but I'm of two minds. The first is to stay here and raise my family, but the other is to go out into the world as blessed Rebbe Menachem Schneerson has taught and become a beacon of Jewish light."

Rabbi Shrenzel thought about his son-in-law's words for several days and then arranged for Aaron, Faygie and their children to live in an empty home that a Chabad family owned in Port Decker.

"Go there with your family," he said. "God will provide a path."

This trip is that path now, he thought. A quiet knock on the door interrupted his thought process.

"Who is it?" he whispered.

"It's Southie. I found someone to tow your van."

CHAPTER 12

Dick McAllister, several inches over six feet and obese, worked the telephone at a cluttered desk in the corner of his store. Between snippets of conversation, he balanced bites of an Egg McMuffin, gulps of coffee, and drags off a cigarette.

"Come on Charlie," he said. "It's not like I haven't had cash flow problems before... Screw Cleveland. You're the fricken' regional vice president!"

As he spoke, Southie and Aaron walked into the store, shook the cold from their bones, and began looking around. In contrast to the desk area, the rest of the shop was tidy and well designed. A cell phone display hung neatly on the back wall, and computers, scanners, printers and faxes made up the middle aisle. iPods, palm pilots and other small computer gadgets were in a glass case opposite the desk area.

"Gotta run, Charlie. I'll see you later at the Rotary Club," he said, hanging up and greeting his clientele with a sweeping motion to come on in. "What can I do for you folks?"

"We're looking for Dick McAllister," said Southie. "Mohammed from the Motel 6 said he would be able to help us."

"Well, you're staring at him in the person."

Dick let out a toothy tobacco-stained smile. A thick roll of fat hung over his belt. Droopy jowls and darkened rings around his eyes made him look considerably older than he was, which was in his mid-thirties.

"Mohammed's a good man. So what can I get you? You need a cell phone? Got some great family packages."

"My cell phone conked out last night," said Aaron.

"That's because you didn't get your phone from Dick's Modern World. Not a dead zone in the entire U.S. of A. No roaming charges either, and free weekends and nights after nine. How's the credit?"

Aaron shrugged. "Could be better."

"Doesn't matter. I got this guy in Florida. Could get a dolphin financed. How about a laptop? Can link up to the information highway anywhere in the world."

"Thanks, really," said Southie, nodding toward Aaron. "But what we're really looking for is someone to pull my friend's van from the ditch at the interstate exit. He slid off it in last night's storm with his wife and seven kids. Mohammed said you might know someone looking to make a few extra dollars with a chain and pickup so we can be on our way.

Dick's face grew thoughtful a few seconds, and then he went back to the messy workstation, picked up the phone and dialed a number.

"Marsha? It's Dick. Gary there? ... Well, tell him to give a holler when he comes back. I got some work for him."

As he spoke, a woman came into the shop, dusting snow off her collar and holding a McDonalds coffee. She looked about Dick's age, but trimmer, wearing blue jeans and a flannel shirt beneath her winter coat. She walked to the messy workstation, dug out a cigarette from a pack half buried in papers and lit one. Meanwhile, Dick stuffed the rest of the sandwich in his mouth and swallowed it down with a few obligatory chews, leaving the fast food wrapper on the desk.

"Hey Peaches," he said through the food after getting off the phone. "Meet our new Dayton visitors. Where you boys heading, anyhow?"

"Las Vegas," said Southie.

"Vegas. Greatest place in the world. Went there last year with ten grand in my pocket. Four days later, I practically walked to the airport. Couldn't even afford a cab."

"That's because we played the crap tables, Dickie. I told you we should have played black jack," said Peaches, digging out a shiny credit card from her purse. "Can you believe it? After ten years at the factory they decided to push my limit to forty-five hundred dollars."

"You be careful with that plastic, Peaches honey."

"That's a scream coming from you," she said, giving Dick a squeeze. "The man who claims there's only two kinds of people in this country - those who have credit, and the chumps that don't."

"What the hey, maybe I was a little harsh there" replied Dick, smiling and looking at his customers. "You boys gamble?"

Southie and Aaron looked at each other and shrugged.

"Just lotto every once in a while when the jackpot's big," said Southie.

"Don't gamble? Then what the hey you doing going to Las Vegas?"

"It's a long story, but suffice it to say, things weren't working out real well in New York for us and..."

"Say no more. I know how it is for you Amish."

"We're not Amish. We're Jewish," said Aaron, touching his facial hair. "The Amish shave their mustache."

"Jewish. I'll be dammed. Say – we have a lot in common, you guys and me. We're both into business."

"That's interesting," said Southie. "But we're just looking to have my friend towed out of a ditch and be on our way."

"No luck on that one today, friend. Everyone with a tow truck is out plowing," said Dick, fishing out another cigarette from the desk and firing it up with a silver lighter. "Say, Peaches, honey. How about coming to Rotary Club with me today?"

"I don't know, Dickie. All them business people and bankers make me nervous. Besides, it's my only day off work this week and I was hoping to do some housework."

"Come on, Peaches, it'll be fun," said Dick, looking at Southie and Aaron. "Maybe our visitors want to come too – meet some of East Dayton's finest. And it's at Mohammed's Motel 6 in the community room. What do you gentlemen say? It's a free lunch."

"Thanks, but I keep kosher," said Aaron.

"Not a problem. Mort Zimmerman who owns Mort's Bagels, is Jewish and he's a member of the Rotary Club. I'll have him hook up something Kosher. You people eat bagels?"

"Bagels, we eat," said Aaron.

"What about the van?" said Southie.

"Tell you what. I'll call my friend and we'll do it ASAP tomorrow. The town's still digging out. It will be 24 hours anyway. So what do you say to Rotary Club?"

"Sure, why not. We'd love to be your guests," said Aaron.

"So it's settled," Dick said, smiling. "Peaches, why don't you head home and put on that dress I like. The one with the flowers on it.

"But Dickie, that's a summer dress," said Peaches, puffing on her cigarette.

"So wear your coat over it," said Dick. "And Peaches do me a favor. When you meet me there, soften up Charlie from the bank. He always had a thing for you since high school. Tell him I'm good for the credit extender."

"I don't know, Dickie..."

"Don't worry about it, Peaches, just go home and get ready."

⌘   ⌘   ⌘

Dick drummed his fingers on the table as the Rotary meeting was called to order. Sharing the table in the back of the community room with him were Southie and Aaron, and two other merchants.

Matt Smith, president of the Rotary and vice president of Dayton Power and Light, called the meeting to order and then recited the clubs mission of holding the highest ethical standards in business and helping the youth of tomorrow.

"Some standards," Dick thought, gnawing on a bagel. Here he was on the brink of losing everything and Rotary preached high ethical standards. Where did these standards come in when people like Charlie, who sat at a table in front near the lectern, were refusing to give him another credit extender. He wasn't all college educated like Charlie, but they went to the same high school together, and Dick felt betrayed by his old chum. Not that he hated Charlie, because Dick didn't hate anybody, and he certainly enjoyed the give and take of the Rotary Club meetings. The networking alone was worth it, and he sold many members their cell phone packages. Yes, business was crumbling, but Dick wasn't about to give up. That's where Peaches came in. Where was she anyway? He told her to be there at three, but she was late as usual.

After going through some old business, Smith introduced a young representative from the box store, Best Buy, and Dick felt his throat go dry. He had heard the rumors that Best Buy was coming into the area, but until now he thought they were just that – rumors.

"I'm just here to tell you how thrilled we are to be building our next Best Buy in Northeast Dayton," said the representative.

It boiled Dick's blood to think this man-child from Best Buy would come in and undermine his own business. The rep looked all of twenty-five, if that, despite his sharp suit, freshly clipped hair and smug attitude. All his life he had busted his butt to make something of himself, and now this kid is coming to try to take it all away.

"So I'm here looking for the Rotary Club's support in our request from the city council for a zoning change so we can build our newest Best Buy right off the Interstate."

"I don't think that will be a problem at all," said Matt Smith. "We can draft a letter if nobody has a problem with that."

"Wait just a minute," said Dick, standing up and trying to keep his voice in even tones. "It may not be in the community's best interest to let a big box store come to our area. I mean they have no roots. I grew up here like all of you. I always support the Little League and Pop Warner football, both of which I played in myself. Bringing Best Buy here will hurt my store and any other digital sales and service shops in the area."

"We at Best Buy understand some businesses may be affected, but after all, this is America," the man said, smiling. "And as for becoming part of the community, we have a great record of joining all member organizations such as the Rotary Club. Best Buy is also bringing over 125 jobs. And we're a big supporter of local Little Leagues. One of Best Buy's teams even went to the Little League World Series two years ago."

"Well, I don't care about your Little League team," said Dick. "I say the membership of this Rotary Club take a month or two to study your proposal."

Dick looked around the room and several people, particularly those with small businesses, nodded in agreement.

"Very well then," said Smith, addressing the Best Buy representative. "We will take your presentation in consideration and get back to you in two months."

As Smith finished speaking, a clattering noise came in at the entrance of the conference room, followed by a pretty woman, who promptly tripped on one of her high heels.

"Sorry I'm late Dickie and everybody else," said Peaches, sprawled on the floor.

"That's quite alright," said Charlie. He quickly walked over to Peaches to help her up, but she pulled her arm away from him.

"Dickie, aren't you going to help me?"

"Of course," said Dick jumping from his chair and helping her to her feet. "You all know my girlfriend, Peaches."

Peaches got up and straightened her attire. Long, shapely legs jetted from a skimpy floral dress. In her arm was her winter coat.

"Where were you?" he whispered, leading her to his table. "I told you to be here at three."

"You know they always plow the trailer park last," Peaches replied in a whisper loud enough for some of the people around them to hear.

Smith regained control of the meeting with a bang of his gavel and under new business, announced the club's annual Wright Brothers Award given to the Dayton high school student who best exemplifies the entrepreneurial spirit.

"Once again, Lee's Floral Shop has generously agreed to sell us roses at cost to raise funds," said Smith.

Lee Wilson, a sturdy woman, wearing gardening overalls, got up from her seat with a broad smile and bowed.

"Which Mr. President, if I may," said Dick, standing up and interrupting the proceeding. "Is why we have to modernize the criteria on giving out the award."

"Modernize criteria?" asked Smith, a quizzical look crossing his face.

"The Wright Brothers revolutionized the world with the airplane, but we're flying on the information raceway now. There's big finance and credit to learn about, and always the need to understand sales. How our entrepreneurs understand these concepts should be our criteria."

"Such passion Dick," said Smith, forcing a smile. "But I'm in the energy business and as my fellow Buckeye Thomas Edison said, 'Opportunity is missed by most people because it comes dressed in overalls and disguised as hard work.'"

"Thomas Edison said that, huh! The man who invented the electric light bulb. Well, what the hey. How can I argue with him? Cause his company is the quickest to shut off your lights when the power bill is not paid."

A strange silence fell over the rotary club meeting save for the bus boy clearing dishes off the buffet table.

Peaches grabbed Dick's pants.

"Pssst," she said. "I think you're having a verbally challenged moment."

Dick looked around at the bankers, real estate people and insurance brokers, realizing his joke didn't go over that well.

"Nah, Peaches," he replied, loudly. "This is what the Rotary Club is all about. Open discussion to make the world a better place. That's why Dick's Modern World wants to be the first in line for the scholarship fund by buying five dozen roses — all for you — the love of my life, Peaches Kilpatrick."

The Rotarians broke into applause and Peaches' creamy white complexion blushed red

"Do me a favor, darling," Dick whispered to Peaches beneath the sound of applause. "Cozy up to Charlie. Tell him I really need that credit extender."

After the meeting adjourned, members of the Rotary mingled, and Peaches made her way to Charlie.

"Had to give it to old Dickie there," Charlie said. "A real jokester."

"Dick may not be college smart like you," said Peaches. "But he's great in business. You know that."

Charlie, wearing a slightly wrinkled blue suit, stared knowingly through his sleek-framed glasses and into Peaches' emerald green eyes.

"I don't know what you ever saw in him, Peaches."

"Just give him that loan, Charlie. You know Dick's good for it. For Christ's sake you two played on the same damn high school football team."

"And you're on the wrong team, Peaches honey. Dick is a dying breed. Even with his modern world."

"I'm just asking you to show some heart, Charlie. Show some damn heart."

"Well you just go tell your boyfriend over there, that we're still looking at his assets. I'll get back to him soon. Now, if you'll excuse me…"

Peaches watched with an awkward smile painted on her lips as Charlie walked over to the buffet table and introduced himself to the gentleman from Best Buy. After a few seconds, she blinked and walked back over to Dick's side.

CHAPTER 13

"Shalom. Come in," said Aaron, scratching the yarmulke on his head, and greeting Southie, Dick, and his friend, Gary, at his motel room door. "I'll just be a minute. That is - if I ever find my shoes."

Upon entering, the men realized finding shoes was a tall order. Especially with two young boys using one of the two beds, pulled to the room's middle, as a trampoline, while a third child orbited it like a moon around a planet. Water was running over the sink like a fountain and three of the youngest were playing patty cake half naked in a puddle of soaked carpet beneath it. The only semblance of order came from the couple's eldest child, Yakov, who had set up the family's beat-up laptop computer on the desk next to the television, and was busy on the Internet. Faygie, seeing they had company, led them to the bed that wasn't a trampoline and where a few chairs were set up.

"Sit, sit," she said. "My husband will be just a moment. So Southie, these are the men who will help my Aaron retrieve our van?"

"Yes Ma'am," said Gary with a smile full of half-rotten teeth. "Got my truck and chain in the parking lot."

The two boys bouncing on the trampoline, tumbled off the mattress, rolled onto the floor and got up screaming at the top of their lungs. Meanwhile, the baby, sitting in the mud puddle and wearing diapers, got up to see what the commotion was about and promptly slipped, landing on her behind, and got up crying like a fire engine.

"Stop it children!" yelled Aaron, climbing out from beneath the bed where he was looking for his shoes, only to clunk his head on the frame.

"But Benji started it."

"I did not."

"So help me God," cried Aaron in a booming voice and rubbing his noggin. "Don't make me count to three."

Natie reached over and slapped his brother upside the head. Benji responded with grabbing a fistful of his brother's hair and yanking it.

"I'm going to kill him," cried Natie, turning red as a beet.

"One.." counted Aaron out loud.

"Rambunctious little tykes aren't they," said Dick, arching an eyebrow.

"One and one half..." counted Aaron. "So help me God, don't let me reach three."

Faygie got up, pried the two boys apart with a stern warning and calmed down the fire engine toddler, placing her on her hip.

"Ah ha!" exclaimed Aaron. "There are my shoes... Under the nightstand."

Aaron retrieved them, and the adults continued talking as he put them on.

"So, my Aaron tells me you bought five dozen roses for your girlfriend yesterday," Faygie said.

"Oh that. What the hey. Put it on company plastic. But then I don't have to tell you people about that, being Jewish and all."

"I hate to break this to you, but not all Jews are good in business," said Aaron, tying a shoe.

"There's nothing wrong with making a few shekels," said Faygie, looking at Dick. "My father always said, rich or poor, it's good to have money."

Dick laughed. "Making money is one thing, but I'm in business for more than that."

"What more could you want from business than to have money to buy your children good shoes, feed them and put them in a nice house?" said Aaron.

"I want to be the fattest cat in all East Dayton."

"The fattest cat?"

"So fat I can't walk. Everywhere I go I want people to stop and say, 'There goes the fattest cat that ever lived.' A man with pockets stuffed with money. Cheeks stuffed with food and all washed down with the finest wine ever pressed from the plumpest grapes ever grown."

Dick stopped speaking and the adults looked at him. It was hard to imagine Dick to be any bigger and fatter than he already was.

"I'm ready," Aaron said, standing up with his shoes on. "Now if I can only find my keys."

⌘   ⌘   ⌘

Outside, the snow started to melt. While the streets were plowed and salted, puddles of slushy snow gathered around the curb and gutters. The four men crowded into Gary's Ford pickup with a plow attached to it, and made their way to the exit ramp. There, nestled in a blanket of virgin snow, was the van. Across the field, in which it was stuck, traffic ran smoothly. on the interstate. Gary pulled his truck onto the shoulder of the road and everybody got out.

"See if she'll start," Gary said.

Aaron half-slid down the embankment and wiped snow away with his hands to clear the front window and door. He unlocked the door, hopped in and the car started right away. Rolling down the window, he gave a thumbs up and put the van in drive, but the wheels began spinning and the van went nowhere.

"Okay, cut it off," Gary yelled. He went back to his pickup and unrolled a long tow chain. Then he slid down the embankment with the hook end and fastened it to a sturdy piece of metal beneath the van's front fender.

"When I get back to my truck, start her up and put her in neutral," he said. "Then don't do anything until you feel the car move a few feet. Then throw her in gear and see if she'll drive up."

Aaron followed the instructions and soon was able to drive up to the shoulder of the road.

"Thanks a lot," said Aaron taking out his wallet. "What do I owe you?"

"Forget it," said Gary.

"No I can't," said Aaron, taking three twenty-dollar bills from his wallet.

"Buy your kids something with the money," said Gary.

Aaron then tried to give the cash to Dick, but he also refused.

"What the hey. Forget about it," he said.

"Then thank you. Thank you very much," said Aaron putting the money back in his wallet.

Southie and Aaron got in the van and went back to the Motel 6.

"Spread the word that we'll be leaving first thing in the morning," Southie said, before heading back to his room to check on Zippy and the kids.

⌘   ⌘   ⌘

Dick, eating a hot dog, arrived back at his office in the late afternoon just as, Sally, his part-time help, was getting ready to lock up.

"You go home. I'll close, Sally" Dick said. "How did it go today?"

"Seven cell phone contracts, including three on the family plan and I'm still waiting on one person's credit app," Sally said, wrapping a multi-colored wool scarf around the winter coat she bought from Wal-Mart. "Oh and Charlie from the bank called. Said he'd be there until six... I left the message on your desk."

"Thanks, Sal."

After she left, Dick stuffed the rest of the hot dog in his mouth and walked to his desk. Between some papers and a cardboard pizza box, he found a stray cigarette and put it in his mouth unlit. Then, still on his feet, he picked up the phone and began dialing.

"Hello, Charlie. It's Dick... Dick McAllister."

"Why hello, Dick... Before I tell you what happened let me start by saying the economy is tough to get extensions, but I went to the mat for you. I even climbed the stairs to the big boys in Cleveland..."

"Cut the crap, Charlie," said Dick, his heart pounding. "What did they say?"

"No dice, Dick. They ordered me to liquefy."

"Liquefy. That can't be. Didn't you tell them I have been making payments?"

"You know as well as me, Dick, that your payments doesn't even cover the interest. You're over your head, buddy."

"Then take my house and car, but let me keep Dick's Modern World. It's a gold mine. I'm nothing without the modern world."

"Listen to me, Dick. See your attorney."

After hanging up, Dick lit the cigarette dangling from his mouth and took a deep drag. Between puffs, he toyed with the idea of suicide. But how would he do it? He owned several guns and a rifle. Nah, too messy, he thought. Wait a minute. There was a rope in the metal cabinet outside the bathroom, and a sturdy elbow pipe jetting out from the ceiling connecting high on the wall. But as he furthered the idea of hanging himself, the phone rang and he answered it by instinct.

"Hello," he said, meekly.

"I thought you said you were going to pick me up from work. Remember dinner? I been waiting at this damn factory for a half hour."

"Sorry Peaches. I forgot. I'll be there in ten minutes."

CHAPTER 14

Snooky's Bar and Grill catered to East Dayton's more upscale clientele. The steaks were oversized and the bar poured heavy. The lighting dim and the tables spread far enough apart for private conversation. At a table against the window overlooking a small pond, Dick ordered a scotch on the rocks and Peaches a white wine. For food, Dick had his usual 22-oz sirloin and Peaches ordered shrimp scampi. After the waitress left, Dick lit a cigarette and it wasn't until his third scotch that his brain went numb enough to talk.

"I'm going to ask you something, Peaches, and I want you to be perfectly honest."

"Truth or dare," Peaches said, sipping her wine.

"Would you still like me, if I lost everything? If all of a sudden I became broke as a cheap watch?"

"What do you think?"

"I wouldn't be asking you if I knew."

"What's gotten into you, Dickie?"

"Answer me, will you?"

Peaches drained her wine and put her thin fingers through Dick's stubby digits.

"Why do you think I've wanted to have your child for the longest time?" she whispered.

"I don't know."

"I swear Dickie McAllister. For someone who's such a genius in business, you don't know much about love."

The waitress brought the food and after she departed, they ate for a few minutes in silence. For the first time in as long as he could remember, Dick didn't feel hungry. Peaches though was starving and in a celebratory mood. Finally, she looked up from her plate shocked to see Dick not eating, but before she could say anything, he beat her to the verbal punch.

"Let's do it tonight without a rubber," he whispered.

"Dickie," Peaches said with a surprised laugh. "But I might get preggars."

"So what the hey." Dick winked at her.

Peaches felt flabbergasted. She had known him since kindergarten, and except for a brief wild period right after high school, Dick was her only lover. If she wasn't so happy about what he said, she may have questioned his mood. Instead she took the new credit card from her purse and gave it to the waitress when she came over with the check.

"Charge it," she said unable to conceal a smile. "My treat."

Dick's roomy SUV was littered with candy wrappers, empty soda pop cans and crumpled cigarette packs. As he drove, Peaches again felt something was wrong. Perhaps it was the doggy bag that was on the seat between them. Dickie usually ate everything, including the remains off her plate. Also disconcerting was his somberness. Usually he was full of words about anything and everything, but now they drove in silence.

"Okay, Dickie what's eating you?"

"Nothing. Just thinking about those Jews passing through town."

"What about them?"

"I figured sure they would be rich and know a lot about money and all, but they're just regular people. You should have seen their kids today — running around like bandits in a room at Mohammed's motel. Reminded me of us growing up."

"Maybe they aren't really poor but just crafty..."

"What ever, but I like them just the same. Beats the Rotary Club types that run our little corner of the world."

Peaches didn't say anything and the car became quiet again until they passed the all-night Dairy Mart.

"Aren't you going to stop for beer before we head to your place?" she asked.

"Yes, sure," he said, looking into his rearview mirror before making a U-turn back to the convenience store. "But I figured maybe tonight we'd go to your place."

"My place? I thought you wouldn't be caught dead ever going back to where we grew up."

"Call me nostalgic," said Dick leaping out of the car for a few six-packs.

⌘   ⌘   ⌘

The trailer park was just how Dick remembered it. The same makeshift street lamps mounted on poles, and bent this way and that from drunken drivers hitting them. The tiny porches filled with toys, clothes and beer cans. Even the teenagers milling around the mailboxes seemed the same. Take away a few body piercings and hip-hop clothes, and Dick saw himself.

Peaches, however, kept her little patch of property looking very homey. Flowerbeds dotted her tiny strip of grass, and the doorway path from the driveway led to an uncluttered porch, punctuated with a welcome mat.

"However so humble, " Peaches said, turning the living room lamp on.

Peaches took the beer and doggy bag from the restaurant and put it all in the refrigerator. Meanwhile, Dick glanced at the photos on the wall of Peaches' mother and brother - both now in Cleveland, and a plaque with a prayer written on it.

Peaches came back with beer.

"Well how do you like the place?" she asked, handing him a bottle.

"Nice. Real nice."

"Here's to us," she said and they clinked bottles. Dick took a gulp, managing only a nod of his head.

"That's it," demanded Peaches. "If you don't tell me what's wrong, Dickie, you can just pick yourself up and leave for the night."

Dick lit a cigarette as he looked at the prayer on the wall. It had something to do with keeping faith.

"I'm done," he said, turning around.

"Done?"

"I didn't get refinanced. They're taking everything."

Peaches lit a cigarette for herself and led Dick to the weathered couch.

"But how can they do that?"

"Credit, Peaches. I borrowed more than I can pay for and now the castle is crumbling. Another month and I'll be broker than you."

"If there's a way into something there has got to be a way out, too."

"No way out except maybe to get the old .45 and blow my brains on the floor."

Peaches looked at Dick with a mixture of concern and shock. She pulled her hair back behind her ears and let the silence set in a few seconds.

"Now Dick McAllister," she said at last. "I've known you to be a lot of things. A liar and bullshit artist – that's for sure. But I never would mistake you out for a pussy."

"You just don't understand," Dick replied.

"Understand shit. That you're gonna let those Rotary Club bastards beat you out of everything you worked so hard to get?"

Dick took a deep drag off his cigarette, then got up and began to pace across the small living room and kitchen area.

"I suppose I could go bankrupt," he said. "Wipe the slate clean."

"You can do that?"

"Shit, yes. I'll pay them ten cents on the dollar of what I owe 'em and fuck the banks. Besides, I'm not really into the modern world of gadgets anymore. I know this guy who accesses credit for cell phones, who's got an in to the next big thing."

"And what's that?"

"Ninety-nine cent shops. It'll replace Wal-Mart one day, I swear. You put up five thousand and get a store full of inventory. Everything goes for a dollar and up. It's the retail wave of the future."

Peaches got up and clicked the radio on, which lay on the counter separating the kitchen from the living room, and a scratchy Red Hot Chili Pepper song played.

"Now can't we just forget about all this business talk for one night?" she asked while gyrating her hips and pulling her skirt up just a little.

Dick grabbed Peaches by the waist and held her tight against him.

"Careful, Dickie," she said, playfully trying to break away. "Remember, I just might get preggars."

"That's what I was thinking," he said and they kissed long and passionately.

⌘   ⌘   ⌘

It seemed a minute later that Dick leapt up in bed, and in the darkness of the room, was lost for a second. Slowly, the shadowy objects of Peaches' bedroom began to reveal themselves. The night lamp and bedroom dresser, their clothes thrown loosely on a rocker in the corner.

"Peaches – you awake? I had this dream."

Peaches groggily awakened and opened one eye.

"What was it about?" she asked.

"It was terrible. I was in this long room, and I had everything I always wanted. Hundred dollar bills stacked to the ceiling and a kitchen table loaded with the most food I've ever seen. Lobster, steak, fifty-dollar bourbon...you name it."

"That sounds like heaven."

"At first I thought it was. Till I tried to eat some of the food and found out it wouldn't go down. It was the weirdest thing. I would chew and chew and chew, but I couldn't swallow. The taste was there but not the satisfaction. And every time I would reach for the money, my hand would just go through it. But my hand was steady and real. It was the money and the food that were the ghosts."

"You're just bugged about your finances," Peaches said, rubbing his large naked back. "Don't let it get to you. Why don't you get something to eat? Shit, half your dinner is in the fridge."

He thought for a minute and as the shock of the dream wore away, he felt hungry.

"Maybe you're right."

"Go for it," she said, taking her hand from his back. "Baby, I got work tomorrow. Let me sleep."

In the kitchen, he tiredly took the doggy bag from the refrigerator and put it on the table. He then fished around the kitchen for a knife and fork. Finally, he sat down, carved out a large chunk of meat and popped it in his mouth without a second thought. After a few obligatory chews, he swallowed, but the meat lodged in his throat. He felt a stringy piece of fat attached to the chunk caught in his teeth and tried to dig it out with his fingernails. Then he tried to swallow again, but the meat only moved down a little further in his throat and felt even tighter. A wave of fear, bordering on panic rose in him as he realized he couldn't breath. He gasped for air. Grabbing the table in pain, he tried to swallow again. Nothing. He got up unsure of himself and felt dizzy. Suddenly he remembered Peaches and took a step toward the bedroom, but tripped on a table leg and fell to the floor. The pain in his throat was unbearable and he felt his face begin to swell and heat up. As in a dream, he saw Peaches standing naked over him.

"Dickie... What's wrong!"

He tried to sit up, but in doing so it seemed all the blood drained from him and he gasped with all his might for air. He fell back down again and clutched his throat. Peaches stood over him sobbing. He began to feel cold. The pain and panic began to fade. The world darkened.

CHAPTER 15

Early the next morning, as Southie's family and the congregants were packing their cars to leave, Peaches pulled Dick's SUV into the Motel 6 parking lot, splashing through a puddle of slush and skidding to a stop in the middle of the group.

"Dickie's dead," she said, bursting into tears.

"What," said Southie, stunned.

"Last night. In my kitchen," she sobbed. "Oh God - I don't know what I'm going to do."

Faygie told her oldest to take all the kids from the van and play in the corner of the lot near the outdoor pool area.

"Did you contact his family?" she said.

"Dickie doesn't have any family. He was raised by his grandmother and she passed away."

The entire congregation looked at each other.

"We're so sorry, but we were about to leave town," said Southie.

"You've got to help me... Dickie liked you people. You are his only friends in this town."

"What about the Rotary Club?"

"He hated those people."

"Perhaps we can make a collection," Southie said.

"I don't need a collection. I need Dickie," sobbed Peaches. "Oh, God. I...I haven't even made arrangements yet. I have to go to the funeral home."

"Southie will go with you," said Zippy, volunteering her husband.

"Zippy," said Southie, a note of protest in his throat.

"We'll help, too," said Aaron. "It's the least we can do. Your Dick? He belonged to a church that we can contact perhaps?"

"No, Dickie hated organized religion - called them spiritual scams, but he believed in Jesus. We both do."

"Then I will help make arrangements and do the eulogy," said Aaron.

So Southie reluctantly told everybody to re-check into the motel and while he went with Peaches in Dick's SUV to a funeral home, Aaron and Mohammed sent a notice to the press about Dick's death and contacted those in town who knew him.

When Peaches and Southie arrived at the funeral home on the outskirts of Downtown Dayton, a slender man in a dark suit greeted them somberly.

"Would you like to see him?"

Peaches nodded and the man led them downstairs to where Dick's body lay on a metal slab waiting for embalming. Dick's already large face looked even more bloated, but peaceful, in death. The smell of rotting flesh, bleach and embalming fluid reminded Southie of his days working at the morgue.

"Oh, Dickie," Peaches sobbed. "Why did you have to go and do this? We had our whole life in front of us."

As Peaches grieved, Southie pulled the funeral director aside and asked how Dick died.

"Choked to death," the man whispered. "Coroner pulled a chunk of meat the size of a softball from his windpipe. Mighty shame."

They were led back upstairs to a small office with a desk and a few chairs. Peaches pulled a tissue from her purse and blew her nose.

"What kind of funeral deals do you have?" she asked.

The funeral director opened a hardcover catalogue with pictures of caskets.

"We have several types of final interments with the cost of services, coffin and cemetery plot all included," he said.

Peaches thumbed through it and after several pages came to a black coffin with gold trim and white satin inside.

"How much for this?"

"With the plot, service and casket it is thirty-eight hundred dollars complete."

"Thirty-eight hundred dollars"? That's a lot of money."

"We have other options," said the man, thumbing through the book and showing her a different casket. "This one here is twenty-eight hundred complete."

Peaches flipped through the book again and then abruptly closed it.

"Do you take plastic?" she asked.

"Yes we do."

"Give me the expensive one," she said, digging out the credit card from her purse. "My man lived on credit. He died on credit. He may as well be buried on it."

The funeral brought together an array of people from the community, from Charlie at the bank and his expensively dressed wife, to Gary with the tow truck, who came in a worn suit toting along his wife and kids. Mohammed and members of his family were there, as well as rotary club members and old friends. The congregants from Port Decker also showed up, minus Aaron and Faygie's children, who were left behind at the hotel to watch each other.

Zippy, on the other hand, insisted that Coree and Billy attend, so each could look death in the eye. And the kids got a close-up view as Zippy took one child in each hand, and walked with them right up to the open casket to see Dick. The corpse looked pasty, and the dark shadowy rings around Dick's eyes were now caked white with makeup.

"Is he really dead, mom?" Billy asked, staring at Dick's body.

Zippy let go of Billy's hand and felt Dick's hardened cold face. "Yes. Do you want to touch him?"

Billy recoiled, but Coree followed her mother's lead and touched Dick's cold face.

After some milling around and paying respects, Aaron made his way to the small wooden pulpit directly behind the coffin. Everybody took a seat in the few rows of pews and became attentive, and Aaron began to speak.

"What can I say here about Dick McAllister that most of you already don't know?" he asked, projecting a low voice and quiet tone. "You who knew him his entire life. Peaches, the woman he loved. His childhood friend, Gary, and everyone else gathered today. Those, for instance, who did business with Dick, buying cell phones and computers from Dick's Modern World."

The Rebbe paused and eyed all the mourners in the room.

"So what can I, a Jew, and stranger among mostly Christians, say about this man, a Christian, whom I hardly knew, but whose eulogy I am now sadly delivering?" The Rebbe paused, took a deep breath and continued.

"As God would have it, a freak snowstorm stranded us here in Dayton. My van was stuck in a ditch, and Mohammed here recommended to my friend to go to Dick's Modern World for help. For Mohammed said that Dick McAllister, was such a man that when his family came to Dayton as Islamic immigrants, he was the first to extend his hand in friendship. That, my friends, was Dick. And this good soul of a man allowed me to also peer briefly into his life. He took me as a guest at a Rotary Club meeting that he so loved, and he spoke of his ambitions in my hotel room."

Aaron paused, and using his fingers, combed his long, dark beard. He then adjusted his black felt hat higher up on his head..

"Now I'm sure most here look at me and see a religious man. A big person dressed in black, with a long beard and funny hat. A Jewish man seemingly very different from Dick McAllister. Yet in our own ways we both cling to God. Me through following God's laws and Dick for his inner godliness. Through Dick's life I have learned something more about God. That God surely has a place in heaven for the soul of Dick McAllister. Dick, who had no particular belief in organized religion, but yet, was a good, kind, fair and just man. There is room for the souls of such people in every religion. There is even such a place for those who don't believe in or acknowledge the presence of God in their life, but who live Godly lives just the same. For God put good souls into this world. People that do for others, regardless of their rank in society – rich or poor, strong or weak, big or small. Dick McAllister was such a soul and God has a place very near to him, and his memory will be cherished by all who have been so blessed to know and love such a man. May Dick McAllister rest in peace."

After the funeral everybody went back to the Motel 6, where Mohammed opened up the community room with food for all the mourners. Here, the Rebbe, who keenly observed the funeral, pulled Peaches aside.

"You were this Dick McAllister's wife, yes?"

"Not exactly," said Peaches. "But we've been together since high school."

"Then you must take care of yourself," said the Rebbe. "And the little one also."

"The little one?" asked Peaches.

"The one in your belly. You are carrying his child, yes?"

"But...?"

The Rebbe nodded toward her belly, and Peaches suddenly recalled her last night with the man she loved.

"Why Dickie McAllister," she said, rubbing her belly. "You didn't leave me all alone after all."

CHAPTER 16

Only patches of snow, tinted gray with soot, remained on the ground from the storm when the congregants left Dayton early the next morning. By the time they crossed the Indiana state line, even those disappeared into the cornfields. The landscape now flattened out like a pancake beneath a cloudless sky. A double-winged crop duster flew low across the plain, which was dotted with wooden farmhouses and fields of withered brown cornstalks. Windmills spun like mad street dancers across the fields to the horizon. Cow pastures sprung up with the massive black and white animals standing around and chewing their cud, or laying lazily in mud while smells of their manure soaked the air. Billboards advertising truck stops, cheap motels and Christian ministries appeared every few miles. Some carried political messages such as stopping abortion. Others had scripture such as, "'God gave his only son to suffer our sins."

As Southie drove, Zippy surfed the channels of the radio, going through various music genres, talk shows and Gospel stations. Finally, she settled on an oldie station out of Chicago, and sang along to Freda Payne's, "Band of Gold." And she kept on singing through "These Boots Are Made For Walking." Then she stopped singing, and the station wagon grew quiet except for the sounds from the radio as they drove around the outskirts of Indianapolis; its steely skyline reaching up like giant mutant cornstalks across the prairie field.

Hearing the Chicago radio station flooded Southie's mind with childhood memories. Of Skokie, where concentration camp survivors, struggling to make semblance of shattered lives, mixed with those like his parents, first-generation American Jews bolting from the Jewish ghetto of

Chicago's west side. Of times spent chumming around with his many non-Jewish friends, where everybody went to public school, played sports in the street, cheered for Chicago teams, and feasted on all-beef Vienna Red Hots and Polish sausages slathered with mustard and raw onions on poppy seed buns. And all the while, everybody listened to the Chicago radio stations like the one blasting on the radio right now.

The caravan roared east across Indiana and its withered brown cornfields as far as the eye could see, and Southie began to think about people from the state. He knew several Hoosiers growing up, starting with the first girl he ever necked with. She was a topless waitress in Chicago, by way of Terre Haute, and lived in a studio apartment near his parent's apartment. He was still in high school at the time, and he would show up to her place after school.

Southie smiled at the memory now, and slid one hand from the steering wheel and onto Zippy's lap.

"Kind of nice these long rides. Jump starts the stick shift, if you know what I mean," he said, thrusting his hips up toward the steering wheel.

"Yeah, right," Zippy said laughing. "What are you going to do?

"Pull the car over on the shoulder, tell the kids to wait in the car and take you into the cornfield."

"And what about the others following behind us?"

Southie winked at his wife. "Tell 'em we'll meet up at the next truck stop."

"There's probably all kinds of snakes in the cornfields."

"Corn snakes, maybe. But they aren't poisonous.'

" I couldn't get comfortable."

"We'll have a real Adam and Eve moment."

"Shit face." Zippy laughed.

Just outside Terre-Haute, the congregants pulled into a gas station and diner to fuel up and use the bathrooms. It was a one-stop exit located just off the interstate where long fields of plowed cornstalks met at four corners. A warm current filtered through the breezy autumn day and the sky was crystal blue without a cloud overhead.

While Zippy and the kids minded the animals, Southie unzipped his leather jacket and strode past the gas pump, manned by two freckle-faced farm kids wearing overalls and sporting John Deer tractor hats. As he edged closer to the diner, Sarah's son David, ran up from behind him.

"Hey Southie. Mind if I ask you something?"

Southie turned until the boy caught up with him. "What's on your mind?"

"What made you fall in love with Zippy?"

Southie stopped walking and sized up the young man, who was as tall as he was, and fairer than his own olive skin.

"Why, you looking to get married?" he said.

David smiled and they continued walking across the parking lot. "No, but I wish I had a girlfriend," he said.

"When I was your age the only thing on my brain was sex. Ever been laid?"

"Almost. I went to second base with a girl back home. She wasn't Jewish though and when mom found out I was grounded forever."

"Well I wouldn't worry much," said Southie. "Your time will come."

"Mind if I ask you something a little personal, Southie?"

"You mean more personal then asking me why I love my wife?"

"Why did you marry her?"

Southie thought a few seconds, trying to arrange ideas on the subject enough to spit out a short answer. They were standing outside the glass doors to the diner now.

"Timing, I guess," he said, "both Zippy and I were ready to settle down at the same time and there was a physical attraction."

"My mom said you married Zippy out of rebellion."

The words caught Southie by surprise, but not shock as over the years he had become used to hearing comments about his mixed-race marriage. "Now how do you think your mom figured that?" he said.

"Because my father, Patrick O'Reily, wasn't Jewish. He was Irish. My mom thinks maybe she married him out of rebellion because my grandparents were very religious."

"Imagine that," said Southie, and as he spoke, Sarah approached them from behind. They were still standing at the entrance to the diner next to news boxes selling USA Today and the local Terre Haute newspaper.

"I thought you were waiting near the van," said Sarah.

"I was, but I had to use the bathroom," said David.

"Yes. That's what your son told me. He had to use the facilities," said Southie. "Oh, and David. Just to answer your question: I didn't marry Zippy out of rebellion. I married her out of love. Can't say it's always been a bed of roses – especially with people's perceptions being what they are – but love is a funny thing and that's why I married her. She is a beautiful black woman and I cherish her!"

Inside, the diner smelled of baked ham. It was a family style restaurant, smaller than the larger truck stops, with white tablecloths spread over twenty wooden tables and matching white curtains shielding light from streaming directly into the dining area. Prints of Norman Rockwell illustrations highlighting a family enjoying Thanksgiving dinners and other American scenes adorned the walls, while local farmers wearing denim overalls sat at four of the ten stools at the counter. After using the restrooms, David and his mother returned to their car. Southie ordered French fries and soda for his family before going to the bathroom. When he came out, he met Sol, who came in for coffee to go for himself and Myrtle.

"Say, Southie. Can you do me a solid?"

"A solid?"

"Myrtle has a cousin in St. Louis. You think we can stop for a quick hello."

"This is no vacation, Sol, we're going to Vegas."

"I know. I know. But Myrtle's driving me crazy about this." Sol gave Southie a desperate look.

"Okay. We'll stop for two hours but that's it. A quick hello and a faster good-by," Southie said.

Sol pinched Southie's cheek, and lit up with excitement. "You're a *mench* you know that, a real *mench*."

Back on the interstate, as Zippy doled out sandwiches she had made before leaving Dayton, along with the French fries and soda, Southie complained to his wife about the burden of leading everyone.

"Now Sol wants to stop in St. Louis to see some cousins. If it were up to me I'd have been to Las Vegas, found an apartment, and be making some money already."

"What's the rush, mister?"

"It's too much. This stopping for Sabbath, and now St. Louis."

"We'll get there when we get there."

"Well it can't be soon enough for me."

The caravan rolled over the muddy Wabash River and into Illinois. For some miles, the cornfields vanished, turning instead into a small forest of oak and hickory trees. Then the forest disappeared and huge corn and cattle complexes appeared. They were more expansive then the smaller farms in Indiana with thin rows of trees separating property lines and large grain silos springing up like country skyscrapers near every farmhouse. How Southie hated these cornfields when he first started hitchhiking out of Chicago. It didn't matter if he was heading south on I-57 past Joliet, west on I-80 toward Davenport or east just out of Gary, the flat cornfields were everywhere, green in spring, golden and high in summer and shriveled brown in winter. The flatness of the prairie landscape, where one could see the horizon in all directions, made him long for the mountains to the west and the oceans to the east, west and south. It was these cursed cornfields that created in him the wanderlust, he thought, robbing him somehow of his youthful innocence. Now though, as the four-lane interstate opened to six lanes, the cornfields seemed inviting in the way they swayed rhythmically in the autumn wind, and he began to miss his parents and brother. They had all separately drifted to California while he spent his years on the road. Then, after he settled down, any hope of becoming close to them was dashed by his choice of wife. Not that Southie thought his family was prejudiced, per se, but he did grow up in a suburb in which many whites fled from growing black neighborhoods.

"You know that divorced woman, Sarah," he said to his wife after turning down the radio. "She thinks I married you out of rebellion."

"Didn't you?"

"No. David just said that because his own father was some Irish guy named O'Reily and his mom was with the fellow out of her own rebellion against her religious parents."

"Humph! That Sarah's got a lot of nerve. Like Jews are better than blacks. She should just remember that blacks might have once been slaves in this country, but they burned ya'll synagogue down."

"Don't start. What matters is why I married you."

"I know why you did that."

"Why?"

"Because I cook in the kitchen and burn in the bedroom."

Southie laughed, but as he did, the car lost power and then surged forward with a hiccup.

"What was that?"

"Probably bad gas."

They drove a little further and it hiccupped again. Then it seemed to vanish, and Zippy began singing along with Ray Charles as he sang *Hit the Road Jack* on the radio.

> *Hit the Road Jack*
> *And don't you come back*
> *No more no more no more no more*
> *Hit the Road Jack*
> *And don't you come back*
> *No more*

Although not having the best voice in the world, Zippy more than made up for it through sheer energy, accentuating some phrases loudly and whispering others. All the while, she laughed and smiled, pointing at Southie every time she sang the phrase, "Hit the road Jack." Coree and Billy joined in, fostering a chain reaction of Buttercup barking and Miss Red clucking. Zippy sang a few songs with the radio in this manner, passing the time, until about 20 miles out of St. Louis, when the car experienced a series of hiccups again and began to lose power. There wasn't much for Southie to do now, except put on his flashers and pull his old wreck, the damn rust bucket, to the shoulder of the interstate with the congregation following suit.

"I can't believe this," he said, slamming the steering wheel with his fists as they pulled to a stop.

"See aren't you glad I make you pay for Triple A every year. They tow anywhere in the country for free."

Southie looked at Zippy and she gave a sly smile. Only his wife would see some light in being stranded on the highway, in late afternoon, and in the middle of nowhere.

"I'll call 'em from Aaron's cell phone," he said, taking the Triple A card from his wife, who pulled it out from the glove box.

Forty-five minutes later, a dirty brown and beat-up tow truck came up on the shoulder of the highway with "Velroy Johnson's Auto Repair Shop" painted in white on the door. The driver came out of the truck with a toothpick sticking out of his mouth and walked toward the station wagon. He was ebony colored with a mustache and a short, thick Afro peppered with white.

Zippy ordered the kids to stay in the car while she and Southie got out to meet the man. Outside, the air smelled damp and swampy. High reeds of green and brown replaced the cornfields without any trees in sight. The weather was fairly warm for an autumn day and trucks whizzed by them on the interstate, leaving gusts of wind in their wake.

"What seems to be the problem?" the man said.

"The car just started losing power," Southie said.

The man looked at Zippy, chewed on his toothpick, and then at Southie, and the kids and animals in the car.

"Pop the hood," he said.

The man looked under the hood a minute and wiggled a few wires.

"Start it up and put it in reverse," he said.

Southie did as he was told and the car moved back on the shoulder five feet.

"Now put it in drive."

When Southie did so, the car hiccupped about two feet and then wouldn't go further.

"Okay, turn it off," the man said.

"What do you think the problem is?" Zippy asked.

"The tranny."

"Can you fix it?"

"Have to put it on the lift and take a look."

Southie walked back to the rest of the congregants to talk the situation over. After some discussion, it was agreed that while everybody else would go to Myrtle's cousin in St. Louis, Southie and his family would go with the tow truck driver to his repair shop. They would meet up once the car was fixed.

After they departed, Velroy, for that was the mechanic's name, hooked the rust bucket up to the tow truck, and Southie, Zippy, Coree and Billy crowded into the tiny cab.

"What happened to the cornfields?" Southie asked as they drove.

The man gave half a smile.

"We're in the Mississippi flood plain. 'Round here we call it Little Egypt."

"Why do they call it that?" asked Zippy.

"Cause its near where the Mississippi and Ohio Rivers meet up, and when it was first settled people considered it like the Nile River delta. Shit, we even got Cairo on the Kentucky border. Southern Illinois has been called Little Egypt since before I was born and then some."

CHAPTER 17

Dusk descended on East St. Louis as the tow truck moved past a Goodwill Shop and beneath dim street lamps illuminating boarded-up storefronts, liquor stores and pawn shops. Soul music spilled out of the Tip Top Bar and Grill, and two blocks further down the strip, teenagers dressed in baggy pants and oversized football jerseys gathered on the corner. As they hung out, thick rap beats and dense poetic lyrics blared from the speakers of a parked Chevy.

When they arrived at Velroy's repair shop, Mary J. Blige's *Sweet Thing* spilled from a radio in the two-lift garage. A half-built engine and muffler lay on the ground against the wall. Awaiting them was an unshaven man, slightly overweight, balding, and dressed in greasy jeans and a windbreaker jacket. He sat on one of two chairs next to a table filled with tools.

"Looky, what warshed ashore from Little Egypt today," the man said, eyeballing Southie, Zippy, Coree and Billy. "What's the problem?"

"Looks like the tranny," said Velroy, hooking the car to one of the lifts.

Before Velroy jacked the car up, Zippy took Buttercup out from the back of the rust bucket on a short leash. The rottweiler sniffed the mixture of grease, oil and antifreeze filtering through the air, and then began growling and barking at Velroy and the man.

"Now calm down old girl," said Velroy, extending his hand slowly in front of the dog's nose.

Buttercup's nostrils twitched as she sniffed Velroy's fingers before becoming satisfied the stranger was okay, and she offered her head up for a pat. Then, she turned snarling toward the other stranger.

"Hold that leash tight, sister," said the man, drawing back in his chair. "My leg ain't no turkey drumstick."

"Dog ain't gonna bother ya' none, Calvin," said Velroy, laughing.

"Maybe so. But them teeth sho' ain't no welcoming committee."

"Calm down Buttercup. Calvin is a friend," Zippy said, coaxing the animal.

"I got enough friends, sister. Really, I do."

Zippy calmed the dog, and then tied her outside the garage. Meanwhile Velroy hoisted the car on the lift and examined it, every so often asking Calvin to hand him a wrench or different size bit for the drill. Finally he motioned for Southie and Zippy to come beneath the car for a look.

"Here's your problem," he said, shining a lamp into the exposed transmission gears. "Teeth are worn smooth as a baby's skin. Gonna have to rebuild her."

Calvin joined them for a look at the problem.

"Yup. That's the tranny, alright," he concluded. "Gonna cost a pretty nickel to fix that."

The group got out from beneath the auto's belly and looked at each other.

"How much is a pretty nickel?" asked Southie.

Velroy chewed on the toothpick in his mouth and studied the family. "Southie was a white and maybe had some money," he figured. Then again, the car was old, and he was with a sister and children.

"Six hundred," he said.

"Six hundred dollars?" asked Southie.

"And that's using junkyard parts. Trust me, you ain't going to find no cheaper."

"Do you barter?" asked Zippy, jumping into the conversation.

Velroy eyed the sister.

"What do you have in mind?"

"I'll do your portrait."

"Yeah," chimed in Southie. "My wife is the best artist you ever saw. That's how we met. She's been doing it all her life."

Velroy looked at Calvin, who shrugged.

"I don't have no time to pose for a portrait," said Velroy, leading the group to his small, storefront office in front of the garage.

"That's the best part. You don't have to," answered Zippy. "Just give me a photo or two to work from. And I must add you're a handsome man with a fine face."

Velroy mulled the offer over. "How much?"

"A hundred dollars and that's for a full oil portrait of your face and shoulders."

"Okay, I'll knock a hundred dollars off. Five hundred flat and you do my portrait."

Zippy looked at Southie whose eyes read approval.

"How long will it take to fix the car?" Southie asked.

"Two or three days, depending if we can find the parts."

"But where will we stay?"

Velroy scratched his head and looked at Calvin.

"Don't look at me. I ain't got no room."

"Well if ya'll don't mind some close quarters, I suppose you can stay with me and mine," said Velroy.

Southie called the congregation to tell them the situation, and found his fellow travelers had been put up nicely by Myrtle's cousins and the St. Louis Jewish community.

"Don't worry, kid," Sol told Southie over the phone. "Get the work done and don't let him overcharge you. We'll wait here a few days."

Meanwhile, seeing that her art supplies were buried in the back of the station wagon, it was decided that Zippy would do the portrait in the front office as Velroy worked on the car. So after securing a few suitcases and the animals in the back of Velroy's truck, the family was ready to leave.

Velroy locked the shop up for the night and Calvin, after bidding everybody good-bye, vanished down the block on foot. Then everyone piled into the tow truck and drove west, back through the downtown area to a dusty and desolate road. Here grassy reeds replaced the buildings beneath dim streetlights. They turned onto a dead end street where there were four wood-frame box houses amongst the tall reeds. Velroy pulled his truck into the driveway where a porch light shined on toys and car parts.

Before taking everyone inside, Zippy found a spot for her animals in the backyard. She also saw to it that they had enough food and water, and were comfortable before everybody went inside.

The simmering smells of turkey wings and greens greeted them at the entrance. An older woman with gray straightened hair, large breasts and smooth, coal black skin sat at the kitchen table. Beside her sat a serious-looking child with glasses, immersed himself in homework. On the living room floor were two other children, eyes glued to BET music videos playing on the television.

"These are the people that broke down on the interstate," Velroy said to the woman.

The woman got up from her chair with a grace that belied her age and weight.

"Call me Momma Docs," she said. "And what's your names?"

"Zippy."

"Humph. That short for something?"

"Zipporah."

"That's a right powerful name. Zipporah!"

Mama Docs eyed Coree and Billy.

"And who are these beautiful children?"

Billy smiled, and one of the two children watching television - a little girl about his age - got up and ran to Momma Doc's side.

"This is my granddaughter, Kenesha," Momma Docs said, and nodded toward the small boy at the kitchen table doing homework. "And that there is my genius in the making, Darryl."

Upon hearing his name called, Darryl looked up from his books. He had a short haircut, nearly to his scalp, with a shaved part.

"Now put away the homework, boy. Don't you see we got company? Momma Docs got to set the table for supper."

The boy quickly picked up his books and vanished upstairs into the house.

"Want to go watch TV," the little girl said to Billy.

Billy looked to Zippy, who nodded. Then the adults all sat at the kitchen table, except for Momma Docs, who spoke as she got out plates and silverware.

"Tell me, Zipporah, how'd you come to marrying a white man?" she asked.

"My husband isn't white. He's Jewish."

Momma Docs lowered her head and raised her eyes taking in Southie. He looked about her son, Velroy's age, with a gray stubble beard and thick, unruly black hair threaded with gray.

"Jewish huh? Sho' looks white to me. How's the in-laws accept you?"

Zippy sucked her teeth.

"I think I'm a little too colored for them," she said. "If you know what I mean."

Momma Docs laughed. "Mmmhmm. I know how that is."

"Come on now," said Southie, protesting. "They love their grandchildren."

"The grandchildren are fine. It's their mother that's the problem. You know how no one wants to hear about the labor, they just want to see the baby?" said Zippy. "Well in this case no one wants to see nor hear about the mother."

"Mmmmhmm. Can't never find a white person admitting dey is prejudice."

"It's not always good for Jews either," said Southie. "The town we came from in upstate New York burnt down the synagogue. That's why we're here."

"Sho'nuff," said Velroy jumping in. "They was leading about a half dozen vehicles filled with other Jews when they broke down in Little Egypt."

"Yes, Southie's leading his people. They went ahead to St. Louis to a Jewish community while we get our car fixed," said Zippy.

"Where ya'll heading?"

"Las Vegas," said Southie. "The fastest growing city in America. I looked it up on the Internet."

Momma Docs stopped setting the table and lifted up her head to stare at Southie and Zippy.

"Las Vegas. The new Promised Land," she said, laughing.

Two teenage boys came into the house. One was tall and lanky, and the spitting image of Velroy, only twenty years younger. The other was shorter and heavier, wearing baggy jeans, a Chicago Bulls jersey, and an afro-comb sticking out of nappy hair. He immediately went up to Momma Docs and kissed her on the cheek.

"Think ya'll can fix an extra plate for me, Momma Docs?"

"Rasheem, you always welcome," said Momma Docs, pressing her eyebrows together as if she was even considering sharing food.

"Where were you all day, AJ?" said Velroy to the thin young man.

"Me and Rasheem were working on our beats."

"I don't want to hear no nothing about beats. You were supposed to come to the shop after school. Not running the streets.

"But pop, we was rehearsing..."

"Listen to me AJ. There's only so many people make money off that rap crap."

"Both you stop it," said Momma Docs, who had finished setting the table. "I won't have the two men in my house disagreeing before dinner. Now let's everybody wash and say grace."

AJ looked around and immediately made eye contact with Coree. She looked his age, with cocoa brown skin, dark-as-night eyes, natural ringlet curls to her shoulders and a curvy, newly matured body.

"Yes'm," he said.

Momma Docs served dinner consisting of pork-tail spiced collared greens, sweet potatoes and melt-in-your-mouth turkey wings where the meat fell off the bones tenderly into a pile of brown gravy, which Southie sopped up with a corn biscuit. In fact, while Zippy had one plate, he took seconds.

"Husband sho' can eat," Momma Docs said.

"Yeah, I got to keep him working every way I can if you know what I mean," said Zippy, grinding her hips a little, and everybody laughed.

After dinner, Velroy grabbed four beers from the refrigerator and led Southie to the backyard and onto a footpath. They walked through a thicket of brown reeds and railroad tracks before coming to the foot of an embankment. Southie saw a half moon at the top of it and beneath it a picnic table. When they reached the top, Southie bent over a second to catch his breath.

When he looked up again, the mighty Mississippi River lay below him, its slow ripples making gurgling noises as it drifted downstream toward New Orleans. Across the river, the lights of St. Louis twinkled into the sky, its mighty arch serving as the doorway, beckoning toward America's west. To their left, trucks and cars whizzed over the Martin Luther King Jr. Bridge spanning the great river between the Illinois and Missouri state line.

Velroy handed Southie a beer and they grabbed a seat at one of several wooden picnic tables overlooking the river.

"Come here many a night to mellow out," said Velroy, cracking a beer open. "Been doing it since I was a kid."

The lights of a large barge appeared ahead, making its way downstream. Water washed against some rocks on the shoreline below them. Southie unzipped his leather jacket. The walk got his circulation going and it was considerably warmer than it was through Ohio and Indiana. Small bugs danced around their heads as the two men talked and fireflies danced all along the waterfront.

"You ever been away from this area?"

"Except for two years in the army, I never left," Velroy said. "My brother did though. Lives in Denver. Doing real well for himself, too. Owns a Toyota dealership. Not me, though. Shit, I couldn't get out if I tried."

"You're not chained to East St. Louis."

"East St. Louie is part of me and I'm part of it. Funny, most people see this corner of the world as full of rundown buildings, crime, crack heads, junkies and prostitutes, and they're right. We got all that, but to me it's something else. I see barbeque shacks, churches and hard-working folks who I've known my entire life and who care about their kids."

Velroy took a gulp of beer. The barge was just a small way upstream now and Southie could make out its rusty color and flattop against the St. Louis lights.

"What about you?" he said.

Southie drank some beer and thought he saw something like a fish fly out of the water with a splash.

"You couldn't anchor me down to any one place if you tried," he said. "It's not that I chose to be this way or even wanted it, but wanderlust has marked me since birth."

"And you married a sister."

"Yes. Never thought I'd wind up with a black woman, but I'm grateful to God for her."

They finished their beers and opened another.

"So you ain't just one of them white boys with jungle fever?"

"Zippy's the sweetest part of heaven when she's going good and the darkest part of hell when she isn't. We've been through a lot together."

"And you say she's a good artist?"

The barge was now passing them, and Southie could make out the human figure in the steering room, above the boat's hulk.

"She's as good an artist as you are a mechanic."

The two men laughed and then Velroy opened his wallet, and took out a worn photograph of himself in an army uniform. On one side of him was a younger Momma Docs, and on the other side was AJ, then a little boy.

"Tell you what. If you can get your wife to do this portrait of the three of us, I'll take another hundred off your bill."

When they arrived back at the house, Momma Docs had already set up sleeping quarters for Southie's family in the living room. She made a soft bed on the floor with several thick quilts for the kids and opened the couch into a bed for Southie and Zippy. Billy watched television.

After Velroy bid everybody good night and Momma Docs finished up in the kitchen, Southie took a seat next to Zippy on the couch-bed.

"Do you know where your daughter is?" Zippy asked her husband.

For the first time Southie noticed Coree wasn't around.

"In AJ's room," she said, answering her own question.

Southie got up and went past the kitchen where Momma Docs was finishing the dishes, through a short hallway near the back door to the stairs.

"Coree, you up there," he shouted.

"Yes daddy," came his daughter's response from behind a closed door.

"Come on down. Momma Docs made a bed for the family."

A few minutes later Coree came downstairs looking sheepish.

"What were you doing in that boy's bedroom?" Zippy asked in a hushed tone.

"Talking and listening to music."

"A young girl shouldn't be going to a young boy's bedroom."

"But mother I didn't do nothing," protested Coree.

"She said she didn't do anything," said Southie.

Zippy turned and pointed a finger right in her husband's nose with clenched teeth. "You stay out of it. This is between me and my daughter." Then she turned towards her daughter. "I saw the way you were eyeballing that boy all through dinner."

"Zippy, please. You're jumping to conclusions"

"Conclusions... Hmm," she said and turned back toward Coree. "Where I grew up in Jamaica once a girl spreads her legs she becomes a woman, and the man she spread them for takes care of her. Where we lived, one skinny, bony chicken would feed the twelve of us for a Sunday dinner, and if a woman spread her legs there'd only be eleven..."

"Zippy, that is ridiculous talk," said Southie, his voice growing loud.

"Southie. This is not your fight. Stay out of this."

Momma Docs came into the room from the kitchen.

"Everything all right with you folks," she said with a laugh.

"Yes Momma Docs," said Zippy, forcing a smile.

Momma Docs looked at Billy, who was now fast asleep in front of the television.

"Ya'll must be real tired. Look at your boy. He's an angel," she said before turning off the kitchen light and retiring to her room upstairs.

Southie turned off the television and lights, and crawled into the couch-bed beside Zippy. Her body felt warm and soft next to his. He laid on his side for a time until he heard the kids make the steady breathing sounds of deep sleep in the makeshift bed on the floor. Then he turned toward Zippy and put his arm around her, but she pushed him away.

"Why don't you go to your daughter? Every time I try to teach her you run and take her side as if she were your wife and I was the other woman."

"Come on, baby. Just relax. You know you're the only woman in my life."

"Don't come on baby me. You've got to back my side in the raising of Coree."

Southie knew from the raspy tone in his wife's voice that any attempt at lovemaking could turn into a cat-clawing fight. Instead, he turned his body away from her and soon fell into a deep asleep.

Meanwhile, Zippy lay awake on her back for a long time, staring at the paint chips on the ceiling. East St. Louis brought up things she had long blocked from her mind. Now the house, the town, even Momma Docs frightened her to the bone. Memories began to flood her mind. The beatings, hunger and abuse. She was such a quiet child and would pretend to sleep when her father touched her, but it seldom worked. And afterward he said he would kill her if she ever told anybody.

Why or why, dear Lord, she whispered quietly to herself, did Southie bring me to this place? All I ever wanted was a better life for myself. A house in the country with a tight, loving, successful, family. Why can't Southie understand? He is white. He can do anything he wants, and I would back him with all my heart and soul. Why dear Lord have you allowed me to escape such darkness only to drag me back into it?

Finally, Zippy fell into an uneasy sleep and dreamt she was flying – fearlessly floating through the clouds with sky all around her; in total control of body and mind. She flew over a scene from her childhood in Jamaica. To Mammy's house in the hills. There was Mammy and one of her cousins feeding the fowl. They looked up to see her, smiled and waved. Then she returned to Kingston, and saw her half-starved brother eating dirt in the yard, and there – there was her father coming up the walk and home from the bar.

Suddenly the sky grew dark and she began to lose control. Now her body flew in total abandon and she tried desperately to stay aloft over the Interstate Highway. It was a strange open road filled with farmer fields and truck stops. There in the middle of the highway she saw their car leading the other cars from the synagogue. She was in the middle seat with Billy. Then she looked in the front seat and saw Southie with his arm around Coree. They were smiling like lovers. Zippy lost all control of her flight – falling, falling, until with a jump, she was awake and on top of Southie.

"What... what is it?" said Southie with a start.

"I had a bad dream," Zippy whispered.

Southie put his arms around his wife and held her tightly. "It's okay. I'm here. I love you."

Slowly Zippy began to relax as he gently rubbed her shoulders and neck, then kissing her soft cheeks, forehead and neck. At last she looked into his face and their lips met with soft, small kisses at first, before turning to longer passionate kisses, where their tongues met, and they gently bit each other's lips. He kissed her neck again and made his way down to her breasts, gently kissing and pulling the nipples with his teeth. Massaging, licking, kissing the entire landscape of her body as if it were the first time, even though he already knew it so well. And every little reaction and quiet moan turned him on more, making his member grow stronger and harder. At last he mounted her and face to face, cheek to cheek, he slid his throbbing penis into her slippery wet pussy. Slowly he thrust deep into her, moving back and forth, in and out, and she began to move with him in syncopated rhythm. After some time, Southie felt his wife's body grow warmer and the two began to sweat. He moved his hands and fingers, which had been on top of her head to leverage his deep strokes down to her shapely hips. Then he slipped his hands under her, grabbing Zippy's soft behind and pressing her tight against him as she ground her hips in a circular dancing motion to get his aching, swollen penis even deeper into her. Finally, his lips again met hers, and they locked in a deep passionate kiss, making his penis even grow harder and longer.

And in the quiet, darkened night, with their own children's breathing beside them, Zippy relaxed even more and mellowed from her husband's love, before finishing with a strong, but stifled quiet orgasm so as not to wake anybody.

"Are you okay?" Southie whispered to her afterward as they lay in each others arms.

"Yes. I'm fine," his wife whispered back. "As long as you are here with me."

"I'll always be with you. I love you."

Zippy closed her eyes and fell into a deep, easy sleep. Before Southie fell into his own sleep, he thought about Zippy's love toward him. How it made him feel that everything was right with the world and that tomorrow promised a sunny day filled with golden opportunities and adventure.

CHAPTER 18

The next morning, Momma Docs made fried eggs, crisp bacon and buttery grits for breakfast along with strong coffee. It being her church day, she quickly cleared the table after the meal and ordered the children to get ready for school. As AJ and the younger children gathered their book bags in the hallway, he met up with Coree.

"Say, there's this park two blocks from my Pop's shop on Fourth Street. We gonna be chilling over there right after school. Maybe you can check us out."

Coree's eyes shined and she licked her full lips. "Maybe."

"Then I'll check you around the way, Shorty."

After the kids departed for school, Zippy looked in on the animals, and after deciding Buttercup and Mouser were comfortable, insisted on taking the caged Miss Red along to the garage for company. When they arrived, Calvin was waiting outside seated on a milk crate with a container of coffee and an egg sandwich.

"What's that you have there, sister?" he asked, pointing to the cage.

"Miss Red. Want to see her?"

Calvin peeked into the cage.

"You got a chicken in there?"

"Miss Red is my hen. Want to pet her?" said Zippy putting the cage down and getting her art supplies from the back of the station wagon.

"The closest I want to come to that bird is Sunday dinner."

Zippy set up her easel near the window in the small front office area facing the main street for more light, and Velroy vanished into the garage to start his work on the tranny. She clipped the picture of Velroy, AJ and

Momma Docs to the top of one of the plain white canvas boards she had packed for the trip and studied the picture for several minutes. Then she dabbed and mixed black and white oils on her small palette, along with several fleshy colors, and began painting with a hair thin brush. Meanwhile, Southie got to reading the *St. Louis Dispatch*, and Coree and Billy took seats next to each other on milk crates. After some time, three outlined figures began to emerge on Zippy's canvas against a hazy blue background as Calvin watched intently.

"That's a mighty fine talent you have there, sister. Where'd you learn to draw like that?"

"Been doing it since I was eight," said Zippy, using another fine brush to distribute a brownish hue on the portrait. "I started with a broken piece of pencil and paper when I was a little girl in Jamaica. After my sister would leave for work, and my chores were finished, I would steal time to practice, drawing for hours. I would do eyes and ears and mouths until they were perfect."

Zippy placed the brush down in a jar with other brushes, and shaded one of the figures, smearing a brownish hue with her little finger and a rag, before continuing her narrative.

"Then in high school I was walking in Times Square and I saw other artists doing portraits of tourists and I said to myself, 'I can do this.'"

"Did you make a lot of money at it?"

"Hit or miss. Sometimes I'd come home with two hundred dollars. Other times I'd be out all night without a penny to my name."

"Why didn't you work the tittie bars?" said Calvin. "A lot of sisters do that 'round here. Supplement their income dancing for them rich white men 'cross the river in St. Louie."

Zippy stopped painting a second and laughed.

"Why don't you kids go out and play," she said to Coree and Billy.

"Can we have a couple of dollars in case we get hungry?" asked Coree, and both children looked towards their father.

There's a hamburger shack and candy store just a few blocks from here," said Calvin.

Southie fished a few dollars from his pocket and gave them to Coree. "Share everything with your little brother," he said, "and watch out for each other."

After the kids left, Zippy continued.

"During the winter hours when things got slow I used to work the peep shows and strip clubs in Times Square. I used to dress proper so nobody would know I was a stripper. A lot of girls were like me. Some even studied to be doctors. Other girls, though, were common prostitutes taking johns into the back room. I never did that, but I did break one rule just once."

"What was that?" asked Calvin.

"Falling in love with a customer."

Calvin looked at Southie sideways.

"Don't look at me," said Southie, peering over the top of the newspaper. "I met her while she was doing portraits. Not at the strip clubs."

He heard Zippy's stories about her working in the sex industry time and again. Marrying a former stripper never bothered him. It even turned him on a little. Either way, a person has to do what a person has to do to make it through life, he thought.

"His name was Denny," said Zippy, continuing the conversation and resuming her painting at the same time. "He was this crazy Irishman — white, white, white like the snow — and he had a wad thick as a baseball bat, if you know what I mean."

Calvin laughed.

"Boy, how I became addicted to it, but Denny was insane jealous. The boy wouldn't let me out of his sight for five minutes. Wouldn't even let me pay the rent. One day after I came back from the store, he accused me of being all over the town. Can you believe it? I wasn't gone more than twenty minutes. He beat me bloody for going to the corner store and choked me till I passed out. When I came to and realized I wasn't dead, I knew it was over between us. At first, I figured I'd kill him to get away. Wait till after we got done screwing and he fell asleep. Then I'd get the biggest kitchen knife, plunge it into his back and twist it in him as hard as I could, but I was scared he'd wake up and kill me. Or that I'd kill him and then have to go to jail."

Zippy paused a few seconds, focusing on one of the eyes in the portrait and then continued.

"So I decided to escape to London, where I did portraits and danced the strip bars for six months. And it wasn't the easiest thing to do, because

I was addicted to his cock, but I prayed to God every day to give me the strength to get over him and I did. When I came back he was gone. Then I met Southie."

"I don't know about you, sister," said Calvin. "But most of the women round here take the white man's money, but when it comes to marrying, they stick with a brother."

"My husband may look white, but he's got black insides," said Zippy.

Southie felt complimented because he truly enjoyed and felt comfortable surrounded by people of his wife's race. After he married Zippy, in fact, he could have easily spent the rest of his life in the West Indian neighborhood of Brooklyn where they had first lived for nearly ten years before moving upstate. Here, even doing the shopping, or laundry along Flatbush Avenue was like a carnival. The smell of the fresh spicy patties and dense white bread coming from the Jamaican bakeries, the fruit stands where the playful West Indian women would haggle with the stern Korean shop owners. He always felt at ease walking among the barbershops, pizza parlors, and Spanish and Arab bodegas with the pulsating sounds of bass-heavy music thumping out of every nook, cranny and window in the neighborhood. And here, even in East St. Louis, among American blacks, he felt very relaxed and at home. Not that he wasn't vaguely aware that outside in the street, dangers lurked in the form of thuggish criminal elements such as illicit drugs, prostitution and gangs, but the other side was the very giving and caring hospitality of Velroy and his family to his own family. Unlike his tribal bond to fellow Jews, and most other whites, he had come to know, American blacks as a people seemed generally hospitable and compassionate to outsiders.

Velroy came into the office from the work area carrying a stripped transmission gear.

"Come on Southie, want to go for a ride to the junkyard for parts?" he asked Southie.

"Sure. Why not."

⌘ ⌘ ⌘

Coree felt the urge for a cigarette as she sat on the edge of a basketball court and watched Billy play in the playground next to it. She hated her parents for making her leave all her friends in Port Decker. They got on her nerves big time. Dad was corny as all hell with his stupid jokes, and mom was crazy, snapping from time to time at her for no reason and quick to slap or dig her nails into her. Now she was stuck with them for one big monotonous journey filled with endless empty miles.

She began to bite her nails, which were already nibbled down to the quick, and really wanted to put on the lipstick and makeup in her bag, but if her mom found out she'd flip. She didn't feel that pretty with it on to begin with, and positively ugly without it. Now, she looked up and saw some kids walking toward the park from down the street, and immediately picked out AJ. He was by far the finest boy she had ever seen; lanky, lean and dark, with smooth skin and short dreadlocks. And he had a really cool gait, a kind of slow dance walk with a certain bend of the knee and tilt of his strait, broad shoulders. This East St. Louis was really cool, she thought. They spoke slower than the people in Port Decker, yet knew all about the latest rap music.

"Hey Shorty," AJ said to Coree, when the gang arrived at the park. "This is the girl I told you about. Her name is Coree."

"So ya'll from New York City?" said one of the kids, who carried a basketball.

"Brooklyn," said Coree. "I lived there until I was nine and then we moved to upstate New York."

"Dag... Brooklyn. That's where Jay-Z is from. Did you know him back in the day?"

"No, but Biggie and KRS came from our neighborhood and we still have a lot of peeps there."

AJ nodded. "Brooklyn, yeah. Forget this East St. Louie bullshit. I'm East Coast all the way."

"Shit AJ, you just East St. Louis ghetto like all of us," said one of the other teenagers.

"Maybe, but me and Rasheem gonna be checking out of this crib cause nobody but ya'll gonna hear our sounds here. Gotta go to the watering hole – New York. Make a name for ourselves in the rap game."

"Yeah," Rasheem said, jumping in. "Me and AJ gonna go to New York to make cash, but we ain't never gonna forget our crew."

Everybody nodded their head and hit knuckles in agreement. Then the teenager with the ball took a shot at the basket, and Billy, who had come over from the playground area, rebounded the missed shot and passed it back to him.

"Anyone got a cigarette?" asked Coree.

One of the teenagers retrieved a pack from his rolled up socks and gave her one.

"I'm telling mom," said Billy, watching his sister light the cigarette.

"If you do, you're dead," said Coree.

"Come on little man," said one of the teenagers. "We'll strike a deal. You don't punk out ya sister and we'll let you play hoops with us?"

Billy smiled and passed the ball to the big kid.

⌘ ⌘ ⌘

When AJ, Coree and Billy arrived back at the garage, Zippy was applying thin coats of flesh-tone colors on Momma Docs' face.

"Hey everybody. My pops around?" AJ said.

"No, he's out with my husband," said Zippy, without looking up from her work.

AJ smiled and looked at the portrait Zippy was drawing. She used a steady hand, coloring around one of the eyes.

"That is really great, Ma'am," he said.

"Yes sir," said Calvin. "That sister got some real talent there."

"You met up with my daughter I see," said Zippy, wiping the brush with a rag and dabbing some white paint on it from the pallet.

"Me and Billy were in the playground and AJ happened along," said Coree.

"AJ is a rapper," said Billy.

Zippy stopped painting and looked at AJ from the corner of her eyes.

"Let's hear something," she said.

AJ smiled sheepishly, but Zippy insisted. "Come on, let's see what you got."

AJ began moving his body from his hips back and forth, while at the same time swinging his arms from his shoulders with his thumbs up.

Here's a story from my kin
And a life where I been
Moved 'round these ghetto blocks
Full of dangers and hard knocks
Ho's giving cootchie, Devils selling hootchies
It's hard to cope with all that dope
But I see a light in my dreams, full of schemes
And things of impossible means
Right there at my side

Lord oh God where have we been
To find us out on the road ah-gin
Back from the fields and through the reeds
I'm destined to seek to leave and believe
They say to do for thy self
Doing that since I been twelve
The rat race has outpaced any pie in the sky
Gimme the rainbow buy and by
Here's a story from my kin
And a life where I been

As AJ rapped everybody moved in their seats to his rhythm except for Coree, whose eyes remained transfixed on AJ.

"That was great," said Zippy after AJ finished. "I bet you have to beat the girls off with a stick."

"I do 'aight," said AJ, smiling.

"You better believe my Coree's fond of you."

"Mo-om," said Coree in protest.

"My daughter's grown some breasts, big as mountains, and now she wants to rub them against any young man she finds."

Everybody fell silent, save for Calvin, who snickered.

"Mother..." stammered Coree.

"You don't want me to get up from this portrait!"

Coree's eyes filled with tears and she ran out of the garage and onto the street just as Southie and Velroy pulled up in the tow truck.

"What is it?" Southie asked his daughter.

"It's mom. She's flipped out," said Coree, teary-eyed. "And she was making fun of me."

Southie felt his head swell with blood and he stormed into the office.

"What did you say to that child?" he demanded.

"Child? That's no child. She's a woman."

Southie looked around. Calvin smirked.

"Don't get me involved in this one," he said. "I ain't 'bout to get between no woman and her daughter, nor between no man and his wife."

Everybody laughed, leaving Southie to scratch his head and let it go.

Later, as AJ helped Velroy unhook the transmission with the sound of music playing on the radio behind them, he confronted his father.

"Hey pops," he said, carefully scraping off the old transmission seal with a razor knife. "Suppose I told you that I wanted to go to New York after I graduate high school."

Velroy stopped turning the wrench in his hand and looked at his son. "New York? What for?"

"To make it in rap music."

Velroy looked at AJ and thought a minute.

"You don't know what you want," he said, going back to work beneath the car. "You'd be better off going into the army like I did."

"I want to be a rap artist," protested AJ. "I want to go to New York and try to make it."

"A rap artist! Now that's a thought." Velroy laughed.

AJ looked away from his father. For months, he and Rasheem had been thinking about either going to Los Angeles or New York City. Meeting Coree and her family now was an omen and they both agreed it would be New York to seek fortune and fame.

"Look, pop, I have a talent. I know we can..."

"We?"

"Yeah, me and Rasheem."

"Look son. It's one thing to have a talent, but something else to make it a cash crop. Rasheem is a good friend, but you two together? New York is a mighty fast town."

"We can handle it, pop. I know we can."

Velroy came out from beneath the car and looked at his son. He was taller than himself, but leaner. He knew the boy would fill out eventually. It was only a question of when.

"Disconnect the exhaust," he said. "We have a transmission to fix."

CHAPTER 19

For the next few days, Zippy's portrait became the talk of all who passed through Velroy's garage. They commented how real Velroy, AJ and Momma Docs looked compared to the photo, and most thought it finished by the second day. Zippy, though, kept finding details from the photo that nobody else saw. The eyelashes of her subjects, and their teeth and mouth were detailed with color and fine lines. Subtle shadows were added to the creases of their clothes. The yellow colors and patterns in Momma Docs' floral dress seemed to jump off the canvas.

One night at dinner, as everybody was talking about the painting, Velroy commented how Zippy worked on it like a man.

"That's because I am a man. Feel my muscle," said Zippy, bending her arm to show a bicep to Velroy.

Velroy felt her muscle and as everybody laughed, Zippy noticed Coree making eye contact with AJ.

"Yes. I could have been a man – I even thought about being gay for awhile, but I made a choice not to be," she continued, and caught her daughter's eye. "People make choices. Like some women choose to spread their legs for anybody, because it feels good. They're called tramps. Other girls learn that there is power by not opening your legs so fast. That's why I always tell my daughter it's better to sell your body than just give it away like a common slut."

Momma Docs and Velroy raised their eyebrows, looking at each other.

"Stop it now, Zippy," said Southie. "Coree doesn't have to hear this lecture..."

"You mister, have to stop defending your precious daughter," said Zippy, turning toward her husband.

"And you ma'am have to give our teenager a little credit. Why are you so hard on her?"

"Hard? A hard life is when you are whipped regularly for no other reason than just being around like I was as a child. Coree has it easy. She is too brash. It isn't love she needs. It's parenting."

"Coree doesn't have to be a tramp or a prostitute. There's more than two choices. There's love."

As her parents quarreled about her in front of everybody, Coree began to shrink with embarrassment. It made her feel ugly. She felt like putting on makeup; so much makeup that she disappeared or perhaps became someone else in another family. Meanwhile, Billy retreated into a world of make believe, where he was an NBA basketball star and everybody looked up to him.

"Both of you calm down," said Momma Docs sternly, putting an end to the quarrel. "I won't allow this kind of talk at my dinner table."

"Yeah, come on, Southie, " said Velroy, getting up from the table and getting some beers out from the fridge. "Let's go by the river."

After Velroy and Southie left with the beer, the younger children were told to get ready for bed.

"Mind if I let Coree come up to my room to listen to rap music?" AJ asked Zippy.

"A handsome boy like you," said Zippy. "You need an older woman not some child like Coree."

"We're just going to listen to some rap music, that's all," said AJ.

"Yes, mother. AJ's going to show me his CD collection."

Zippy stared coldly at her daughter.

"It should be okay. We're all in this house together," said Momma Docs.

After AJ and Coree went upstairs, Billy lay down in his makeshift bed on the living room floor, where he read a kid's book about basketball legends until his eyes grew heavy and was soon fast asleep with dreams of one day playing for the New York Knicks. Meanwhile, Momma Docs and Zippy cleaned up the table and the kitchen together.

"How long you and Southie been together?" Momma Docs inquired.

"For 17 years."

"Seventeen years is a long time. You know your daughter is still only a child."

"Only a child?" said Zippy. "She is a child of age to bare a baby. And that's what's wrong with our people. We have too many children having children."

"Our people are coming up," said Momma Docs. "We have to learn to trust our children."

"Children don't know what they are doing. They do things that make them feel good without thinking. Where I grew up, a child that wouldn't listen was made to feel with the strap."

"There is God as well, Zipporah. You must always remember that. That things happen for a reason, and try as we might, it's all in God's hands."

Zippy nodded and grew quiet. She believed strongly in God, but also remained adamant that she would raise Coree as she saw fit. And she had dreams for Coree to become a doctor. Dreams that were slipping away due to Southie always meddling and spoiling her. Perhaps, it was more than mere spoiling, she thought, and wondered if perhaps he was attracted to her. If so, that was Coree, not Southie's fault. Look at the way her daughter dressed and always wore makeup. It would be enough to attract any man. That was Coree. Always seeking attention.

"Your daughter is very beautiful. She takes after you," said Momma Docs.

"I was much prettier than Coree when I was younger," said Zippy. "My sister would sometimes take me out on Sundays and everyone would comment about my pretty hair. Strangers would give me money or buy me ice cream."

Momma Docs laughed. "Lord have mercy. We were all young and pretty once. Time and God has its ways though, and there's a season for everything and everyone."

⌘ ⌘ ⌘

Southie followed Velroy outside, stopping to take Buttercup who was chained in the backyard, and they walked through the reeds and up the hill to the picnic table. The lights of St. Louis twinkled across the dark expanse of water. The archway to America's west lit up against the darkened sky like the rings of Saturn.

"That wife of mine just drives me nuts," said Southie, as the two popped open cans of beer. "I can count the times she has hugged Coree and told her she loved her."

"Maybe you're being too hard on your wife," said Velroy. "She's an artist."

"Zippy's a great painter, but so's Coree. She is really smart if she puts her mind to it, and you should hear her sing."

"Daddy's little girl," Velroy said, laughing.

Southie took a gulp of beer and looked upriver. The water bent north, leaving behind a hilly shoreline that case shadows from trees billowing in the breeze beneath a white-half moon pockmarked with blue-green craters.

"Yeah, those kids will drive you nuts with their computers and rap music," continued Velroy. "Me though, I'm old school. Better to learn a proper trade where a man can earn a decent living than to rely on boyhood dreams like making it in rap music."

"Zippy told me your son has some top notch talent as a rapper."

"Everybody's got talent, but it takes luck to make it in music."

"Maybe he's like Zippy with his art. Some people just have to express themselves."

Velroy took in Southie's words and the two men finished their beers, mostly in silence, with the lapping river making a soft clapping sound as its waves hit the wall of a levee.

CHAPTER 20

By mid-Friday the transmission was rebuilt and the portrait completed. As the Sabbath was coming on in the evening, Southie realized that meeting with his brethren and traveling would again be problematic. So he called the others in St. Louis and told everybody to be ready to journey first thing on Sunday morning. This was all fine by Momma Docs, who insisted that Southie, Zippy and their children stay an extra day for Saturday was Velroy's fiftieth birthday and they were having a barbeque to celebrate.

So on Friday night everyone returned to the house from the garage with the finished portrait, now in a classy second-hand frame bordered in wooden sculpturing. Velroy hung it proudly on a wall between the dining area and the kitchen where there was good light, and the smells of collard greens and chicken on the stove, and sweet potato pie in the oven, filled the house as Momma Docs prepared for the great event.

The next morning Southie and Velroy made a run to the liquor store, a shop not far from the garage. Outside, a few old drunks sat on the curb with several wearing pork pie hats, and inside the merchant filled liquor orders behind thick, bulletproof Plexiglas. When they returned around noon, family and friends had already began filling the house, and Southie and his family were introduced to cousins, nephews, nieces, aunts, uncles and friends. Some in the group were already on the levee setting up barbeques, and AJ, Rasheem and other teenagers began making their way through the backyard and thickets up to the levee to set up a sound system. It was a warm day with a clear blue sky, and slight breeze blowing downriver from the north.

Soon, every able-bodied person began carrying things up to the picnic
area. Some held marinated ribs for barbequing. Others big bowls of potato
salad. The older children were in charge of carrying up folding chairs and
tables, and the younger ones, plastic silverware and plates. In no time,
there were upwards of seventy-five people on the levee with the Mississippi
waters rippling below and an R. Kelly song spilling over the river and
drifting south with the breeze towards Memphis and New Orleans.

Step step

Side to side

Up and down

Dig it now

Separate

Bring it back

Now lemme see

You do the love slide

While the adults sat around eating, laughing and talking near the
barbeque and picnic table, kids of all ages gathered a little further up the
levee near the sound system – dancing and playing. Even Buttercup and
Miss Red, both tethered to a bushy shrub on top the levee, seemed to enjoy
themselves.

That is everybody but Zippy, who as always, had one eye out for her
children. And right off, she noticed Coree missing. Billy was there all right,
playing with some kids his own age near the music, but no Coree. She
eyeballed all around, from adults sitting around and eating, to the younger
ones dancing near the sound system. Still no Coree, and AJ was missing as
well. Southie seemed to be enjoying himself mingling with Velroy's family
and friends, and filling up with liquor and food, so she didn't mention her
observation to him. Instead, she sipped soda and waited.

After about an hour, as the sun began to set leaving an orange sky above
the St. Louis skyline, she spotted Coree and AJ coming up the levee from
the house through the thickets. Her daughter tucked in her blouse as she
walked and Zippy saw her face with fresh mascara and lipstick on. Coree,
though, didn't see her mother watching her. At first she went to where the

music was playing and started to blend in with the other kids, occasionally glancing toward her parents with a growing confidence she wasn't spotted missing.

Finally, she walked to the food table, but as she passed Zippy, her mother grabbed her by the arm and dug her nails into the flesh.

"Where were you?"

"Ouch mother! That hurts!"

"And where did you get that make up. Take it off, now."

With Zippy's free hand she lunged for Coree's handbag, but her daughter yanked away from her grasp. Zippy, in trying to hold her daughter's arm, left a giant scratch that immediately turned white for six inches along Coree's inside forearm.

"Ouch, mom! I didn't do anything!," cried Coree with a yelping sound.

All the adults turned around. Southie, seeing what was happening, put down his plate of food and drink, and jumped into action.

"What is going on here?" he yelled, getting between them.

"Your daughter is a slut, that's all."

"I am not," cried Coree, tears running down her face. The white scratch had turned deep red and now dripped with blood.

"Give me that pocketbook," Zippy said, lunging for the pocketbook and this time grabbing the strap.

"No, mom, no!" said Coree, holding the pocketbook tight.

"Zippy, what are you doing?" Southie said, grabbing the pocketbook and trying to separate his wife and daughter.

"Why must you defend your slut daughter?"

"She's not a slut," said Southie.

"Oh, we'll see about that." Zippy yanked the handbag with all her might, ripping it in half. Onto the ground spilled its' contents including makeup, cigarettes and condoms.

"My purse! My purse!" cried Coree, falling to her knees in a desperate attempt to collect her belongings. Zippy, though, with cat-like quickness, picked up a cigarette and condom that had fallen from the handbag, and nodded her head toward Southie like a detective who had just solved a case.

"Your slut daughter smokes cigarettes and I bet she knows how to fuck better than you and me combined."

Southie recoiled in disbelief. Could this be true? Could his innocent Coree have been doing all this under his eyes with his not knowing? As if on queue the music stopped and the entire party watched the drama unfold.

Coree, sobbing now, looked up at her father completely disheveled and embarrassed. "I'm sorry, daddy."

"Stop it. Stop this nonsense now!" demanded Momma Docs, rising from her chair like a queen.

Zippy and Southie stopped looking with anger at each other and turned to the elderly, heavy-set woman. Coree though, continued sobbing, failing to listen.

"All week long ya'll been fighten' like sleet and rain bringing the whole world down," said Momma Docs. "Can't you two see that you is special. I mean really special."

Southie and Zippy now looked at each other with quizzical looks.

"I couldn't figure it out at first," Momma Docs continued. " but then it all came together starting with you, Zipporah. You have a gift from God with your art and have made a beautiful family and gave Southie two beautiful children. And the way you love and care for them animals of yours."

"I hate those animals. Too, damn many of them," said Southie.

Momma Docs laughed. "And you Southie. You blinder than a Mississippi catfish who can't see the water for the mud. You can't even see your own blessings, let alone that God has picked you."

"Picked me for what?" asked Southie.

"You're the American Moses leading your Jewish brethren across America to the new Promised Land of Las Vegas."

Southie laughed. "That's a funny idea, but I'm hardly a Jewish leader. All those I travel with know more about Judaism in their little finger than I in my entire soul."

"Leaders are not born – they are chosen," said Momma Docs. "You must get your people to their new Promised Land. That is you - and your wife, Zipporah."

"Zippy?"

"Yes, just like Moses, you have a black wife."

"Are you sure?" asked Southie, "That Moses had a black wife?"

Momma Docs narrowed her eyes toward Southie. "One thing I know is my Old Testament. And it is written, after Moses fled Egypt he took a Kushite – a black woman." Momma Docs paused a second and looked at Zippy. "And her name was Zipporah."

Southie looked at Zippy, and thought about the biblical Moses being married to a black woman. Perhaps poor Moses had his miserable domestic moments as well.

"I believe in God and all," Southie said. "But it's funny how others see Jews. That we're the chosen people and all."

"Who said anything about Chosen People? Ya'll Jews not the chosen people. Least not in this country," said Momma Docs.

"Then who are the Chosen People?"

"Us black folk that's who. We came here as slaves just like them ancient Hebrews in Egypt. But we came at the same time as the white man so we was on the same footing as our masters in this so called New World. And we toiled for the white man. We learned more about the soil than he did because we were often knee deep in it. Still, they enslaved us, sold our children – broke up our families, lynched us, maimed us, and we cried out to God and he heard us and set us free. Still we suffered through years of Jim Crow, but we kept our faith and God heard us. Now we've gotten more educated and have moved up on the pecking order. The meek will inherit the earth. It is the black man who is the Chosen People of America. Praise God, the almighty."

To this several people shouted out, "Amen."

"Now you two stop the fighting, and Coree get up and wash your face," said Momma Docs. "I'll not have dark clouds blotting out my baby's fiftieth birthday celebration. And where's my grandson, AJ? Let's hear a rap.

AJ came forward with Rasheem, and the boys put a CD into the stereo that had syncopated rhythms and a catchy melody played on flute. Then AJ half sang, half rapped.

East St Louis rumblings
Coming from underneath
Everyday I redeem myself standing on this street
The ghetto now is hooked up with all these Internet wires
Preacher always talken 'bout consumption by a fire
Four billion grains and more
make a desert sand
Is the messiah God or is the messiah man

I did not create the time or place that I was born
Yet I enjoy the sunlight breaking at early dawn
I alone am responsible for decisions that I make
And if I travel to some strange land
It's there that I will wake
Why we live and die
I can hardly but understand
Is the messiah God or is the messiah man

"That's my baby," shouted Momma Docs hugging AJ as everybody clapped and laughed when they finished.

Soon, the entire party was back in flow, with people dancing, drinking, talking and eating. Velroy, who was sitting, at the picnic table with family, caught AJ and Rasheem sitting together nearby and overlooking the river. He excused himself, got up and walked over to the boys.

"That was a mighty good performance," he said. "Mighty good."

AJ turned around and looked at his father. It was the first time he ever acknowledged that he could rap.

"Thanks pop."

Velroy turned toward Rasheem. "AJ tells me that you and my son have plans to go to New York City after high school and pursue rap music?

"Yes sir,"

Velroy narrowed his eyebrows.

"New York. The Big Apple. Supposed to be a mighty fast town. You boys think you could go there and do old East St. Louie proud?"

The two boys nodded and Velroy's stern face eased to a smile.

"Well I guess there's a time for everything and for everything there's a time. You boys finish high school and give it a try for a few years. Just make sure ya'll take care of each other." Velroy hugged his son and shook Rasheem's hand.

⌘   ⌘   ⌘

Coree sat on the ground and waited until the party was in full steam again before getting up and making her way back to the house. Here, she looked in the bathroom mirror and saw a tear-stained face with mascara running down it. She washed off the makeup, and waited in the bathroom another twenty minutes, looking at herself in the mirror and watching the long scratch on her forearm form a thin scab. Finally, she made her way back to the party, and along the path through the thickets, again ran into AJ, who was returning to the house to retrieve pies.

"Hey, how ya' doing, Shorty?" he asked, softly.

"I want to go to New York City with you," she said, firmly.

"But I thought you was heading out west with your family."

"I made up my mind. I'm running away."

"But I'm not going until I finish high school in June."

"So I'll stay here. I'll find a job."

"That's not possible."

"But you said you love me and would have my back."

AJ looked at Coree.

"Listen, Shorty," he said, gentle as he could. "Your place is with your family, and me and Rasheem, we have a dream to follow."

⌘   ⌘   ⌘

The next morning, Southie's family woke while it was still dark and began to pack to leave. Momma Docs, too, rose early to make them something to eat, and Coree helped her clear the table.

"What's wrong child?" asked Momma Docs.

"My parents fight all the time and it's all my fault."

"Your parents both love you and only want what's best."

"I just feel so ugly and dirty," said Coree, a single tear running down her cheek. "And my mother. She hates me."

"You listen to me, child," said Momma Docs. "Your mother only wants what's best for you. What's more, God loves you no matter what you look like, because we're all created in his image. You're beautiful inside and out. There aren't any flaws."

Zippy came in and ordered her daughter to get the animals from the back yard and into the car.

"Take care of that family of yours," Momma Docs said to her. "I'll pray for ya'll."

"I will and thanks for everything," said Zippy, hugging the old woman, and slipping an envelope with a hundred dollar bill inside her apron pocket.

CHAPTER 21

Myrtle's cousin in St. Louis, as it turned out, was a reform Jew, and belonged to a thriving temple with an active membership. Rabbi Miriam was the spiritual leader, and her husband, Merv, was the congregation president. After hearing of the traveler's plight, they jumped into action, calling the city's orthodox and conservative leadership. This was no easy plight with the orthodox Jews, who took issue with the reform movement's female rabbi and open embrace of mixed marriages between Jews and non-Jews. But Rabbi Miriam, a slim, pretty woman in her forties, was persistent, and soon all the travelers had a place to stay until Southie caught up with them.

Aaron and his family found lodging with Tevye, who ran the kitchen at the St. Louis Chabad *Yeshiva*. Tevye and his wife, Sadie, had five young children, who mingled easily with Aaron and Faygie's brood, doubling and tripling up in bedrooms, the living room couch and the floor. The religious Rebbe stayed at the home of Rabbi Nocham Weiss, a recently widowed Talmudic scholar. Sarah and David found shelter with a family belonging to a conservative synagogue and Sol, Myrtle and Isaac all stayed with Myrtle's cousin.

The St. Louis Jewish community was also generous with funds. After hearing about what happened in Port Decker, they took up a collection for the travelers so they should have some money in case trouble came their way. A little more than fourteen-hundred dollars was raised and Isaac held the money among his belongings in trust. And by the time Southie and his family arrived across the river in St. Louis they were greeted in near celebrity style. Southie, though, came prepared to leave, until Sol quickly pulled him aside.

"What's the hurry," he said with a wink.

"We were only going to stop here for a few hours. Remember?" said Southie.

"But everybody wants to schmooze a little with you."

"It's been almost a week, Sol."

"That's because your car broke down," said Sol.

Southie was silent a few seconds.

"What? A little socializing is going to kill you? The people here even put together a going away brunch for us. Smoked fish, lox, bagels. The whole schmeer."

Southie scratched his head. "Okay, a quick schmooze."

So Southie and his family followed Isaac to a Jewish community center, where a huge buffet table was spread with food, juice and coffee. When they arrived, Isaac, Aaron's family, Sarah, David and the Rebbe greeted them as did members from each of the Jewish sects.

"It is such a pleasure to meet you both," said Rabbi Miriam after the blessings were made over the food and everybody was eating.

"And so nice to meet you," said Zippy, breaking into a smile. "I didn't know there were women rabbis."

Rabbi Miriam threw back her head with a laugh. "Like all humanity, Jews come in all shapes, sizes and genders."

"Here in St. Louis we have the oldest reform temple west of the Mississippi River," Merv explained, jumping into the conversation. "It was started by some of the original German Jews who came to America."

"Southie, have you ever told Zippy about reformed Judaism?" asked Rabbi Miriam.

"Not really."

"Well our brand of Jewry is progressive," she said. "We openly embrace the modern world including women's' rights, interfaith couples, feminists and people of color who wish to become Jewish into our congregation."

"The Rebbe here told me a lot about you, Shmuel," interrupted the orthodox Rabbi Weiss, calling him by his Hebrew name. "That you were a *Bar Mitzvah* boy."

"Yes. I was quite the scholar in Hebrew school until my parents split up," said Southie. "I even learned to read Hebrew - phonetically that is."

"Perhaps then you'd care to learn something about your religion with the Rebbe and me tonight. I was hoping that your family would be guests in my home for one night before you continue on your journey."

"Now please don't hog our friends here," protested Merv and he addressed Southie. "My wife has already prepared rooms for your family to stay at our house. We can keep your animals in our yard."

"Thanks, but we were planning on getting started right after lunch," said Southie.

"Oh come now. It's already past noon and Las Vegas will still be there a day later," said Rabbi Weiss. "Southie, perhaps you can come to my house this evening, and afterward the Rebbe, you, and me can study some Talmud together. Then I'll give you a ride back to Rabbi Miriam's house. What do you say?"

Southie looked at Zippy and her shrug left it up to him.

"One night. But we've really got to get a fresh start in the morning."

⌘ ⌘ ⌘

Rabbi Weiss' living room smelled of pine cleaner and included a small couch and chair set, complete with a coffee table filled with photos of Rabbi Weiss' dear departed wife, along with their children and grandchildren. A dining room table and several stacked bookcases took up the rest of the room. Southie thumbed through the book titles, finding most religious and more than half-written in Hebrew. However, he also spotted books on Jewish mobsters, entertainers and athletes as well as Isaac Bashevis Singer novels.

Rabbi Weiss took out a bottle of schnapps, and after the three men had a shot, he asked Southie what he knew about the Talmud.

"It's a group of books related to the bible," Southie answered, vaguely.

"It's the written account of oral discussions and biblical interpretations from the most learned rabbinic sages throughout our history pertaining to Jewish law, ethics and customs," said Rabbi Weiss.

"For instance, it debates questions concerning night and morning," chimed in the Rebbe.

"What does the question of night and day have to do with being a Jew or even religion for that matter?" asked Southie.

The two rabbis smiled at each other, and Rabbi Weiss took from the bookcase three identical books of the Talmud and spread them open on the dining room table. They were large books and the text was mainly written in Hebrew with English phrases mixed in. The design of the writing included a square patch of text in the center of each page, then several lines of larger text wrapped around the square, followed by an even larger text filling out the page. Southie was instructed to read aloud from the middle of the page out. His reading level was like that of a third grader as he stumbled through the Hebrew phonetically. After he read, the Rabbis translated.

"This passage has to do with the prayer affirming that there is only one God. Jewish law requires this prayer be said the first thing in the morning and the last thing at night," he said and looked up to see if Southie was following him.

"Okay, I'm with you so far," said Southie.

"But here the sages started arguing over what constitutes night and morning so the prayer can be said at the right time," continued the Rebbe. "A baker works during the night so perhaps his morning is another person's night, says one sage. Another points out that it was dark before God said, 'Let there be light,' meaning that night is mentioned in creation before morning. This, they decided, contributed to the reasoning of all Jewish holidays beginning at sundown.

"Then one of the sages broke down the night into three watches. During the first, a donkey brays. During the second, a dog howls, and in the final watch, a mother nurses her infant while speaking to her husband."

As the two rabbis proceeded rather quickly through the Talmud, Southie's thoughts became fixed on the three watches of the night. A donkey brays at dusk, he thought, perhaps in an instinctive ritual calling to hunker down for sleep. A dog howling, however, reminded him of the part of night when the bars are full and carnal desires come to the forefront. But the night ends when the wife speaks to the husband, and Southie recalled the many nights when he made love to Zippy as the gray dawn seeped through the sheer curtains, and the birds outside peeped.

Southie's mind was brought back to the Talmud when the two Rabbis began discussing how to pray when traveling. The sages agreed that stopping to pray somewhere off the road in ruins was not Godly, and secondly, as a practical matter, it is more possible to be waylaid in ruins off the road. Thus, it was determined that the prayers should be said on the open road, and in a short abridged fashion. The sages concurred this was a better means of praying than a full service as the road has inherent dangers in itself.

By the time, Southie was driven back to Rabbi Miriam's large ranch home, everybody was asleep, save for Merv, a prominent estate attorney, who was watching sports highlights on the large, flat screen TV in the den just off the kitchen.

"How was your little Talmud study," he said.

"It was interesting. I'm not much of a Jewish scholar, though."

"Talmud is interesting, but I've never considered them holy writings," said Merv. "To me, it's more about historical Jewish interpretations spread over several centuries and civilizations."

Merv walked to the kitchen, which had an island countertop with stools, and took down two glass tumblers and a bottle of whiskey from an overhead cabinet. "Care for a nightcap? I've some really rare scotch. A gift from one of my clients."

"Sure."

Merv poured two fingers of scotch, and offered up a toast to life. Southie found the alcohol strong, but very smooth with a clean finish.

"I've been thinking about that incident that set you people traveling to Los Vegas," said Merv. "The synagogue burning down and all. Believe me, these things would never happen in St. Louis."

"People do stupid things sometimes," said Southie.

"Well, I can assure you that if such a things happened here there would be hell to pay. My family in St. Louis goes all the way back to the 1860s, and helped establish the city's first reform temple. Everybody gets along. We even developed a fruitful relationship with American Muslims here."

"I'm not much into politics," said Southie. "I just react when things happen."

Merv smiled and rolled the scotch around in its tumbler. "How much do you know about the reform Judaism movement?"

"When I was a kid in Chicago, I had some cousins who were reform Jews. I remember the services were all in English and nobody wore yarmulkes. My father never liked them. Said it wasn't real Judaism. That's why he forced my brother and I to go to an orthodox Hebrew school after public school until our bar mitzvah. My family never kept kosher though, and my dad seldom went to synagogue himself."

Merv smiled and sipped his drink.

"Yeah, I remember those days when all the services were in English. But the reform movement has changed since then. My wife keeps a kosher home and insists that the congregation's children learn Hebrew, and she leads half the prayers in Hebrew. Most reform temples do this now."

"So reform Jews are becoming more religious?"

"Yes and no. It's more that America's changed and we have changed with it. The melting pot has melted down and that makes it a more comfortable environment to practice Judaism in a more traditional form. Embracing modern customs and practices is what we do. We are the Jewish representation to the modern world."

"I don't know how comfortable I am with assimilation," said Southie. "Jews who thought and acted most like Germans were among the first to go to the gas chambers in the Holocaust."

"The Holocaust is one of the reasons most reform temples now embrace the state of Israel. At one time, most didn't because we thought it took the moral imperative out of our religion. But since then, even reform Jews understand that Israel is necessary. But an Israel with liberal values reflecting the modern world and its global cultural diversity. Your family, Southie, would feel very welcome in a temple such as ours."

"Maybe."

"Well you think it over."

Southie nodded and Merv raised his glass for a final toast. "Well, here's to surviving," he said, and the two men clinked glasses.

After he turned in for the night, Southie tossed and turned until Zippy, ever the light sleeper, opened one eye and asked him what was the matter.

"Maybe you should convert to Judaism." It was a suggestion he had put to Zippy several times in their marriage.

Zippy turned and faced Southie from in the hideaway couch bed in which they slept. "I love you, Southie, and I love your people, but I believe in Jesus Christ as the son of God."

"Well I'm not exactly a good Jew."

"A good Jew? What's a good Jew? I always thought Jews were Jews."

"I don't know. A religious Jew. One who learns Talmud and embraces God and the study of the laws taken down by Moses. Or even a reform Jew – one who does not turn from their religion, but allows for a secular vision embracing the modern world."

"I don't know what a good Jews is, but I know if you pray to God – if you ask God for help, good things will happen," said Zippy, and then turned away from him. "Now, you can debate what it is to be a good Jew by yourself. We've got a long day tomorrow and I'm getting some sleep."

In the stillness of the night, Southie took his wife's advice and silently prayed in an abridged version as he was, after all, on the road. He started by asking God to watch over his family, and ended with his asking God for help in leading his brethren across America. Then he drifted into a sound sleep.

CHAPTER 22

The congregants departed early the next morning, and by the time the sun lifted into the eastern sky, the Missouri interstate smoothed out into a freshly paved six-lane highway. Green leafy trees replaced the Illinois farmlands, and the terrain turned hilly, its dark brown soil glistened with moisture.

From the middle seat of the station wagon, Coree felt the long scab that formed on her forearm. When she made a fist, the sharp crusty edges of the dried blood pinched her arm. Not that she minded the scratch or even what happened in East St. Louis. Maybe now, she thought, her father would stop lecturing her about being a good girl. Her mom was right about her father being a fool, and she deeply loved her, even if she was crazy. She recalled the times they cared for the animals together and went picking wild plants and flowers. Her mother also took her side when she got in fights with outsiders, no questions asked. This was unlike her father, who always had to hear the other person's story first. He would say he was there for her, but he never was really. Even the times when her mother beat her, burned her, tied her up and made her sleep on the cold kitchen floor. Her father would yell and scream about it, but then run out of the house and do nothing to stop it. Between her mother's craziness and her father's stupidness, it was to the point where she couldn't live with them anymore.

⌘ ⌘ ⌘

"Look at that," said Zippy pointing to a billboard reading, "Come in Thru Jesus..."

"Bible thumpers," replied Southie. "They're all over the place."

"Yeah, but look at that one," said Zippy, pointing to another reading, 'County's largest Triple X Peep Show - next exit.'

"These people can't seem to make up their mind," said Southie, smiling. "They are either religious fanatics or perverts."

"They're both. I remember working the peep shows in New York's diamond district. Our biggest customers were religious Jews, who used to come in with those curls and black hats, and then used to beat off. Used to pack the place at lunch. Men like Aaron."

Southie thought about Aaron, Faygie and their kids. "Nah, Aaron doesn't seem the type. Besides, religious Jews don't corner the market on beating off. You just see it more because of what they wear. Men of all stripes and cultures love to beat off. That's why porn is so big here. They allow it."

Between her parents' conversation and the billboards, Coree thought about losing her virginity. It happened after her mother beat her and threw her out of the house. She was fourteen at the time and decided to hang out with her friends for a few days until her mother calmed down. Then her father came along and spoiled it all. He started yelling at her on the street in front of everybody. Like it was her fault her mother was crazy! Then, when the shouting was over, she convinced him to let her spend one more night out anyway. That was the night she drank apple wine and lost her virginity on a basement couch to Carlos, the brother of a friend.

Coree spotted a billboard reading, "Trust in the Lord with all thine heart. In all ways acknowledge Him, and He shall direct thy paths" and she began to think about what Momma Docs said. That God loved her no matter what she did and the thought comforted her.

The billboards gave way to promoting tourist attractions like the hideout for famed train robber Jessie James and his gang. Then they advertised the Missouri Ozarks, with wide-mouth bass, wriggling and splashing outside the billboard frames. Nothing though compared to the billboards advertising the show town of Branson. Here some of the biggest names in country and western music were appearing. There was Dolly Parton, Kenny Rogers, Alan Jackson, George Strait and others.

As they passed, Zippy blasted a country station and sang to each song being played, adding in her own click sounds for more percussion. All in the car enjoyed Zippy's merriment, until Coree tapped her on the back to point out a billboard advertising Dolly Pardon, one of her mother's favorite artists. At this, Zippy turned around without missing a beat, and pointed right in Coree's face while singing:

Don't you tell me what to do
I'm your mother
Don't you tell me what to do
I'm your mother
If you tell me what to do
I'll give you a crack or two
Don't you tell me what to do
I'm your mother

While everybody else in the car laughed at Zippy's made-up song, Coree seethed. Although she was deathly afraid of her mother, she was now as tall as her and very strong for her age. Things were not getting better, and she felt like she would burst if she didn't let her anger out sooner or later.

Across the Oklahoma State line, the earth dried out, and small, thirsty looking trees sprouted up from the dusty brown topsoil. Shacks and trailers appeared sporadically along the Interstate, some with longhorn cattle grazing on the little vegetation around, while others housed horses in small corrals. They passed through the Cherokee Indian reservation along the Will Rogers Turnpike, and across the Arkansas River, whose banks were cracked with mud. They passed Tulsa, getting caught in a hot sticky afternoon rush hour, with the sun shimmering and glaring down, bouncing off the metal cars on the interstate. Meanwhile, the radio blasted country music with a slick DJ hawking used cars between songs.

"Ya'll come down to Frank's Motors for the best previously owned vehicles with low, low, low miles. Got no credit? Going through a sticky divorce? Not a problem, we'll get you financed. So bring the kiddies. Bring granny. We have free hot dogs. Free, free, free..."

On the other side of Oklahoma City, talk shows about the local high school football teams dominated the radio airwaves along with more evangelism and country music. The flat parched earth disappeared into shadows and the sun set behind grey clouds as the congregants pulled into an Econoline Motel about 90 miles from the Texas border. After everybody checked in and got settled, Southie took the family across the parking lot to check out the truck stop complex.

Inside the restaurant, big-bellied truckers wearing turquoise belts, Levis, cowboy hats and boots, feasted on greasy food and mugs of coffee. While Southie and Zippy browsed in the gift shop, Coree and Billy snuck away to check out the rest of the truck stop. They soon found a corridor leading to a laundry room, a small movie theater and a tiny chapel. Outside the chapel a group of a dozen young Christians took turns preaching about how Christ died for the sins of others. Billy had little interest for the subject, and tugged on his sister's sleeve to go to the movie theatre where 'Hellboy' was playing, but Coree told him to run ahead and she fastened her gaze on a charismatic young black evangelist.

"For only through Jesus can your sins be washed away. I know because I come from a horrible childhood filled with demons and destruction to build a personal relationship with God. A relationship that will never be broken," said the youth.

As he spoke, Coree remembered again what Momma Docs said about God loving her no matter what had happened in her life. Then the teens broke into a song that her mother used to sing around the house, and she sang along with it:

And he walks with me
And he talks with me
And he tells me I am the one
And the cross we bear
As we tarry there
None but him has known

"Have you accepted Christ as your lord and savior?" asked the young black man, approaching Coree after the singing stopped.

"I believe in God," she answered. "But..."

"I wouldn't be talking to her," said Zippy, coming down the corridor with Southie. "And where's your brother, Coree?"

Coree jumped backward in fright.

"He's watching the movie."

"You left him alone again?"

"No mother. My eye has been on the movie theater door the entire time." Coree, motioned to the movie theater.

"Go get him now," said Zippy, "And you – you wouldn't be talking to my daughter if you knew how many men she has slept with."

"Every saint has a past and every sinner has a future," replied the boy.

"Maybe, but this sinner better get her younger brother this instant."

Back in their motel room, Zippy demanded to know why Coree wasn't watching Billy.

"Come on Zippy, she said she had an eye on things," said Southie.

Zippy stared at Coree.

"Where did you get that makeup?" she demanded.

"It's just lip gloss. I bought it in the gift shop."

"God damn it, Zippy," shouted Southie. "If I didn't know you better, I'd think you were jealous of your own daughter?"

"Jealous! Do I have reason to be jealous?"

"That's ridiculous."

Zippy's eyes grew large as saucers, and she grabbed Coree and dug her finger nails into her ear lobe.

"Have you been sleeping with my man?"

"Ouch! Mom, you're hurting me."

"Stop it. Stop it," shrieked Billy, hoping his scream would stop the argument.

"Let go of her now," Southie demanded.

"Have you and Coree been fucking?"

"This is crazy talk," yelled Southie.

"Crazy talk. We'll see crazy talk," said Zippy, digging her nails harder into Coree's ear.

Southie lunged forward, caught his wife's hand and twisted it until she let go of their daughter's ear. Coree seized the opportunity and quickly bolted out the door.

"Coree," yelled Southie, letting go of Zippy's wrists, but now it was her turn to yank on his shirt.

"Stop chasing your daughter," she said.

"But she's our child."

"She takes dick. Believe me she can take care of herself."

⌘ ⌘ ⌘

Two hours after Coree left, Southie took Buttercup for a last walk on a patch of grass at the end of the Econoline Motel. He wanted to go to the truck stop as he felt sure Coree was there, but he didn't. After everyone went to bed, Southie could not fall asleep and at two in the morning, he got up to use the bathroom.

"I only wished you worried as much about your wife as you do about your daughter," said Zippy, forever the light sleeper.

At daybreak, Southie told Zippy he was going for coffee and searched high and low for Coree, but she was nowhere in sight. He reported this back to his wife, and by this time, the rest of the congregation was roused and preparing for a day of driving. Southie told them that Coree was missing and everybody fanned out to have one more look before calling the police.

Finally, Aaron came across a janitor mopping the floor outside the bathrooms who said he saw her.

"She left with the Christians last night just as my shift started," he said. "They belong to a Born Again Christian school just past Arapaho up Route 183."

CHAPTER 23

The entire caravan raced north along the two-lane highway as clouds floated low and westward in the dawn sky. After several miles they passed a Wal-Mart and a few subdivisions of small shanty ranch homes and then drove through Arapaho, a two-stoplight town with a gas station and general store.

A few miles later, Southie saw the landmark he was looking for: a huge metal cross reaching out into the sky. As they neared it, he could see one side of its three-sided beams gleaming, and floodlights aimed strategically from the base to light it up at night.

Just past the cross, the caravan turned onto the dirt road entrance to the Christian compound. It ran past a worn football field and weathered basketball court to a cluster of cabins. In the center of the cabins was a parking lot facing a large wooden tabernacle building. The congregation got out of their cars and examined the situation. A gust of wind kicked up the dust and it swirled around them.

"For this we left Port Decker?" Sol cried, throwing his hands in the air. "I must have been drunk, I tell you. May God throw a lightening bolt at my head like a fastball."

"Cork it, Solly," said Myrtle, poking at her husband while checking out the surroundings. "So what? We're in the middle of nowhere. There's a cross the size of Mt. Everest, and we're about to confront a bunch of Christian fanatics. What's the big deal?"

"Only two things I want to know about Jesus, Myrtle," said Sol "Where was his bar mitzvah and who catered the affair?"

"Enough," said the Rebbe, quieting down Sol and Myrtle. "They have Southie's daughter."

Southie felt a mixture of anger, sadness and resolve as he led the others, with Zippy, and little Billy at his side, up the steps of the tabernacle. From inside the tabernacle he heard the end of a song.

> Jesus loves the little children
> All the children of the world
> Whether black and white,
> They are precious in his sight
> Jesus loves the children of the world

Then he heard the preacher begin:

"It is only through Christ our lord that you can enter into the gates of heaven. For the lord gave us his only son, who died for our sins so that we can live in eternal light."

The preacher was in his twenties and a little overweight with a thin goatee. Behind the pulpit was a video screen flashing various pictures of Jesus, the cross and other religious symbols. Two huge speakers were hooked up on either side of the stage area.

"I see we have visitors," he said, upon seeing Southie lead the congregants through the back of the of the tabernacle. The young Christian congregation turned around from their wooden pews.

"You have my daughter," Southie shouted.

"Your daughter?" the preacher asked, surprised.

"Coree, where are you?" Southie bellowed.

"Here," came a voice from the first row of the prayer room. Coree stepped out from among the kids.

"Get your stuff. We're leaving," said Southie, moving toward his daughter with Zippy on his heals.

"I'm not going with you," Coree mumbled.

"What do you mean not coming..."

"I'm sick of you both," she said with a voice that surprised herself. "You keep treating me like some virgin queen. And mom, she's bugged out..."

"Bugged out!" Zippy shrieked and grabbed her daughter. "I'll show you bugged out. I brought you into this world, and I damn sure can take you out of it. Now come on. We're going!"

"No," Coree cried, and she pulled away from her mother's grasp. "Help me, Jesus! I've accepted you into my life! Help me now!"

Southie and Zippy surged forward, but several of the young Christians interceded.

"What is this?" came a voice from the podium. It wasn't the young preacher, but an older man of medium weight, with a salt and pepper goatee, receding hairline and glasses perched half way down his nose.

"They came for her, Reverend Watkins," said one of the Christian kids motioning at Coree. He was a white boy with sandy blonde hair. "She came with us yesterday from the Flying J Truck Stop. She's born again."

"No she's not. She's a Jew," said Southie.

"Not exactly," interrupted Sol. "Because her mother's not Jewish. You see if the mother..."

"Whatever," Southie said. "Either way, she's with us. That's our daughter."

"I'm staying here," said Coree, resolutely.

Zippy pursed her lips together and gnashed her teeth. "I said get in the car now," she whispered angrily.

"Okay, it appears we have a problem here," said Reverend Watkins, stroking the whiskers on his chin. "Maybe we should take the main parties and go somewhere a little more private. Perhaps my office."

"How about my daughter is underage and we call the police," said Southie.

"How about we talk in my office and if things don't get resolved, we'll call the police - who, by the way - are my God-fearing Christian friends."

Southie quickly mulled the offer over, figuring that police would probably complicate matters.

"OK," he said.

⌘ ⌘ ⌘

"Are you people familiar with the gospel?" the young preacher asked the congregation of Jews as they waited for Southie's family to resolve the issue. They were sitting on one long pew against the wall and surrounded by Born Again Christians.

"I know you're not talking to us," said Sol.

"Yes... Yes I am," said the preacher. "Have you been saved?"

"Saved?" said Sol, his voice raising. "Am I drowning?"

"Yes, my brother. You are drowning in your own sins, but becoming born again can wash them away."

"That's it," said Sol, getting up. "I mean I'm all behind Southie and getting his daughter back, but I'm not about to let some kid tell me about the messiah."

"Oh, Solly. Stop it. If the boy wants to believe that this Jesus fellow was the messiah, let him believe," said Myrtle, turning to the young preacher. "My husband. He's such a kidder."

"This is no joke. I am a fisher of men and it is only through Christ that we can enter the kingdom of heaven."

"Listen kid," said Sol, standing. "You ever hear of something called the Hebrew tribes? The Jews? You know, Moses and the people who wrote the bible? Well that's us. We're them."

"Yes, but you were cast out and are now returning to the Promised Land for the final days..."

"Cast out, shmast out," said Sol. "We been around for centuries. When the Egyptians built the pyramids, and when Caesar made his salad. We were there through the Ottomans, the Turks and all the Islamic empires. All that time we had Israel, lost Israel, had it again and lost it. Right Rebbe?"

"Well," said the Rebbe. "The Talmud says..."

"Exactly my point," interrupted Sol. "You think this messiah of yours cuts the cheese through the Torah and Talmud that we have studied and followed for thousands of years?"

Several of the younger Christians began to take notice of what Sol was saying.

"But Jesus was prophesized from the Old Testament. That he would be a descendent of King David..."

"Now how can that be?" questioned Sol. "I thought Jesus' father was God the almighty. An immaculate conception!"

"Yes, but his mother came from David's lineage."

"There you go," said Sol. "In the Jewish religion the lineage is determined by the father and not the mother. Therefore this Jesus fellow did not come from David's lineage as you say. Isn't that so Rebbe?"

"Well, the prophets say..." said the Rebbe.

"Exactly, the prophets say the messiah will be born a normal man and live a normal life. That he will arise from Israel and rebuild the temple in Jerusalem and gather the banished to Israel. Did Jesus Christ do any of that? No. Maybe he was a great leader of the poor and gave a sense of God to the pagan world. But the Messiah? He doesn't fit the criteria."

"No, it is you who are wrong," said the young preacher. "The only way to the kingdom of heaven is through the father, son and holy ghost..."

"There is no trilogy. There is but one God, the almighty and creator," said Sol.

The young preacher smiled. "The trinity is the wisdom of the father, the will of the son and the power of the Holy Ghost," he said.

"The expression of a trinity is a fundamental error, for wisdom is not an external element of chance in the creator," said Sol. "For God and God's wisdom are one. God and God's will are one and God's power is all one. Even if God were affected by external chance, the almighty would still not be three, but one. Isn't that right, Rebbe?"

"It's a funny thing you mention this because the Ramban said..."

"Forget it Rebbe. You said enough."

⌘   ⌘   ⌘

Rev. Watkins' office was outfitted with a living-room-type area several feet in front of his desk. He sat in an oak chair at the head of the living room set up and beckoned Southie, Zippy and Billy to sit on the couch, and Coree on a sofa chair across the coffee table from her parents. On the table was a bible, along with a worn copy of The Power of Positive Thinking and the latest Oprah magazine.

"Now. What is the problem here," said Rev. Watkins.

"This really is a family dispute, Reverend, so if you don't mind we'll be on our way," said Southie. "You have your things, Coree?"

"I'm not going."

"Get your stuff," said Southie, sternly.

"I can't live with you guys anymore," said Coree, resolutely. "I made up my mind,"

"Good," said Zippy, gnashing her teeth. "You've been trouble to me ever since you were in my belly."

"Zippy, please," said Southie, weakly.

"You stole all my make-up and now you've been trying to steal my man…"

"I never stole anything from you, Mother. And I don't want your fucken man!"

"Coree! Stop talking that way to your mother!"

"Okay," said the Reverend. "I see we have some issues here and…"

"There's no issue here, Reverend. My daughter is a tramp. That's all there is to it."

"Damn it, Zippy. Will you stop calling our daughter a tramp."

Zippy looked straight into the preacher's eyes.

"Reverend, I can't say for sure, but I suspect my husband and daughter are sleeping together."

"You're nuts Zippy," said Southie, standing and looking at the minister. "I swear she's off her rocker, Reverend. Tell them Coree. I've never touched you."

"Like I say, Reverend, I've never seen them together, but I highly suspect it."

"Mom's not nuts. She just a fucking bitch," said Coree, anger rising in her voice. "I hate you both! And Mother, why would I want your sorry-assed man - my father? This man who just stood by or ran away all the times you beat me and threw me out of the house."

"Reverend, please. Our daughter is a little troubled," said Southie, embarrassed.

"My only trouble is you two," shouted Coree. "I'm so sick of you both. In fact, Mother, I have a little song for you:"

I hate you
You Fucking bitch
Every time I see you
My nerves start to twitch
I'll soon be gone
Without a care or hitch
Cause I may not be a virgin
But at least I'm not a witch

Zippy got up and grabbed her daughter.

"Let go of me now," screamed Coree, and with a surge of strength pushed her mother away. Zippy fell off balance and back into the couch, knocking the Oprah magazine off the coffee table on her way down. Billy let out a shriek with fear and terror to stop the confrontation.

"Help me Reverend. Help me. I've accepted Christ into my life!" Coree screamed. "I can't stay with my parents anymore. I want to stay here."

"No, Coree. You don't know what you want," yelled Southie.

A loud knock came on the office door and everyone became quiet as the Reverend got up and answered. It was a young man from the assembly hall. He told the reverend that one of the Jews was beginning to make problems, and some of the other Christians were listening to him.

"All this bickering is not doing anybody any good," said Reverend Watkins, returning to the living room area and sitting back down in the oak chair. "Now you are Mr. And Mrs.?"

"Lewis. Mr. and Mrs. Lewis. I'm Southie and this is Zipporah. And these are our children, Coree and Billy."

"Yes, Mr. And Mrs. Lewis. May I tell you something about us? We are one of the oldest Christian schools around here. We are not a sect or some strange cult. We are associated with a network of churches in Tulsa, Stillwater and Oklahoma City. Our students typically go to one of the many Christian Colleges in the area like Oral Roberts and Texas Christian to name a couple. Many graduate in secular studies and go on to become lawyers, doctors and other professionals. We teach Christian doctrine, but we also teach secular studies, and pride ourselves in turning out fine young men and woman."

"I'm sure you have a really fine place here," said Southie. "But what's your point?"

"That if you two say it's okay, we will gladly accept your daughter to live here," said the reverend and then turned to Coree. "And young lady, we are Christian here, but do not accept your style of speech. We have rules and they must be followed."

"That's right you never followed the rules at home, Coree and now see how real life is," said Zippy.

"Zippy, what are you saying?" cried Southie.

"Some people leave home at twelve, others at sixteen and good girls go off to college," said Zippy. "It's time Coree makes her choice."

Southie smelled the shellac in the wood and noticed a modern looking painting of the crucifixion on the wall.

"I'll be okay, Daddy."

"Your daughter, Mr. Lewis is free to leave here at any time she wishes, and you and your wife are always welcome to visit," said Reverend Watkins, handing him a card. "Our address, phone number and e-mail are on this card. Feel free to contact your daughter or me any time of day or night. Perhaps she has some clothes?"

"Clothes. She's lucky to have the clothes on her back," said Zippy.

Despite her anger and decision to stay, tears now formed in Coree's eyes. She was glad to be leaving her parents, but never in her wildest imagination did she think it would come like this.

Southie embraced his daughter, but she quickly broke away from him.

"Can I get a hug, Mother?"

Zippy got up with tears running down her face. "Let's go," she said, grabbing Billy's hand.

Coree tried to hug her younger brother.

"Don't you touch him," said Zippy, pulling Billy away.

"Please, Mother," Coree pleaded.

Zippy faced her daughter.

"Don't ever call me mother again," she said. "For now on, if we ever speak, my name is Zipporah."

Although her mother's words hurt, Coree wouldn't let them stand. "Fine Zipporah," she said. "Then I hope I never speak to you ever again!"

CHAPTER 24

Southie, Zippy and Billy returned to the large meeting hall, and Southie told his fellow Jews that they were leaving.

"But where is you daughter?" Isaac said.

"She's staying here."

"You're leaving your daughter? What kind of craziness is this?" said Sol.

Southie gave Sol a hard look. "I said let's get in our cars."

Outside, the wind remained gusty, swirling dust around the congregants as they all got back in there cars, and drove out of the parking lot past the giant cross brazenly towering into the sky.

"Coree's not coming with us?" said Billy, sobbing from the middle seat. "I want my sister."

"Maybe she would have come if her father stopped chasing her like a dog on the loose," said Zippy.

"Our daughter is not a dog," said Southie, loudly. "Coree was a good child."

"A good child wouldn't have condoms in her purse."

"Maybe if you wouldn't have constantly berated her...."

"Berate her? I always told Coree she could be whoever she wanted to be. But you always got in the way lusting after your own daughter."

"I never lusted after Coree. Never!"

"Face it. Your daughter's a slut."

"Shut up! Just shut up for once," yelled Southie.

Zippy burst out in tears and sobs. "You turned our daughter into a slut. Ohhhhh! I should have never married you. You should have let me raise her, but you always got in the way. Every time I tried to discipline her you protected her. I wanted her to be a doctor. I had plans for her. She is my daughter and now I've lost her. She's a woman now. I can't help it Southie if she spread her legs..."

Billy let out a scream and also began sobbing. "Ohhhhh! I want my sister."

Southie could do nothing but keep driving with a heart heavy and emotions torn to shreds thinking how his daughter left.

The caravan sped back on the interstate and across the cracked and half-dry Red River into the town of Erick with the station wagon radio blaring an old Roger Miller song:

> *Trailer for sale or rent*
> *Room to let for fifty cents*
> *No phone no pool no pets*
> *I ain't got no cigarettes*
> *But four hours of pushing a broom*
> *Buys a four by twelve two-bit room*
> *I'm a man of means by no means*
> *King of the road*

They crossed the Oklahoma border into Texas, and the altitude began to rise with the flat plains growing into small, sandy mounds. Shrubs emerged between patches of dirt and tumbleweed blew sporadically across the landscape. Gullies appeared. Some were wide and deep. Others were slivers as if somebody sliced the earth open with a pocketknife.

As they climbed, the western sky blackened and stretched across the horizon from north to south. A flash of lightening blinked. Seconds later, a boom of thunder sounded, echoing across the plain in every direction. Off the road, Southie caught sight of a giant jackrabbit sprinting up a hill and disappearing into a hole. Low-flying black clouds now swept the dust all around the empty, dry land. A gust of wind made the rust bucket swerve on the interstate, and Southie clutched the wheel firmly and heard a honking sound.

He turned his head to see Isaac driving in the next lane over and frantically pointing to the southwestern sky. He followed his colleague's finger, seeing a funnel cloud race toward them. He stepped hard on the gas, thinking to outrace the wind, but quickly decided that wouldn't work. So he slowed to a crawl, thinking the funnel would race over the interstate before he got to it. But the funnel stalled in the sky, like a bull scratching the ground waiting to attack, and it turned into a twisting tornado from the sky to the ground, a mile wide. Quickly, he pulled to the shoulder of the interstate and everybody followed suit.

"Everybody out," he shouted, flying out of the station wagon with his family, and helping Zippy and Billy grab the animals. He led everybody down the elevated Interstate and into a ditch. Isaac and Sarah helped Aaron and Faygie with the kids. David helped Sol, Myrtle and the Rabbi. Meanwhile, the twister hesitated about two football fields away from them, kicking up dirt like a wild bronco. Then it reared back and raced across the plain toward them.

"Everybody down into that gully!" shouted Southie, with a hoarse voice, and he raced them over to the cut in the earth ten feet off the interstate. The congregants jumped down into it, bracing themselves against its south wall as wind and dust swirled all around them.

Southie ordered everybody to lie down flat, but he peeped over the gully wall as the tornado passed. Swirling around in its gust were pieces of houses and other debris, as well as two longhorn steers and several large plants and trees. Suddenly, he saw a giant cross swirling in the wind and he recognized it as the cross from the school where they left Coree. And then there was Coree herself, flying round and round in the twister.

"God, no. My daughter, Coree. Come back to me. God, please no!" he shouted only the storm was louder and nobody heard his cries.

The tornado hesitated again as if smiling and beckoning for Southie to watch. There Coree was, her arms and legs extended as if being torn in every direction, and she had a look of terror on her face.

"Help me daddy, help me!" she screamed

"Hold on, Coree, I'm coming." Southie cried, tears running down his face as he lunged up toward the funneling twister, but Zippy saw him and grabbed his legs.

"Somebody help me!" she shouted until Isaac, Aaron and David pitched in and the four of them grabbed Southie.

"Hang in there, Coree." yelled Southie.

"Daddy. I am scared and now I am gone. Gone with the world," Coree cried, and a giant gust swept her up into the funnel, and the tornado moved away into the northwestern sky.

Southie, sobbed and struggled to get loose, but the others held him down tightly until the tornado had passed safely out of sight.

"Are you sure you saw Coree?" Aaron asked Southie after the tornado passed and they let go of him.

"Yes. It was Coree. I'm sure of it."

"Why don't you call her and find out for sure."

Aaron handed him his cell phone and Southie dug the reverend's card out from his pocket before dialing with trembling fingers.

"Hello," he said. "Is this Reverend Watkins? This is Coree's father... Yes. Is everything okay there?"

"Everything is fine," said Reverend Watkins. "Your daughter has joined the choir and everybody is at practice."

"Are you sure there was no storm there? We just saw a tornado and..."

"Oh, yes. I heard about the storm on the radio, but it completely bypassed us. Do you want me to have someone get your daughter?"

"No. That's alright," Southie mumbled and hung up the phone.

"Is she all right?" Zippy asked.

"Yes. She's fine."

"You are too much in love with your own daughter. That's your problem. You lust after her more than you want me. Love me. I am your wife."

Southie ignored her and climbed out of the gully, dusting himself off. The congregation followed suit. Construction debris along with wire fencing, siding from a house and sign posts lay scattered on the prairie floor. Aaron coughed from the dust and then proclaimed it a miracle that not only was everybody safe, but their cars were intact.

"Are we ready to go, Southie?" he asked.

"Why are you asking me?" Southie replied, "Can't you people think for your selves? I'm sick and tired of all this. I want out. I can't lead you. I can't even lead my family!"

"Listen to me, Southie," said Zippy.

"Listen to you? You are not my wife. You are a stranger to me."

Everybody looked at Southie stunned. Tears formed again in Zippy's eyes. The dark clouds of the tornado had moved north and the sky overhead was again clear and blue as if nothing happened.

"That's it. I'm out of here. You all want to go to Las Vegas. Go ahead. Be my guests."

Southie walked back up to the edge of the interstate and began to cross it.

"Where are you going?" asked Zippy.

"Away," said Southie. "Take care of Billy."

He crossed the four-lane interstate and leaned against a guardrail, sticking his thumb out as a truck passed by.

"What do we do now?" said Isaac, scratching his head.

"Stay. Let me talk to him," said the Rebbe. Then he carefully crossed the interstate and took a seat on the guardrail next to Southie.

"So," he said, sticking out his chin and stroking his long gray beard. "Where are you running off to now?"

"You just don't understand," Southie blurted out. "I'm a simple man. I spent many years drifting and then God gave me a family. Now it's torn apart. My daughter is gone forever and to Christians no less..."

As Southie told his story, the Rebbe listened patiently, twisting strands from his beard and occasionally raising an eyebrow.

"To console you about your daughter would be impossible," he said at last. "Except that God does everything for a reason. Take me, for instance. One of the greatest blessings in all Jewish life is the blessing of children. Yet I never had any. My wife, what a great woman she was. Forty-three years we were together. Such a cook you've never seen, and the way she kept house. The best. But God never blessed us with children and then He took my Rachel. It's been twelve years now."

Southie straightened his shoulders.

"I'm sorry to hear that."

"Don't be," said the Rebbe. "God has a reason for everything. Perhaps mine is to be on this trip with you now."

A few trucks passed them, but Southie didn't try thumbing them down.

"Tell me, Rebbe. Do you believe I saw my daughter swirling around in that tornado?"

"Remember what I told you after the Sabbath in West Virginia? Miracles of magic happen all the time. Like the Golem that comes to Jews in times of need."

"But the tornado didn't even pass that Christian school where we left Coree."

The Rebbe glanced across the Interstate at the rest of the congregation.

"You know Southie, wise men don't live on mountaintops, and mystics, prophets and magic aren't only in fairy tales." The Rebbe knocked on the guardrail lightly with his knuckles, producing a hollow metallic sound. "Miracles and magic happens all around us. If you say you saw your daughter in that tornado, what's not to believe?"

Southie looked at the Rebbe from the corner of his eyes. He gave Southie a certain pride in his Jewish wisdom.

"Then there is my wife," Southie lamented. "We are two tormented souls, she and I. Her for her madness, and me for letting it all happen. What kind of life have I lived? I married out of my faith and now I lost my daughter."

"Yes, you're wife, she is a problem. I see that. It hurts me to see one of our own marry a black woman."

Southie's tongue felt the inside of his cheek, and his thoughts drifted back to Momma Docs and what she said about Moses' wife being black. The Rebbe was wise all right, but he was also prejudice, pure and simple.

"I see what you mean," he said, playing the conversation without expressing these thoughts.

"The commandments, you're familiar with them?" said the Rebbe. "Do you know what the first one was?"

Southie thought a second. "Honor and love God above all else," he said.

"Not exactly," said the Rebbe, smiling. "It's to use your *Seychel*, which is Yiddish for brains, because if you don't, it's difficult to love and honor God above all else. You'll know when it's time to leave your wife."

It was Southie's turn to knock the guardrail. A few more trucks passed them eastbound, but Southie didn't stick his thumb out. Traffic on the westbound side of the interstate began to get congested.

"So, Mr. Atlas – with the world on your shoulders. Where do we go from here?"

"We?" asked Southie.

"Yes… we. All of us. Should I tell the others to turn their cars around? You said you're taking us to Las Vegas – no? Is this some kind of short cut?"

Southie let out an exasperated breath. All he had were the clothes on his back and a few hundred dollars in his wallet. Also, as pissed off as he was at Zippy, he certainly couldn't leave her and Billy in the middle of nowhere.

"Nah, forget it," he said, getting up. "The way to Las Vegas is westward and that's the way we're heading."

⌘   ⌘   ⌘

Back on Interstate 40, the westbound traffic slowed to a crawl for about ten miles as the setting sun glared through the windshield glass. Finally, they came upon a Texas State trooper standing beside his flashing car at an overpass close to an exit leading to Route 70.

"I'm sorry folks," he said to Southie through sunglasses. "The tornado tore up the interstate down yonder. Got road crews working on it now, but it will most likely take the night to clear the road."

"Where do you suggest we go?" asked Southie.

"There's a Flying J Truck Stop at this exit. No motel though, but considering that twister, I reckon they'll welcome y'all with real Texas hospitality."

CHAPTER 25

Southie's mind drew blanks and he didn't say a word all the way back to the Flying J Truck Stop. Then, after arriving, he bolted from the car to the coffee shop, while Zippy and Billy cared for the animals. Inside the restaurant, he found a lone stool between a trucker and a salesman, and was doled out free coffee due to the tornado. Slowly, the numb mix of loss, anger and natural disaster began to wear off, and he began thinking about the two constants in his life – God and Zippy. While he sensed God's eternal presence would always be there with him, he suddenly wasn't that sure about Zippy. They traveled many miles together, both literally and spiritually, but what type of soul mate would spread falsehoods about him and Coree. His thoughts were interrupted by the woman herself as he spotted Zippy coming toward him.

"I made up your bed in the front seat," she said, softly.

"I'll be along," he said.

"Why don't you talk to me?"

"I have nothing to say."

"All our married life, I looked up to you because I wanted you to be a man. My man. But the way you left after the tornado shook me to my core. Now I love you, Southie, and I'm true to my marriage vows under God, but I won't spend my entire life brooding nor running. That's not me."

"Those accusations about me lusting after Coree. You know those aren't true?"

"All I know is Coree was an unruly and ungrateful child, but she makes friends easy. She'll be all right."

Southie stared into his wife's eyes. The whites now washed in red from crying and her dark brown pupils seeming to mask her soul.

"You do love Coree, don't you?" he asked

"Remember those dresses I made her? I stayed up all night sewing them on that broken down machine. And the times I played ring around the rosy with her on the front lawn. What do you think?"

"But I want to hear it."

"I will always love Coree. She's my child, too."

"If I had only been a better parent," whispered Southie.

Zippy took hold of his hand. "Come on. You look tired. Billy's in the car alone and we both need you now more than ever."

Southie gently pulled away from his wife. "You go ahead. I'm just going to stay here awhile longer. I'll be along soon."

After Zippy left, Southie motioned the waitress over for a coffee refill. She was in her early twenties and shapely. Streaks of bright red dye highlighted her dark hair, and she wore her waitress uniform tight with the top three buttons of her blouse undone.

"More coffee?" she said, coming toward him with a pot of coffee.

Southie shook the silver creamer holder. "You're out of cream."

The waitress topped off Southie's coffee, and then reached up over the counter behind her to get more cream, and in doing so her blouse lifted revealing a pierced bellybutton. Then she smiled at him while refilling the creamer, and his eyes followed her as she returned down the crowded counter pouring coffee refills. Then, she stopped in front of Sarah's son, David, of all people, and put her hand on his arm, laughing.

Southie gulped down the rest of his coffee, threw two dollars on the counter and went to the truckers' lounge and watched television. The news from Amarillo was on, and watching it made him realize how close they were to Las Vegas. He wondered what kind of work was out there, and considered maybe listening to Zippy, and going into business. Then after getting settled, perhaps send for Coree.

Fatigue finally began to overtake him, but as he was getting ready to turn in for the night, David stopped him near the gift shop outside the diner.

"I think she likes me," David said.

"Who?"

"The waitress."

"I noticed."

"Do you think she's pretty?"

"She's a looker alright."

"She's getting off work soon and wants to show me where she lives."

Southie looked in David's youthful eyes, wide with excitement.

"What's your mother say?"

"She doesn't know. I told her I was keeping you company, with your daughter being gone and all. Will you cover for me?"

"I'm not your mother."

"Please, Southie. My mom would have a seizure if she knew I was out with a girl and a non-Jew at that."

"Where does she live?"

"She said her cabin is near the Dixie Roadhouse – north on Route 70."

Southie looked at the clock above the gift shop cashier. "I won't say anything unless your mother asks. Just be careful, and be back in two hours."

⌘   ⌘   ⌘

David and Dawn, for that was the waitress's name, hopped in her 1988 blue Chevy pick-up and headed north on Route 70 toward Pampa. Indian beads hung from the rear view mirror and the cab smelled of lilac. Outside, the full moon illuminated the dirt prairie, casting a silvery white light on shadowed shrubbery and the occasional chugging oil well.

Along the way, Dawn filled David in about all kinds of details from her life. How she went to Panhandle High School where all anybody cared about was football, but her love was the drama department. How she had gotten the lead in *Cats* her senior year. Then she talked about how most of her friends either ran off to college, or worked in the cattle yards of Amarillo. Some had just run off period, and that's what she was fixin' to do as soon as she saved enough money from her crummy job and lousy boss.

"Ahma' fixin' to go to Hollywood... Be a big star jus' like Reese Witherspoon," she said. "Or maybe I'll go to Las Vegas like you."

"Why Las Vegas?" David questioned.

"Because it's a show town and gambler's paradise and ahma risk taker. Got some friends there, too. One deals blackjack, and the other's a stripper. We all went to high school together."

"Do they have tattoos and piercings like you?"

"Who?"

"Your friends in Las Vegas."

"Probably."

"Did it hurt when they did it to you?"

"No, not really." Dawn threw back her hair with her left hand, and lifted her blouse exposing her pierced navel. "Want to touch it?"

David recoiled a little and Dawn laughed. "Go ahead. Ain't gonna bite you none."

David gently touched her flat mid-section with his left hand, and then fingered the thin silver ring through her navel, and pulled it gently.

"Ooooh. Gentle now," Dawn moaned softly.

"Why did you get your belly pierced?" David asked, gently pulling the silver loop.

"Because it made me feel free. I go where the spirits move me. I cry with the rain and dance with the wind."

David removed his hand and sat up straight.

"Maybe I should call you Wind Dancer."

Dawn laughed.

"Wind Dancer. I lahke that."

The road flattened out and Dawn turned into the dusty parking lot of the Dixie Roadhouse. Country music spilled out of the tavern and several cowboys were hanging out near their pickups. They went through the lot and behind it, where a dirt road, shaped like a horseshoe, had about a dozen small cabins around it. Several of the cabins were dimly lit by stark light bulbs outside of them. A dog barked.

"Home sweet home," said Dawn, pulling up to the front of one of the cabins. Outside it was quiet except for the country music coming distantly from the roadhouse, and the chugging sound of an oil well drilling on the prairie. Then, a howling laugh echoed off in the distance behind the cabins.

"What was that?"

"Coyotes, but they ain't gonna botha' ya none," said Dawn. "Look out for them scorpions, though. They've been plentiful this year. Always are when there's a drah spell."

"Scorpions?"

"Especially the red ones. Ain't as bad as rattlers, but they pack a ra'ght powerful sting."

Dawn flipped the switch to her cabin and a soft light with a red hue illuminated the room. They moved past the kitchen area with its small stove, sink, and refrigerator and counter space before coming into the sleeping quarters. Colorful dream catchers, and other macramé's and beads lined the walls, as did a framed picture of an Indian village with teepees all around. A computer and CD player took up most of the space on a small desk. As for a bed, it was a futon, which now was made up as a couch.

"Make yourself at home," she said, taking clean glasses from the dish drainer. "Wanta' drink?"

David picked up a bottle of Jack Daniels near the sink and saw the kosher seal on it. "Sure, why not."

"Ice?"

"No, I drink my whisky straight," he said, trying to act older and more experienced than he was.

"Suit yourself."

Dawn put some ice in her glass and took a sip. David threw down the whiskey in a gulp. It felt like a roar of fire traveling down his throat to his stomach and he made a face.

Dawn laughed, put a few ice cubes in his glass and poured him another.

"You don't have to drink it all in one gulp. Sip it."

She put on a CD and led David to the futon and sat him down as the music played.

Everybody's going out and having fun
I'm just a fool for staying home and having none
I can't get over how she set me free
Ohhhh lonesome me

A pipe lay on the coffee table next to the futon and she picked it up, lit it and passed it to David.

"What's this?"

"Texas tea," Dawn laughed. "Whacky ta'backy."

The whiskey settled in David's stomach and warmed him. After several puffs of the herb, he felt even more light-headed and numb. The lighting grew even softer, casting pleasant shadows around the room. Meanwhile, Dawn lit some incense and sprayed herself with fruit smelling body mist. David got up and touched the mouse of the computer and the screensaver lit up showing the Hollywood Hills.

"I see you like your computer," he said.

Dawn got off the futon and followed David to the computer, near the window.

"It's slower than sin, but keeps me connected and off this big old prairie."

Dawn spread the curtain from the window and moonlight drifted in upon her fair face and freckles. As she walked to the window, she brushed against David and he took in her sweet fragrance.

"Tell me something, David, what do Jews believe in?"

David laughed and the sound of his laughter surprised him, making him laugh more.

"We believe in one God as the creator of the universe. God created everything and made a world where anything is possible. For instance, God was smiling on me tonight in meeting you."

Dawn turned and faced him.

"I swear by Jesus, your mouth is sweet as honey."

"And your hair. It's so beautiful and thick."

Dawn took David's hand and ran it through her hair. Then she caressed his finger and put one of them in her mouth, sucking it gently. She then guided his hand up her blouse and David felt her soft breast and hardened nipple. He kissed her parted lips and felt her tongue probe the roof of his mouth.

"Tell me, David, are Jews allowed to make love to girls like me?" she whispered into his ear.

"Well I…"

She walked him to the futon and David felt her tongue in his ear and then he felt her hot breath.

"Take me. Fuck me. I'm all yours," she whispered.

⌘ ⌘ ⌘

Southie woke to the sound of Buttercup barking and he looked up to see a panic-stricken Sarah outside the rust bucket.

"Do you know where my David is? He was supposed to be keeping you company inside the truck stop."

Southie got out of the car and calmed down the frantic woman as best as he could.

"David's all right. He'll be home soon. I'm sure of it."

"Home soon?" she shrieked.

"Shhh you'll wake everybody up," Southie said, and sure enough Zippy was up and out of the car in a jump.

"What is it?" she asked.

"David is missing and Southie knows where he is," Sarah said. "Go get him."

"Okay, okay… I'll go get him," Southie said, turning toward Zippy. "Don't worry I'll be back soon."

With that Southie went over to Isaac's car and tapped on the window.

"Mind if we take a ride?"

Isaac pulled away the blanket under which he was sleeping and unlocked the passenger side door.

"Where to?" he asked after Southie slid into the front seat.

"We've got to go get David - Sarah's son."

"You know where he is?"

"He's on a date with the waitress from the coffee shop."

"You mean the one with the pierced bellybutton?"

"You bet."

"I should be so lucky," said Isaac, starting the car.

CHAPTER 26

Southie and Isaac entered the smoky Dixie Roadhouse to several dozen cowboys and cowgirls whooping and hollering to George Strait's, *All My Exes' Live In Texas,* blaring from the CD player. They squeezed up to the bar and Southie ordered a few Lone Star Beers. The floor was lined with peanut shells and sawdust, and the bar smelled like it was stained in whiskey.

"Okay. What's the plan?" Isaac asked.

Southie led Isaac to the back of the roadhouse where two cowboys were shooting pool and a few more were on a bench or leaning, with one cowboy boot against the lower half of the wall, which was painted black. Then he walked over to a chalkboard, also on the wall, which had several first names on it. Standing next to the chalkboard with a beer in his hand was the only other man in the bar not wearing a cowboy hat. He had a ruddy face, red hair, green eyes and a body thick and solid as concrete. He wore a soiled T-shirt, greasy jeans and construction boots.

"This the sign-up list to play?" Southie said

"Yup," said the main nodding his head.

"Thanks." Southie took a piece of chalk, which was attached to a string and the chalkboard, and wrote his name at the bottom of the list.

"Ain't my business none, but you fellers are strangers to these parts," the man said to Southie and Isaac.

"We're looking for a friend of ours. Actually a boy. He ran off with the waitress from the truck stop on the interstate."

"Doesn't sound like a boy if he run off with a waitress," the man said. "Just an observation, I mean."

"His mother is worried sick and we were sent to get him."

"Jacob... Jacob Farlen is my name, but everybody 'round these parts call me Cain 'cause of all the hell I raise," and he held his hand up for a slap of flesh. When Southie returned it, Cain caught his hand with a calloused grip before letting it back go. "Sounds as if you fellers could use a little help," he said.

"Be much obliged," said Southie.

Cain took a gulp from his Lone Star beer, walked over to the pool table and raised his voice just loud enough over the music so that those gathered around the pool table could hear.

"Any ya'll knows the waitress over at the Flying J?"

"Ya'll mean Dawn," said one cowboy sitting on the bench. He was tall and strong, but staggeringly drunk. "We're childhood friends. Lives just yonder in the cabins. Why something happen to her?"

"Nah, she's fine, just my friends here are looking for some friend of hers."

Cain came back to Southie and Isaac and told them to drink up slowly, and when the drunken cowboy got up to use the bathroom, they slipped out the door. He then led them through the parking lot and to the horseshoe-shaped dirt road. They walked quietly listening to the sounds coming from the cabins. Some were dark and quiet, others louder with sounds of radio, laughter and conversation spilling into the night. Suddenly, David's voice filtered through one of the open cabin windows.

"One in the morning! I must have fallen asleep. Where're my pants?"

"On the chair by the desk. I'll get ready to drive you back," said Dawn.

"That you David?" said Southie, knocking on the door.

"Southie?"

"Yeah."

David and Dawn quickly threw on clothes and came to the door. When it opened Southie saw a sheepish grin across David's face.

"Your mom is worried sick," said Southie.

"I'm getting ready to drive David back to the truck stop now," said Dawn.

"It's alright, Dawn. You have to work tomorrow and my friends can take me back," said David, suddenly thinking about the trouble he'd be in with his mother.

Dawn's sky blue eyes grew large. She threw her arms around him and gave him a passionate kiss.

"Then good-bye my special Jewish friend. Maybe I'll see you one day in Vegas."

She opened the screen door to her cabin and saw in the porch lights, three drunken cowboys walking toward them from the roadhouse.

"Hey Dawn... It's me, Clarence. Everything alright?"

Dawn threw her hands halfway up in the air and exhaled. "Ye-ah, 'Ahma alright."

Clarence and the men approached until they stood under the same naked light bulb in front of Dawn's cabin. Both men were smaller than Clarence with stubby beards and cowboy hats.

"I thought you boys came to shoot pool," said Clarence stepping into Southie's shadow. "But 'stead you come round her' messen with Dawn.

"What in tarnation?" interjected Cain, stepping between the two men. "Sounds if'n ya'll boys been jumping to conclusions."

"This is all a misunderstanding," said Southie.

"You stay out of this, Cain," said one of the cowboys – a wiry man.

"Shat up, Morgan," said Cain. "You got yar fat head so far up a longhorn's ass the shit is flying out your mouth."

Morgan stammered a second trying to think of a verbal comeback, but nothing came to mind. Instead he rolled his fingers into a fist and let fly a powerful roundhouse. Cain, Southie and Isaac could see the punch coming from the interstate and ducked, but the knuckle sandwich caught David clean in the eye, and he fell backward, landing in some flowers that Dawn had planted in a pot.

"Stop it! Stop it!" Dawn shrieked. "You fellers are crazy and stupid in one big old bag. I swear."

"You sure you're okay, Dawn?" Clarence asked.

"Couldn't be rah-ter. These guys are my friends, Clarence. Get that through your concrete skull. Do I hafta' spell it out any clearer? F-R-I-E-N-D-S."

Dawn helped David get up. A red swelling was already forming beneath his eye.

"Ya'll all raht, baby?"

"Looks like you're going to have some shiner, bud," Morgan said, a boyish smile crossing his face.

"Shat up, Morgan," said Dawn. "You just clocked my friend and I'd say ya'll owe him a whopper of an apology."

The three men apologized with a snicker and then Dawn went back in her cabin, returning seconds later with some ice in a washcloth.

"Dag gan it! It's cowboys like ya'll that makes me wanna beeline out of this panhandle here. I swear to Jesus Almighty, I do," she said putting the ice over David's eye.

"It okay, Wind Dancer. I'll be alright," said David.

"What's that he's calling you Dawn – Wind Dancer?"

"Shat up Clarence. If David wants to call me Wind Dancer, let 'em call me Wind Dancer. I think it's sweet."

"If you think so…. ah Wind Dancer," said Clarence, and the three cowboys broke into guffaws, which carried into the night as they made their way back toward the Dixie Roadhouse.

David assured Dawn again that he was all right and after a final hug and kiss, Southie, Isaac, Cain and David headed back toward the Dixie Roadhouse.

"Think you can spare me a lift back to the Flying J?" asked Cain, when they had reached Isaac's car. "Fact is I just got off a roustabout gig some two miles from here and I'm looking to get back to the Interstate. My bedroll's behind the bar."

Isaac and Southie caught each other's eyes with a nod. "Not a problem," Isaac said. "If you can squeeze into my escort."

The four men loaded themselves into the Ford and started back.

"Well, how was she," Cain said, poking David in the ribs as soon as they hit the two-lane.

"Who are you?" David responded, holding the washcloth full of ice over his eye.

"Jacob Farlen, but folks 'round these parts call me Cain 'cause of all the hell I raise."

Southie, who was riding shotgun, looked in the back seat and nodded at David.

"So how was she?" Cain asked again.

"Who?" David said.

"Wind Dancer, that's who. Fine looking piece of woman, if you ask me."

David looked at Southie, who shrugged and David considered his adventure. Though his eye still throbbed, the whiskey and Texas tea lingered, as did the lilac smell of Wind Dancer and her cabin.

"Women are God's greatest creatures," he said, and the car exploded into laughter.

"You're a man now," Cain said.

"No, I was a man when I was bar mitzvah. Every Jew becomes a man then."

"Maybe so," said Cain. "But if you ask me, there's only two kinds of people in this world - virgins and non-virgins. Innocent or guilty as charged."

They arrived back at the truck stop parking lot, and Sarah, Zippy, Aaron and Faygie were out of their cars waiting for them. When David got out of the car with an ice-filled rag over his eye, Sarah let out a powerful shriek.

"Oh my God! What happened?"

"It's nothing Momma, really," said David, lifting the rag to reveal a puffed up welt surrounding his eye.

"Oy vey! Hold me. I'm going to faint," she said, falling back into Isaac's arms.

"Chill out there a little, Momma. It's only a black eye," said Cain. "If you ain't never had a shiner or two in life, I reckon you ain't really lived."

Sarah straightened herself up.

"What is this? Who is this goy? Southie?"

"The names Jacob Farlen, but folks 'round here just call me Cain 'cause of all the hell I raise," said Cain.

Sara's eyes narrowed into slits and stared like a laser down at Southie. "What happened? I demand to know what happened," she said.

"Let's just say, your son tripped on a wind dancer," Cain snickered, and poked Southie and Isaac, who both held back smiles.

"Wind Dancer? What is this? I won't take lying, especially from a *goy*. Southie, what happened?"

Southie squared his shoulders and looked at David.

"You going to tell your mother or should I?"

"It was a girl, Momma," David blurted out. "The waitress. I went home with the waitress."

"The waitress!" Sarah shrieked and grabbed her son's head, ignoring the throb in his eye. "Did she hurt you? Oh, God in heaven!"

"No Momma. It's okay, really," said David, pulling gently away from his mother's grasp.

"Trust me, your son couldn't have been in finer hands - or should I say arms," said Cain, bursting into rip-roaring laughter.

At this point, Sarah became so excited that Cain stopped laughing long enough to see his welcome wearing thin. So he grabbed his bedroll from Isaac's car and vanished into the truck stop.

"It's all your fault, Southie," Sarah said after he left. "You have been a curse to us all. We should have never come with you."

Southie couldn't meet Sarah's eyes. Behind her a breeze came off the panhandle floor, kicking up dirt and he saw it blowing across the parking lot.

"Now don't be talking trash about my husband," said Zippy, jumping into the conversation. "Unless you can explain how my husband made your David go with that girl."

"He's a bad influence. That's how. He sees how Southie flaunts his own lack of religion in everybody's face like it's the thing to do."

"Well you did it too, didn't you...Mrs. O'Reily? What happened? You couldn't hold on to your man?"

Sarah's mouth opened and she took a few seconds to gather her thoughts.

"I've made my mistakes," she said, softly. "But I've learned from them. Now look at your family. Branches without roots. Scattering in the wind. Look at your daughter. Where is she now? With strangers and Christians no less."

"I'm a Christian," said Zippy. "And as for my daughter, I was there when she was born. I carried her in my womb. She is my blood and a strong black woman."

Zippy paused and glanced at her husband. "Right, Southie?"

Southie was speechless. The thought of losing Coree broke his heart every time it entered his mind.

Sarah lifted her chin and took her son by the sleeve. "We'll be ready to leave at daybreak," she said.

After everybody went back to their cars, Southie and Zippy stood and faced each other in silence.

"Well, you can stand here and brood over your daughter all night, but I have another child asleep in the car to take care of," said Zippy.

She walked off to the station wagon, leaving Southie alone in the parking lot, listening to the murmurs of truck generators, oil drills chugging, and the distant interstate whistling.

CHAPTER 27

At dawn, Southie woke in the front seat of the station wagon, and took Buttercup for a walk, maneuvering her on a short leash between sixteen-wheeler trucks, cars and recreational vehicles. They walked through the parking lot, across the two-lane, and once there, Southie let Buttercup's leash out so she could run into the open Texas prairie. However, the dog had hardly gone ten feet when she began growling and barking at a figure lying down where the sandy earth dipped a few feet below the roadway grade.

"Take it easy. It's only me," said a man, quickly sitting up from a sleeping bag in the grayness of dawn.

"Cain? What are you doing here?"

"Camping."

Cain got up stretching his thick, strong frame. Then he put his construction boots on and began rolling up his sleeping gear.

"Think I'll get to the truck stop and have a coffee before I get going," he said, attaching his bedroll to the bottom of a small rucksack with elastic chords.

They began walking together toward the truck stop.

"That was quite a barnstormer last night," said Cain with a guffaw. "That boy's momma was mighty pissed at you."

"Yeah," said Southie, grimacing at the memory of his confrontation with Sarah. Then he took notice of Cain's dirty jeans, beat-up old Levi's jacket and stubble of a red beard.

"What kind of work you do anyway?"

"Mostly roustabout'n. Setten' up speculative oil fields from here to the Gulf of Mexico, but I'll do anything when things get slow."

"You don't have a car?"

"I travel light if you know what I mean." Cain cracked the bones in his neck. "Then again, a car could come in handy now and again. Say, you folks wouldn't be heading west would you? Cause I got some friends outside Santa Fe lining me up with hotel work for the ski season."

Southie pulled Buttercup's leash in tight. Cain didn't seem totally trustworthy. Then again he did help with David, and that counted for something.

"I'll take you as far as the Santa Fe turnoff, but that's where we part ways. Understood?" he said.

"Understood, boss. Understood."

They arrived back at the car, where Zippy repacked the bed supplies, and her and Billy took care of Mouser and Miss Red. Southie took his wife aside and quickly explained they would take Cain as far as Santa Fe.

"Morning misses," Cain said to Zippy.

"Come on, Cain," said Southie, handing the leash to Zippy. "You come with me. I'm getting some coffee and hot chocolate for the family in the truck stop."

As the two men walked away, Zippy played in her head for the hundredth time Coree's leaving. The girl was an ingrate, she told herself. After all she had done for her and trying to teach her right from wrong. Still, as she repacked the car with Billy's help, tears formed in her eyes. Port Decker now seemed a lifetime ago and this wandering across America made her feel like a bird without a nest, flying from tree to tree, emitting more of a cry than a song; a cry for a lost child and no home to go to on the horizon.

"It's okay, Mom," said Billy, seeing his mother saddened. "I'll always be here for you."

Zippy looked at Billy. He was a skinny boy, lighter in skin tone than Coree, favoring his father. She now grabbed him and put him in a light, loving headlock.

"You're my superman," she said, kissing the coarse, tight hair on the top of his head. "You will listen to your mother. You're my champion."

Billy smiled and grabbed his mother around the waist. "Always. Mom."

When the men returned and the caravan was ready to leave for the day, Zippy insisted she sit in back with Billy, and let Cain ride shotgun. This way she could keep an eye on the stranger and a distance from her husband, who also seemed a stranger to her now.

"Sure is good to be heading west again," said Cain, as they hit the open road.

"And where's home to you?" Southie asked.

Cain smiled, "Texas sometimes. A little bit New Mexico and Utah always."

"Utah?"

"Yeah, from a little town in the mountains called Ephraim. That's where my kin is. I'm a Mormon. Proud descendent of Joseph Smith. Our people got persecuted across America until we founded the Great Salt Lake – the American Jerusalem.

"If you don't mind me saying you don't seem the religious type to me."

"Call me the prodigal son. I come from a family of sixteen and always went my own way. See, we Mormons are required to go out preaching for two years right after high school. I kind of went out and never came back. That was some twelve years ago"

"So you believe in God, then?"

"I believe in God, alright, but most times I don't really think about him," said Cain. "Some of my best adventures come that way – lovers, bar room brawls, good times. Ain't none of that would ever happen if I was all righteous and holy."

The barren earthy landscape began to give way to shacks. North across the plain, Southie saw the Santa Fe Railroad chugging parallel to the interstate, and also heading west. Billboards advertising places to visit in Amarillo began appearing off the interstate. Several baited travelers to take the Texas challenge at a steakhouse, where anybody who could eat an entire 72-ounce steak would get it for free. The railroad train now came closer to the interstate and Southie could make out cattle and lumber cars. They drove past subdivisions of housing made of gray stucco and wood, and then stockyards filled with cattle on their way to slaughterhouses, supermarkets and butcher shops across America.

Shortly, the interstate narrowed to four lanes and moved right through the center of flat Amarillo as if it were Main Street. It was now noon and as the sun baked the city, the radio blared:

> She's the diamond of the desert
> Golden flower of spring
> The yellow rose of Texas
> Can make a man a king

On the other side of the cow town, America's west opened her wide thirsty mouth, with a flat dusty horizon visible in all directions. Las Vegas now seemed in reach and Southie's stomach fluttered with anticipation. Perhaps he could smooth things out with Zippy, and again he thought about Coree. Perhaps, once they got settled he could settle this big family mess, and they could all be together again. The more he got to thinking about Las Vegas the more anxious he was to get there, and the more his foot grew heavy on the gas pedal, with the rest of the congregation keeping pace.

About thirty miles out of Amarillo, as they came flying off a hilly stretch of land, a Texas Ranger, who hid on the other side of an underpass, took pursuit. He pulled up along side Southie and motioned him to pull off to the shoulder of the road. The rest of the congregants followed suit. Southie, looking in his rear view mirror, watched as the highway cop got out of his car and strolled toward the rust bucket. His light brown uniform matched the Texas dirt around them, and he wore sunglasses and a police hat that looked almost like a cowboy hat, but the brim was stiffer and shorter. He stopped a second before reaching the car, tilted his head and slapped a bug dead that landed on his neck.

"Something wrong, officer?" Southie asked, rolling down his window.

"Ya'll boys from New York, I see," said the cop leaning down to see inside the vehicle.

"Yes, officer. Just passing through. On the way to Las Vegas."

The cop pushed his forefinger against the bridge of his sunglasses, lifting them further up his nose and against his eyes.

"I don't know if ya'll New Yorkers think you can just fast talk law enforcement, but in Texas we don't take to speeding lightly. Specially on the interstate."

"Speeding?" said Southie incredulously.

"Ya'll was going nearly 80 in a 65

"Nearly 80. Are you sure officer?"

The cop pulled his glasses down his nose and peeked out over the dark lens.

"You got a license, boy?" he asked.

The cop studied Southie's license for a minute. Meanwhile, Southie heard the whizzing sound of traffic passing on the interstate. That and Miss Red, who decided now was a good time to do some clucking.

"So what do we do now?" Southie asked breaking the silence.

"Got to run y'all into town in front of the justice. Let's see, that's six vehicles going 80 in a 65. That will cost dern near a thousand dollars, I reckon," the cop said.

"A thousand dollars," Southie said, lifting his eyebrows up.

"Excuse me, officer," said Cain. "Would you be so kind as to let me interject a thought or two?"

Cain took the ensuing second of silence for a yes and continued.

"See I met these people here in Oklahoma and they ain't just your regular New Yorkers. These here are Jews – religious people on their way to Vegas."

"You mean speeding their way to Vegas," said the officer. "And we're good Baptists 'round these parts. We don't take t' no fancy religions."

"Maybe, but if you been to church lately you'd know these here people are children of God and they have a special talent as well."

"Special talent?"

"Namely football. Pig skin. You do know the game, officer? Don't you?"

"Football," the cop said, peering into the window and giving a smirk. "Y'all look as if the Texas A & M cheerleaders could whup y'all asses."

"Maybe so, but I'm willing to wager that thousand dollars in fines and say another five hundred that a group of ours can beat a group of yours in a game of two-hand touch football."

The cop gave a boastful, loud laugh. "Y'all yanks against us Texans. We'd make barbeque meat out of y'all.

"What are you saying?" said Southie, turning suddenly towards Cain. "We don't have that kind of...."

"I'm saying this Mormon from Utah here, plus a couple of these here Jews can kick your Longhorn asses all the way to Tulsa in a winner-takes-all game of touch football. We win, you let us go, you win and you get the fine plus bragging rights. You get your best six and we'll get ours," Cain said.

"Done. First one to score six touchdowns wins," said the cop with a start. "And I know just the place to play. Follow me."

Southie told the rest of the congregation to follow the squad car, which they did, turning off the interstate at the next exit onto a two-lane. They traveled south several miles along the dusty panhandle road, passing oil wells and several ranches until they came to a large building with a sign reading, "Jericho High School, Home of the Jericho Bobcats." Behind the school was a football field with enough bleachers to hold several thousand people, and in its dirt parking lot, the Texas Ranger pulled to a stop.

"Y'all wait right here. Our shift ends in another hour. And just to make sure, let me have your keys. I feel like feasting on some Yankee asses."

After everybody gave the trooper their car keys, he sped off with a smile, leaving behind a thick cloud of brown Texas dust and a bewildered congregation.

"What happened?" asked Aaron.

"We were all speeding and the cop was set to take us all in until Cain here committed us to a game of football."

"Football? Are you crazy?" said Sol, his voice growing excited. "These guys will make chopped liver out of us."

"Shut up Solly," said Myrtle, poking her husband in the ribs.

"Listen. We can beat these red necks, I just know it," said Cain. "Have faith."

"Faith we have. Football players we have not," said Sol.

Cain looked around at the group. "Look, all we need is five able bodies plus myself."

Everybody in the congregation was taken a back. Many of the men stroked their beards or scratched the back of their neck.

"Okay. Count me in," said Southie. "I wasn't a bad street player as a kid back in Chicago."

"Me too," said Isaac, thick as a log from unloading Wal-Mart dog food.

"What about the kid?" Cain said, motioning to David with his black eye.

Sarah grabbed David's arm.

"My David is not risking his life anymore with your shenanigans."

"Don't worry, Momma, I'm alright," said David pulling his arm away, and touching his eye. "I owe these Texans here a little pay back. Count me in, Mr. Cain."

"I used to play some baseball and football back in Atlanta. I'm fast and can catch pretty good," said Aaron. "Count me in, too."

Cain looked at Sol then the Rebbe and back to Sol.

"That makes five players," he said. "We still need one more."

"Don't look at me. My bones will snap like peanut brittle," said Sol.

The Rebbe's eyes were old and tired, and he had a paunch. His long, thick beard curled at the sideburns and lay halfway down his chest.

"Count me in," he said.

"Rebbe," protested Southie. "I can't let you do this."

"God makes miracles," the Rebbe said. "I'll be okay. Besides I grew up in Baltimore. Home of Johnny Unitas, the greatest quarterback who ever lived."

"Okay, that makes six," said Cain, rubbing his hands together. "Now let's come up with a game plan."

"You fellows strategize. Let me go pray and enlist God's help that we will win this contest," said the Rebbe, and he walked down the field, vanishing beneath the empty bleachers.

For the next hour Cain devised a game plan. It was decided that he would be the quarterback, while David and Aaron would run the longer pass routes, and Southie and Isaac the shorter ones. No sooner than he explained everybody's positions than three pick up trucks pulled into the parking lot and out hopped a bunch of Texas cowboys wearing tank tops, sporting arms like boa constrictors, and tossing a football in the air. Following them were several women in halter tops, who started taking out all kinds of picnic equipment from the back of their pick-up trucks.

"Welcome to Bobcat Stadium fellers," said the cop who stopped them, tossing the football at Cain with a perfect spiral.

"Well, I'll be derned with a branding iron!" said one of his teammates. "You was right, Donny. Our wives and girlfriends could beat this scrap pile."

"Let's say we just go over the rules of the game," said Cain, gripping the football.

"Sho' nuff," said Donny. "We play on the field sideways with the end zone line and the twenty-yard line being out of bounds. Two-hand touch and three complete is a first down. Everybody is eligible and the rusher gotta count five Amarillo like this – one Amarillo – two Amarillo – three Amarillo and so on, before he rushes in. First team to score six touchdowns wins."

As the teams went over the rules, one of the young women, wearing cutoff jeans and a halter-top offered Myrtle a seat.

"Come on momma," she said with a drawl. "Pull yo'self up a chair and let's watch us some football."

"Why thank you young woman," said Myrtle, taking her up on the offer. "You got an extra one for my husband."

Another young woman came forward with a chair and set it next to Myrtle and Sol took a seat.

"If y'all want beer, they're in the cooler. Help yo'self. Let's see us some pig skin," said the young woman.

"Pigskin. You mean pork?" said Sol.

"Yeah. That's what a football is made from."

"For this I left Port Decker? God in heaven, why do you do this to me!" said Sol pointing to the sky.

Meanwhile, Donny pulled a coin from his pocket and flicked it six feet in the air. "Call it."

"Heads," said Cain.

The coin twirled a few times high up in the air before the Texan caught it with one hand and slapped it on the back of his other hand. "Tails! Looks like you boys can't even win a coin toss. We'll take the ball first," he said. "But wait a minute. Where's your sixth player. I count only five."

"I'm here," yelled the Rebbe coming out from beneath the bleachers. "With my nephew, Golem."

Southie, Cain, Isaac, Aaron and David looked up in astonishment. Walking with the Rebbe was a six-foot-one Jew wearing a yarmulke, sweatpants and a tank top t-shirt. He had a hairy chest, strong arms, a sinewy build and eyes that darted all around before locking in on his opponents.

"Rebbe, but how did you ...," Southie whispered..

The Rebbe winked at Southie.

"But, he went behind the bleachers alone," said Cain.

"No, you were mistaken," said Southie, rubbing his chin. "Golem was riding shotgun with the Rebbe."

"Shush, my nephew is ready to play," said the Rebbe and he went back to the sidelines to watch the game. "I'll be the substitute."

Cain kicked the ball off with a pretty good foot and everybody ran down the field with a burst of energy toward the Texan returning the ball. Southie saw a gap between two other Texans to the runner, but as he tried to squeeze through, one of the Texans lunged forward blocking him hard and he went flying on his behind. He looked up to see the runner moving around him downfield. Suddenly, Golem cut across his peripheral vision, hopping like a jackrabbit in the darkened night, and made a perfect two-hand touch on the man with the ball.

Cain raced over to Golem and slapped him on the back. "That was one hell of a play, boy. Now we got us some more defense to play."

The teams lined up, man against man, with Isaac, keeping an eye on the line of scrimmage. The quarterback hiked to himself and saw one of his Texans in the flat. He threw the ball, but out of nowhere Golem reached in, grabbing the interception and raced it to the end zone for the game's first score.

"Man, where did he come from?" the quarterback said.

"That's one score," Cain said.

"I thought you said they was all a bunch of sissies," one of the Texans said to Donny.

"What the hell?" replied Donny. "There were six cars of people. I didn't have time to size each and everybody up raht."

The game seesawed back and forth with Golem making one great play after another. At last it came down to five touchdowns each and the Texans had the ball. Cain called a timeout. Meanwhile, the Rebbe brought some water to the huddle.

"Come on, now. You have to let me play," said the Rebbe.

Everybody looked around at the Rebbe.

"No, Rebbe," said Southie. "It's too rough out there and you're old. I don't want to see anything happen to you."

"What are you talking about?" asked the Rebbe. "Before I became religious, I used to play on the streets of Baltimore. Look, I got my nephew Golem to play, didn't I, and hasn't he played great so far?"

The team looked at Golem. Although everybody on the team was winded from the game, he hadn't even broken a sweat.

"Let the Rebbe play," he said in a monotone voice.

Cain looked around and saw Aaron looking the most tired.

"Okay," he said. "Aaron, you played a great game, but we're going to put the Rebbe in. Rebbe, you rush the quarterback. Keep some pressure on him. I feel it's going to be a trick play. Watch a pitch back and throw to the quarterback."

Sure enough, when play resumed, Donny hiked the ball to himself and then pitched the ball back to a teammate who threw the ball back to Donny at about midfield. While Donny eluded Southie and was about to catch the ball, Golem again came out of nowhere and batted the ball back toward the line of scrimmage. The football fluttered in midair seemingly in slow motion until landing in the Rebbe's arms. Then the old man huffed and puffed his way to the end zone for the winning score.

"Well y'all boys sho' made fools of yo'selves. I suggest you give 'em their car keys back," said one of the Texas women.

"Well how's I to know that these here Jews can play football, Mary Lou?" said Donny.

"Come on lets go," said another of the women. "It's hot out here. Why don't you boys take us to Dairy Queen?"

After the Texans left, the congregation continued rejoicing on Bobcat Field.

"It was only an act of God that we won," Southie said.

"I don't rightly know if there is a God, but I do know that we won one hell of a football game today," Cain said. "And we owe it all to our most valuable player, Golem. Where is he?"

"My nephew? He had to leave."

"But where could he have gone? I didn't see him leave."

The entire congregation turned and looked at the Rebbe.

"My nephew, Golem, is a bit like you, Mr. Cain. He comes from nowhere in a time of need and is often gone just as quickly," he said.

CHAPTER 28

"It's true what Grand Pappy used to tell us," said Cain as the congregants crossed the state line into New Mexico. That us Mormons and you Jews have a special bond."

He had been talking about the game for a while, going over many of the best plays and how they unfolded.

"How's that," said Southie.

"That we're part of the lost tribes of Israel. The Chosen People of America and Salt Lake City is the American Jerusalem. So fer as I'm concerned, I been traveling with kin."

"I guess so," said Southie.

"And that's why that Gollum character came out from behind the bleachers. Cause when Mormons and Jews get together it's something special. Miracles happen."

The appearance of the Golem bothered Southie as well. Too many strange things began happening, starting with Momma Docs calling him the American Moses, then losing Coree to the Christians, seeing her again later in the tornado, and now the Rebbe making a golem appear and disappear in seemingly midair. He looked now at Cain, and wondered if he too, was not sent from God. Then again, Southie had seen his types and then some. And while Cain seemed a good enough chap, he took a few too many risks for Southie's taste. Plus it was always risky traveling with a stranger, especially with a wife and kid in the back seat to look after.

Just past where the interstate crossed Route 285, Southie pulled to the shoulder of the road and everybody followed suit.

"Why you stopping?" Cain inquired.

"This is the turnoff. You said you were heading to Santa Fe."

Cain turned around in his seat and saw the ramp north onto Route 285.

"So it is," he said, smiling. "If you can just pass me my rucksack and bedroll, ma'm, I'll be on my way."

Zippy passed Cain his gear and watched as he went from car to car in the caravan uttering final good-bys to the rest of the congregants. Then, after he vanished down the ramp heading north to Santa Fe, she got back into the front seat, and they took off in silence along the flat desert floor. In the distant west, a hulking mountain range loomed from behind darkened brown shadows as the sun began setting in the western sky with a burst of tangerine orange behind a gathering of puffy clouds.

Try as he may, Southie couldn't stay angry at Zippy. True, her temperament played a role in the family breaking apart, but he too came from a broken family. Perhaps that's what families do, he thought, come together and drift apart, like breathing. And for better or worse, he and his wife had endured a lot together. As for Coree leaving, it felt like a hole with sharp and jagged edges had been ripped into his soul, but there was little more he could do now but move on.

"Doesn't the sunset look beautiful," he said, laying his right hand over Zippy's hand, and locking his fingers into hers.

"I'm sorry we ever left Port Decker," Zippy said softly.

"Sorry?"

"Ever since I came to America at fourteen all I ever wanted was a home in the country. A home with a yard and property. Something to look after and attend to. We had all that Southie and more."

"But we didn't have money and Port Decker is a racist little town."

"We had each other, Southie and we had our children..."

"Why didn't you tell me that when we were packing and getting ready to leave?"

"I tried to, but I saw how much you wanted to go," said Zippy. "You're my husband and I follow you. At least that's what I thought, but now I wished we had stayed in Port Decker. Then nothing like this would have happened. We'd still have Coree."

The mountain range was now before them. It's brown and barren boulders jetting out from steep inclines like the tears of a sullen woman. They began climbing through a winding pass. Road signs appeared warning of sudden wind drafts and falling rocks. Strong wire fences lined parts of the interstate to catch falling boulders from the mountains surrounding them, and Billy cried out from the back seat as the rising altitude made his ears pop.

They reached the mountaintop plateau, and as then descended, into Downtown Albuquerque, where they Interstate turned into an eight-lane. Here they entered again into a world of big box stores as a Wal-Mart, and Target lined the exits of the highway. Then the interstate narrowed to four lanes, and once more they were on flat desert terrain. Cactus plants looking like thorny three-pronged forks popped up and thick boulders began appearing, sticking out of the barren red-brown earth. And in the distance, another mountain range loomed.

The congregants drove though the Laguna Indian Reservation, and up the San Rafael Mountains across the continental divide, where water coming off the mountains now began to run west toward the Pacific Ocean. The sun now disappeared behind the mountains, leaving a watermelon-colored western sky in its wake. The dusk lit up as they passed the Giant Truck Stop with flames from a nearby oil refinery spitting up thirty-five feet into the air from two large chimneys. Then they wound around a canyon, that even in nighttime looked ghostly white, and into the town of Gallop, where Southie exited and pulled into one of the many lodges along Main Street.

"We'll check in here for the night," Southie told the congregation as they stopped in the parking lot. "Tomorrow, we should make Las Vegas."

As Southie walked with Zippy and Billy to their second-floor room, he took in Gallop from the wrought iron veranda. Rusty old cars and pick-up trucks traveled the main thoroughfare of red stucco stores, bars, restaurants and hotels.

The lodge in which they were staying shared a parking lot with a Mexican restaurant that had a video arcade attached to it. Several green picnic tables were in front of it on a small patch of stones, around which several dozen teenagers gathered. One – a pretty, brown-skinned girl, was pregnant.

"Look at her," Southie said, nodding to Zippy. "Poor girl."

"You really like those young girls, don't you. Just Like Coree?"

Southie, who had just approached their room door, set down the suitcase he was carrying and came within an inch of Zippy's face.

"Can't you ever let anything go? Ever?"

"It's your fault that Coree left because you lusted after her."

"Damn it, Zippy. Can't you see just once that I'm not your father. You're father molested you, but that's not me. I only loved Coree as a daughter and nothing more."

"My father only touched me when he was drunk and I always was able to avoid him."

Southie opened the door to the hotel room.

"What your father did was not normal. He victimized you and now you have victimized you're family. I would never touch our daughter the way you were touched by him. Just consider once the possibility that you are wrong about Coree and me."

"What have I ever done wrong as your wife, but put you first. You wanted to leave and chase some dream to Las Vegas and I went along with you. Everything you've always wanted I've done."

"You're a hard woman to love."

Tears welled in Zippy's eyes. Then she sat on the edge of the motel bed and sobbed.

"I'm sorry," Southie said, walking over to his wife and putting his hand on her shoulder.

"Damn it Southie, all I ever wanted was a home and a place to raise a family, and you destroyed it all."

"And all I ever wanted was for my family to stay together. Something I never had as a child."

Zippy dried away her tears and looked at Billy, who had taken a seat at a desk in the corner of the room.

"It's always about you, isn't it Southie?" she said, grabbing her son's hand and making for the door. "Come on, Billy."

"Where you going?"

"Out! The same way you always do when you get mad."

"Fine," said Southie, and he was glad for the peace when they closed the door to the hotel room and were out of sight.

After leaving the room, Zippy and Billy checked on Miss Red and Mouser before taking Buttercup for a walk behind the Mexican restaurant and near the video arcade. They stopped at one of the picnic benches and sat for a minute, and Billy asked his mother for a quarter to play the video games.

"Listen to me, Billy," she said to her son. "You're a good boy and you have a good brain. Playing videos is okay for an average child, but not for mine."

As Zippy spoke to Billy, a painful shriek came from one of the teenagers at a nearby table between the arcade and the fast food restaurant. She turned to see a teenage boy standing over the pregnant girl sitting on a bench, her face twisted in pain.

"What is it? What is it?" said the boy, alarmed.

"The baby. It's coming," the girl cried, through clenched teeth.

"Shit, what do we do," said a boy.

Zippy quickly gave Buttercup's leash to Billy and ordered him to hold it tight. Then she ran to where the pregnant girl sat, wearing a baggy basketball jersey over jeans. Zippy saw the jeans darken near the crotch area. "She broke her water," she said out loud.

"Someone call a doctor," one of the teenagers yelled.

"It's too late for that. Give me that jacket," Zippy ordered.

The teenager handed her the Levi jacket he was wearing and Zippy quickly used it to wipe the picnic table clean. Then she shook it off as best she could, and told the girl to lay on the table.

"Go to the restaurant and see if they have any clean rags and get some scalding hot water."

As one of the kids ran off to do the errands, Zippy covered the girl with a poncho that one of the teenage girls handed to her, and gingerly removed the jeans from the pregnant girl. She then looked beneath the poncho to see the girl's birth canal fully dilated; but there was no sign of the baby's crown. The girl let out a painful screech again. Her face was beaded in sweat and her dark red skin appeared pale. Zippy touched the girl's head, which was hot as a match. Next she reached down and felt the girl's stomach, and with the sensitive hands of an artist, felt the outline of the fetus.

"Ouch!" said the girl, sucking air in through her clenched teeth.

"It's okay. You're baby is lying sideways. I'm going to turn it. Take three deep breaths and than hold your breath and count to twenty."

One of the teenagers came back with clean cloths and a pot of hot water. Zippy put several of the cloths in the steamy water and let it soak, before she quickly reached for one and rung it out. Then she used it to wipe the entrance around the birth canal clean. She then took another rag and wiped her own hands clean, before locking eyes with girl, giving both a determined and reassuring stare.

"You ready?"

The girl nodded through furrowed eyebrows.

Zippy reached with gentle fingers up the girl's birth canal until she found the baby's armpit, and then gently guided it headfirst near the birth position.

"Okay. Push," she said, and as the girl pushed, Zippy guided the infant's head further into place and saw its crown engaged. Zippy took another cloth and wiped her hands as well as the sweat off the girl's head. The thought of her own hard labor with Coree flashed in her mind. She had been in labor with her more than twenty hours before coming into the world, but now she quickly refocused on the crisis at hand.

"Okay, let's see your baby," she said, sternly. "On the count of three, push. One... two... three"

The girl pushed again until Zippy saw the head, eyes, nose and mouth appear out into the world and a second later an entire newborn child slipped into her waiting hands. She quickly took it from beneath the jacket and cleared its nose and mouth of blood and fluid and then she slapped it, but the baby was quiet and looked blue.

"No, no. You will not die on me," she cried and opened the baby's mouth and breathed into it. The newborn gave a cough and then started to cry. Zippy wrapped the infant in a blanket, looked at it for a second, and then gently put her in her mother's arms.

"It's a girl. A beautiful girl," she said through her own tears of happiness, and the teenagers broke into applause.

⌘ ⌘ ⌘

Southie showered and turned on the TV – half watching a situation comedy rerun, and half reading The Navaho Times newspaper, which he had picked up in the lobby. After finishing the paper, he flipped through the channels of the television without finding anything of interest. Finally he settled on the news out of Albuquerque and drifted off to sleep. An hour later, a used car commercial startled him awake and he sat up in the flashing television light to realize that Zippy and Billy had not returned. He looked at the clock on the nightstand. It was past midnight.

Alarmed, Southie quickly dressed and made his way to the parking lot. The station wagon was still there, but Miss Red, Mouser and Buttercup were missing, as was a suitcase. He rubbed his face and looked out from the car in all directions. Down the street were a few bars, but that wasn't Zippy's style. So he walked across the parking lot to the picnic tables where a half dozen teenagers were still hanging out.

"Did you happen to see a black woman with a child and a dog?" he asked one of them.

The teenagers eyed him for a second and then each other.

"Why? What do you want with them?" one of them said.

"She is my wife and that is my child," said Southie.

The teenagers grew quiet again.

"She delivered a baby for a friend of ours," one of them said.

"You mean that girl hanging out here on the picnic benches?"

The boy nodded and Southie felt a surge of pride for he knew if anybody could deliver a baby it was Zippy.

"She told us you would come looking for her," said another one of the teenagers. He was brown skinned and had eyelids arching downward.

"Where did she go?" he asked.

"To Window Rock on the Navaho Nation. That's where the girl's family lives."

Southie got directions to the girl's home and went back to the lodge to tell the others. When he walked through the parking lot, he spotted the Rebbe sitting in his car and reading the Talmud.

"Rebbe," Southie said. "Zippy has left."

"I know. She delivered a baby and left with the Indians. I saw."

"And you didn't say anything?"

The Rebbe put his arm on Southie's shoulder.

"Listen to me Southie. Let her go. God makes things happen for a reason. Remember the first commandment. Don't let your emotions take control."

Southie gave the Rebbe a hard look.

"I'm going after her," he said. "Meanwhile, take everybody to Flagstaff in the morning and wait at the first Flying J truck stop you come to. I'll catch up with you there tomorrow."

CHAPTER 29

Southie checked out from the lodge and headed north onto the Navaho Nation. A full, silver moon lit the desert in an amber haze as he veered west of the town, Tohatchi. The altitude began rising, testing the old rust bucket engine, which revved, but stayed strong and true. Giant rock formations and three-pronged cactus cast shadows in the metallic light, and the landscape appeared alive as if watching him.

About a half-hour later, he pulled into a gas station and got further directions. He proceeded further west past a rock formation that framed stars in the night against boulders balanced on cliffs. Then past a cemetery, where burial mounds draped in American flags were visible beneath white streetlights. The road forked left until at last Southie came to the adobe complex gate for which he was looking. Inside, small adobe homes and trailers lined the narrow, dirt streets. Southie stopped near a group of teenagers playing basketball with a makeshift hoop set up against a light post.

"I'm looking for the Begay family," he inquired of them, reading from the directions he had written on a scrap of paper.

"Well you found us," said one teenager, and they all laughed and nodded.

The teenagers led Southie by foot through a group of homes and tiny fenced-in yards with horses, cows and chickens, until they came to a porch lit by a naked light bulb. One of the teenagers opened the front door. There sat Zippy on a wooden chair, sketchpad in hand and drawing a young Navaho woman nursing her baby on a more comfortable chair across the room. Next to her an older couple sat on a couch covered over with woven earthy fabric. Watching television and sitting on the floor were two younger children.

"Are you and Billy all right?" said Southie.

"We're fine," said Zippy, not looking up from the sketchbook. "Mr. and Mrs. Begay. This is my husband, Southie. And Southie, this is Alvino," she said, nodding to the young woman nursing the child. "And this is the baby that I helped bring into the world."

"It is indeed an honor." said Mr. Begay, beckoning him to sit.

Southie took another wooden chair that was in the corner near the door and pulled it up next to Zippy.

"Why did you leave without telling me, Zippy?"

"Alvino insisted," said Zippy, continuing to draw. "They named the baby, Zipporah."

"Your wife did a very special thing," said Mr. Begay. "We owe her two lives. She delivered and saved my granddaughter, and I am told she also saved my daughter."

Dim lamps scattered yellow patches of light throughout the room. Meanwhile, the television threw off its own blinking lights, and murmured softly as the sound was turned low.

"Zippy is a special person," said Southie, proudly.

"We gave your wife a gift in return," said Mr. Begay. "It is our way."

"What kind of gift?"

Zippy put her sketchpad down and got up.

"I want to show you something," she said.

"Wait," Mr. Begay said. "I have a gift for your husband, too."

Mr. Begay went to a small closet and pulled down a folded, red wool blanket and opened it to reveal a circular shape with arrows and tribal designs on it.

"This blanket has been in our family for five generations. It tells of our journey to the horizon and back," he said, handing it to Southie. "Give it to your next generation for we are now connected."

Southie took the blanket, nodding with respectful thanks. Then Zippy led him out the front door and across a lot to a fenced-in yard with a small adobe house on it. He followed her up to the doorway where Buttercup greeted them at the door with a wag of her stump. Billy lay asleep on the floor in front of a tiny television in the small living room, with Mouser curled up beside him.

"Shhh, don't wake him," Zippy said and she showed him around the house – the kitchen, the bathroom and through a bedroom, where she stopped at the window.

"Well, what do you think?" she said with a broad smile.

"Nice."

"It's ours," whispered Zippy, trying to hold back excitement.

"Ours? I don't understand."

"Mr. and Mrs. Begay gave it to us as for delivering their granddaughter."

Zippy spread the sheer white curtains and motioned for Southie to look out the window where he saw the silhouette of a horse in the silvery moonlight.

"And look, Southie," said Zippy, turning around. "They gave us a horse!"

"But what about Las Vegas? That was our plan."

Zippy took her husband's hand.

"That was your plan."

"And what about Coree. Do we just forget she ever existed?"

Zippy turned stern. "Now look here. Coree is not a bad person, but she is your daughter and I am your wife."

Zippy put her drawing pad on the dresser as Southie glanced out the window at the horse. The night was cool and a desert breeze blew through the window, which was cracked open.

"Stay with me here, Southie," she whispered. "This is an opportunity to start over."

"In the middle of nowhere?"

"If two people love each other they can live in a cave," said Zippy.

Southie faced his wife and studied her. Her eyes steadfast like a ship on calm seas.

"I'm so proud of you for delivering that baby."

Zippy smiled. "The whole ordeal gave me a cramp in my neck. If you know what I mean."

Southie stepped behind his wife and began to rub her shoulders, and after feeling her relax, he gently bit the back of her neck. She turned and he pulled her close, their lips meeting in a full, deep kiss.

"Let's undress," she said, and he watched as she shed her homemade dress, the white one with pink flowers that fit loosely around her body. He now studied her shapely hips and behind, and her narrow waist and breasts, which were large, soft and beautiful.

"Come hold me. I'm freezing," she said, and he put his own naked body against her and she shivered in his arms. Then she slipped beneath the sheet and blanket of the bed while he closed the window, before following her into the bed with his own shiver. They pressed flesh to flesh against each other for some time until they both warmed. Slowly and gently he began playing with her breasts, sucking, kissing and gentling biting her nipples. She reached down and gently stroked his hardened penis and then stopped.

"Check on our son," she said. "Make sure he's warm."

Southie picked up the blanket Mr. Begay gave him, off the edge of the bed, and walked naked through the house to the living room, where Billy was curled up on the floor sleeping in front of the television. Buttercup, who dozed against the door, opened her eyes and after seeing it was Southie, closed them again. He picked his son up and carried him to the couch, and then put a chair against the couch to keep him from falling. Then he unfolded the blanket and his son opened an eye.

"Hello, daddy," he said.

Southie hugged Billy and tucked him in, throwing the colorful woven blanket over his son.

"Sleep well," he said before returning to the bedroom.

"Everything okay?" asked Zippy.

"Everything's fine."

He crawled back beneath the covers and pressed his flesh against Zippy until he became warm again.

"I have always loved you my husband," Zippy whispered into his ear.

The couple again kissed deeply and they began caressing each other, trading messaging rubs, pinches and kisses until at last he mounted her with long gentle strokes, each one going deeper inside her.

"I want to see your face," she said.

He propped himself on his elbows and looked into her eyes. Then he reached behind her, and with spread fingers, grabbed her soft behind in a firm grip. In and out he went while she kept her eyes on him and studied his face. Then she watched intently as he exploded with ecstasy.

Afterward, they lay a few minutes in silence. Out in the desert, a coyote howled and Southie got up and looked out the window. The horse was still against a fence, and the stars looked so close he could reach up and grab one. The boulders in a nearby formation, even in the dark of night, had a red hue.

"Stay with me here" Zippy said.

"I can't," replied Southie. "I told the Rebbe we would meet up tomorrow in Flagstaff,"

Zippy sat up in the bed. "I've left one house for you. I'll not leave a second."

"This is your journey, not mine," said Southie.

"Why are you always running? Look at the gift we've been given."

"I'm not running. My calling is out there somewhere. I just don't know where or what it is."

"Momma Docs was right about you," said Zippy. "You are the American Moses. Go lead your people to this Promised Land of Las Vegas. But as for Billy and I, we're staying. These people here love and want me."

Southie looked at his wife in the darkened room.

"But I'm scared to go on without you."

"Listen to me. Fear nothing for God is always with you."

Southie crawled back into bed and soon fell asleep, but Zippy lay awake for a long time. First Coree abandoned her and now Southie was about to do the same. Maybe he wasn't like her father. But what could she do? She refused to stop him from leaving. A person does what a person must do. Then there was this house. Never in her wildest dreams did she think somebody would actually give her one.

At dawn, without sleeping, Zippy got up and made a breakfast of eggs, bacon and toast that the Begay family had left in the refrigerator. She then woke Southie and Billy, and they ate silently at the small kitchen table. Afterward, Zippy put fresh water in a plastic bottle for her husband.

Southie then hugged his son while Zippy picked up her drawing pad and a pencil.

"Before you leave, I want Coree's phone number."

Southie looked lovingly at his wife, then pulled the church school card from his wallet and handed it to his wife. She jotted the number down on the pad and handed it back to her husband.

"Zippy..."

"Don't explain," said Zippy, pushing him gently out of the door. "Take your people to their Promised Land. I'll wait. But listen to me, Mister. I won't wait forever."

CHAPTER 30

"See everybody. I told you Southie would meet us here," said Isaac, when Southie arrived in the parking lot of the Flying J truck stop just outside of Flagstaff.

"Where's the family?" asked Sol.

The edges of Southie's mouth turned downward.

"See, Myrtle. I told you she would leave him. That's what you get for marrying out of your faith," said Sol.

"Put a finger in that dyke you call a mouth, Solly. It's got more leaks than a rusty basement pipe."

"What, I can't talk!? God gave me a mouth and I can't talk unless Myrtle tells me."

"Let's get going," said Southie. "We can make Vegas by nightfall."

The congregants descended from the thin mountain air of Flagstaff, and traveled west across the glistening white valley. In the distant north the Grand Canyon's south rim rose up in the shadowy horizon through the gassy desert heat. As they drove Southie felt a dry longing for Zippy. He missed her happiness and how the whole world would light like a star when she was cheerful. The way she took care for and loved her animals. Gods little creatures, she used to call them. He kind of missed even that old clicker, Miss Red. He turned on the radio, but the country song coming from the car speaker also reminded him of Zippy. That funny way she would sing, alternating in a soft and loud voice, depending on the syllables and words. He fumbled through several radio stations until coming to an old Jamaican song that he and Zippy used to sing around the house. He also knew the lyrics from Hebrew school as a child growing up.

By the rivers of Babylon, there we sat down
ye-each we wept, when we remembered Zion.
By the rivers of Babylon, there we sat down
ye-each we wept, when we remembered Zion.

The song finished and Southie let down all the windows. Hot, dry air rushed in, all but drowning the sound from the radio, and blowing his hair like scattered hard spaghetti. At least he had the rust bucket, he thought, and took a mental inventory of the old station wagon. While the air conditioning barely blew cold air, he never minded opening the window, and loved the softness of the burgundy leather interior. If worst came to worst he could fold down the middle seat and live in it like a turtle in its shell.

Just outside Kingman, signs pointing the way to Las Vegas began to appear. They veered north onto the two-lane Route 93, passing a sign reading, 'Las Vegas 100 Miles'. Southie's hands began to sweat and his stomach jumped at the realization that their destination was finally within reach. The thoughts of his future now crowded Zippy out of his mind. He had given her practically all his money before he left except for a few hundred dollars. The Rebbe had a point about using his head instead of always relying on his heart. Perhaps he could borrow some money from the others until he could get on his feet. Then he could figure out his next move.

The Sacramento Valley desert floor was littered with tin desert shacks, trading posts and cactus. Then they began to climb the Black Mountains with the snow-capped Cerbat Mountains to the east. Southie's ears began to crackle and pop as the rust bucket engine revved and chugged beneath the hood. Up further they climbed through rock formations carved out from blasting to make room for the road. And as the sun began to set, bright as an orange peel, between two peaks, he saw the Colorado River snaking down several thousand feet below them at the bottom of a canyon.

At last they reached a rest stop overlooking the great Hoover Dam, with its muscular concrete sheet several hundred feet high, staving off the Boulder Basin waters from spilling into the Colorado River. Huge steel girders branched out like a spider web bracing up the blasted-out rocky mountain walls, and keeping boulders from falling into the dam. Although the sun had now set, the entire dam area was lit with floodlights, keeping the black early night painted in the background between the gaps of the rock walls. Meanwhile, tourists strolled footpaths surrounding the dam, snapping photographs and staring down the concrete chasm to the waters below.

The congregants drove down about a hundred feet, winding around the dam and then they began to climb to the west again, past a sign welcoming them to Nevada and declaring Las Vegas to be 22 miles away. Although drunk with anticipation, Southie stopped in the first parking lot inside the state line. It was the Hacienda Casino, its' entrance lit like a Christmas tree with neon lights advertising $2 black jack, a night's lodging for $29.99, and prime rib dinners at $5.99.

"Why did you stop?" asked Sol after everyone got out from their cars. "We could be in Vegas in a half hour."

"We need a scout," said Southie.

"A scout?" said Sol.

"Yeah someone to drive ahead and check out Las Vegas while we stay here and hold onto our money. We'll send Isaac forward with three hundred dollars from your cousin's synagogue in St. Louis. He'll find out about the housing market, and the Jewish community and then he'll come back and tell us. Today is Tuesday. He'll return by Friday before the Sabbath."

Everybody agreed that this seemed like sound advice, and shortly afterward, Isaac commenced for Las Vegas in his Ford Escort.

The rest of the congregation went into the hotel check-in past a casino full of people playing black jack and slot machines. It seemed everyone in the place was wearing white, black and brown cowboy hats. The check-in clerk informed the congregants that the lodge was temporarily short on rooms due to a cattle rancher's convention. As a result, everybody found a room except Southie. While several of the others invited Southie to stay in their room, he politely declined, especially after the check-in clerk recommended the Lake Meade Campground just two miles further down the road.

"Come back Thursday in the afternoon. The convention ends, and I'm sure a room will be available," the clerk said.

So Southie borrowed a large Styrofoam cooler from Aaron and Faygie and half filled it with ice. Then he bought three six-packs of beer, a loaf of bread and sandwich meat from the small Casino general store. As night fell, he drove a few miles towards Vegas and entered Bolder Basin State Park, where he followed the dimly lit road signs to the desolate campground, save for one trailer parked on the far side of the grounds. He parked in a bay close to the entrance and began drinking beer with the cool night air seeping into the car. Across the darkened flat basin before him, Southie could make out lights, but they were distant and appeared only as twinkles, barely different than the symphony of stars that played across the expansive sky.

After several beers, Southie put on the car radio to some country music and slumped behind the steering wheel, melting into the burgundy interior. "How's my Rust Bucket?" he asked the car out loud, patting the car's dashboard. "I know you're tired but once we get to Las Vegas, I'll change your oil. How's that? I promise."

After finishing a six-pack, he got out of the car and walked around the little patch of land in which he parked. The bay was in a small clearing and equipped with a water pump and barbeque pit. At the edge of it, the nocturnal basin stretched out beneath a darkened sky. As he took a few steps into the basin, rustling sounds seemed to scamper away at his feet. Distantly, he heard howling coyotes, and an owl hooted from one of the campground trees. After relieving himself, he went back to the rust bucket, and after taking off his shoes, stretched out in the middle seat, with the doors locked and the windows cracked open.

The cackle of crows woke him and he pulled the jacket from his head to see the sun rising up over the glistening Boulder Basin and a few tiny sailboats in the distant horizon on Lake Meade. After stretching, he went to the water pump and splashed cool water over his head and face, which opened his nostrils to the sweet smells of white, pink and fuchsia cactus flowers. Then he noticed the occupants of the trailer across the grounds walking toward the shared bathroom and shower area, so he walked up a small incline to meet them. When he reached the common area, he found they were an older Asian couple.

"Hello," he said, feigning a Chinese accent. "It is nice to meet you."

"And it's nice to meet you, too," said the woman in perfect American English. "I'm Lee Young and this is my husband, Kim. "We're from Seattle, and you?"

"Chicago originally."

"This is a beautiful campground. Are you a regular campground rat?"

"Not really. I'm waiting for a room to open up at the casino not far from here."

"Well you're in for a real treat. If you get a chance hike on the foot trail that the Nevada Parks Department made in the basin. You can walk down to the lake."

When Southie got back to his car, he drank some water from the pump, and enjoyed the solitude of the cool morning, but by noon it grew hot. He pulled the station wagon beneath several trees for shade and rolled down all the car windows, had a sandwich, and cracked open a beer. On the other side of the basin, he watched the sailboats, which appeared as small specks, floating across the horizon on Lake Meade.

As the sun lowered itself in the western sky, the day started to cool down and Southie began thinking about Las Vegas and what he would do once he got there. The first thing, he thought, was finding a place to live. He could max out his credit card to pay for it and then he could find a job. While he really missed Zippy and Billy, he knew that she would not be keen about moving to Las Vegas. It took a lot for Zippy to leave their house in Port Decker, and leaving a second one really wasn't her nature.

For the first time, Southie pondered a future without Zippy. While the house on the Navaho land was nice, he was a city boy and Las Vegas was at hand. A new sense of freedom gripped him. He could leave behind the stress and responsibility of being a husband and father. Not that he wouldn't send money once he began to make some, but now was his chance to start over in life. As he pondered his future, night fell and the sailboats on the lake in the distance became the twinkling lights he had seen the night before. They sailed as only lights now, flickering across the horizon as he finished the last beer.

He awoke at daylight with a fierce hangover. Overhead, birds cackled across the basin and he pumped some cool water on his head and face making him shutter. Across the campground, the Asian couple had left and now he was alone in the completely desolate campground. A few more hours and there would be a room available. Then he looked across the basin to the sailboats and suddenly his eyes spotted the narrow two foot wide trail to the lake that the couple had told him about. It wasn't more than a hundred feet in front of him. A few minutes later, he ventured onto it.

The trek started pleasantly with Southie noticing cactus plants and desert flowers, along with occasional rocks and boulders littering the grainy basin floor. But it soon grew roasting hot, and Southie wished he had brought some water. It was a very dry heat, making it hard to sweat and the sun bore down on his head and face. The further he went the more the desert seemed to jump and dart around him. He thought the movement as optical illusions created by the gassy heat rising from the valley floor. After an hour of walking his mouth became dry and he considered turning back. However, he was now closer to the lake then he was to the campground so he trekked on.

Finally, Southie reached a desolate patch of the lakefront with a parched throat and a blister forming on one of his toes. He immediately took off his sneakers and socks and waded into the water, scooping handfuls of water over his head and into his mouth, swishing it around his teeth and cheeks before spitting it out. Some distance away, fishermen in small boats were casting their lines and further out on the water, sailboats drifted across the lake. The water looked clear enough to Southie, so he reached down and took two small gulps before resting some minutes on a patch of grass beneath a shady tree planted near the water. After some minutes he thought about making it back through the desert, first to his car and then the casino. Before starting though, he waded back into the water and took two more gulps. Then he picked up a stick that had fallen from the tree and decided to use it as a third leg for the trek back.

The deadening desert heat continued to rise, and the darting movements became more pronounced. Southie now made out the trees lining the campground and old Rust Bucket appeared as a speck in the distance. Feeling to weary to make the hike in one fall swoop, he decided to rest a few minutes against a large rock just off the foot path. Once there, he leaned the walking stick up against it to his right, and wiped dried grime from his face with his soiled t-shirt. A gust of wind picked up some dust and he thought he heard it whisper, "The Creator has sent me."

Southie's tongue turned pasty, his stomach knotted and he resisted the urge to vomit.

"Who are you?" he managed to say.

"The Creator gives us many names," the dust whispered.

Southie looked down and two inches from his shoes was a giant beige lizard, its slinky tongue darting in and out of its mouth. Suddenly, he realized the desert floor was full of lizards, darting about and crawling along sides of rocks.

"Woah! What the fuck," said Southie, jumping back from the first lizard he saw and the animal darted away.

"There's a lot of things in the world to see if you are willing to look," said a calm voice just to his left.

Southie jumped away from the voice and then turned toward it to see a haggard-looking fellow leaning against the rock.

"Who are you?" he asked.

"The Creator sent me," said the man. "We spoke at the Dunkin Donuts. Remember in New Jersey. The night your car swerved off the road."

Southie closed his eyes and recalled the day he quit his job at the morgue. Then he reopened his eyes and the man was still there, leaning against the rock. He had a stubble beard, and patches of unkempt gray hair spilling out the sides of a light green desert hat.

"Okay," Southie said. "If the Creator sent you I don't suppose he gave you some water."

"I'm not here to give you water," the man said. "I'm here to tell you that you've completed your mission."

"What mission?" he said.

"You've made it to Las Vegas."

The long journey from Port Decker now flashed through Southie's mind, but so did a simple fact.

"Technically, I'm not in Las Vegas. I'm just outside of it," he said.

"This trip had nothing to do with you," the man said and he beckoned towards a brown scorpion lumbering across the desert floor. Overhead, Southie spotted a red tail hawk with a squeaking rodent in its claws.

"This trip has to do with the animals in the desert?" he said.

"I'm speaking of Rebbe, Sol, Myrtle, Isaac, Aaron, Sarah and the others. The congregation of people you led to Las Vegas. Now they're here so you're mission is accomplished."

Southie stood up thirsty as a bucket of dust and with fresh blisters burning his feet.

"Oh, I get it. I'm the American Moses!"

"You are who you want to be," said the man.

"Okay, so what's the fatal flaw?" Southie replied. "What mistake of biblical proportions did I make to not be able to enter the Promised Land of Las Vegas? Moses struck a rock for water and that's why he never entered the Promised Land. What did I do?"

Southie grabbed the stick and struck the rock. Silence followed and then a ticking sound came from the rock. Southie half-expected water to come gushing out from it, but instead a rattlesnake slithered from its shadow and down a hole.

The man stood up and walked a few feet out in the desert before facing Southie.

"There's no fatal flaw," he said. "You can go backward. You can move forward. You could spend the rest of your life here in this desert. It's up to you. Enter Las Vegas or don't."

The man paused and tilted his ear toward the desert as if listening to it speak and looked into the horizon towards the lake.

"...but I'll tell you one thing," he continued, "You don't need what the others are after. They seek the Promised Land and it's not where they think it is. You can reach a higher ground."

"Where is it?" said Southie, squinting into the horizon. "Where is the Promised Land?"

The man stuck a finger into Southie's chest and then against his brain. "The Promised Land is in your heart and in your head."

The man walked out into the desert a few steps and turned transparent with a large round head.

"Tell me, if you are a messenger of God, why am I here in this place and time?" Southie asked.

"You are here to be who you are." The man's words trailed off and his body became lighter and wavy like the gassy heat rising off the desert. Two lizards slithered from his mouth and crawled up his face before disappearing into his eye sockets. Then he burst into deep orange flames, neither hot nor consuming, before vanishing into the dry air.

CHAPTER 31

Southie's room at the Hacienda Casino had cigarette burn marks on the desk and dresser, and despite freshly made beds, and clean linen, it carried a musky scent. After throwing his bag with some clothes on one of the two beds, he went to the casino downstairs, past rows of ringing slot machines and blackjack tables, to a small restaurant where he sat at the counter.

"Whacha having, honey?" said the waitress. She was an attractive middle-aged woman with worn fingernail polish and a few strands of grey in her dishwater blonde hair.

"A coffee," said Southie, "And two glasses of water, please."

"You get stuck in the desert or something?" she said, pouring the water.

"Something like that."

The waitress smiled. "Where you from, honey?"

"New York by way of Chicago, but I'm on my way to Vegas."

"Aren't we all," she said. "Left my husband on a farm in Iowa to come here eight years ago."

"Did you ever regret it?"

"My momma used to say better to run from a bad marriage then stay in a sick one."

"So what's your advice about Vegas?"

"You can do real good out here. Start over, live comfortable. Just don't start gambling. Once you start that you're done for."

After the waitress vanished down the counter to wait on other customers, Southie noticed Aaron exiting the casino general store. So he quickly downed the second water, ignoring the coffee, and put two dollars on the counter. Then he caught up with Aaron, who was paying for a two large bottles of Pepsi.

"Southie. When did you check in?"

"About an hour ago. They finally had a room for me."

Aaron followed Southie to his car in the parking lot, where he retrieved the cooler and then followed Aaron up to his room to give it to Faygie. When they arrived, the couple's eldest, Yakov, was surfing the internet on the family's battered old personal computer. The rest of the children were either bouncing on one of the two beds or playing in the bathroom.

"Southie," said Faygie, taking the soda from her husband at the door.

Southie handed her the Styrofoam cooler. "Thanks for letting me use this."

"My pleasure," she said, and led the two men to a few chairs near a small hotplate, where soup, thick with beans, was simmering. She then called the kids to lunch with only Yakov on the computer responding.

"Your mother called you," Aaron yelled with a booming voice. "Don't make me count to three."

After much cajoling the children all sat around the beds and everyone was served in worn plastic bowls.

"If you don't mind me asking," Faygie asked Southie after the prayers were said and everybody was eating. "Do you miss Zippy?"

"Zippy's my other half and the love of my life," replied Southie, softly.

Faygie exchanged glances with her husband. "Not to worry, Southie. I'm sure there's a nice Jewish girl in Las Vegas we can find for you. There's even an online site for Jews in Las Vegas. I saw it on the computer today. They have a dating service, you know."

"Faygie, let the man breathe awhile. He'll find another woman in good time."

"It's okay, Aaron. I'll be fine."

"We just want you to know, Southie, we appreciate everything you've done, and we are now here for you to reconnect to the Jewish chain."

"I appreciate it," said Southie and kept quiet through the rest of the meal.

After Southie got back to his room, he took a long shower and then lay in bed with the television on, but couldn't focus on any shows. Instead he thought about Zippy, and how they would whisper in the middle of the night before making love as the sun would come out and the early birds chirped. He remembered her always saying a man could have all the gold in the world but it meant nothing without having somebody to love. The memory saddened Southie and he tried to fall asleep, but after tossing and turning for several hours, first with the television on and then with it off, he gave up. So at two in the morning he dressed and went out.

The casino downstairs was half-full and many of the gamblers wore jeans and blazers, while others wore orange Hoover Dam worker uniforms. Southie made his way back to the coffee shop hoping to see the waitress, but he found a pot-bellied Mexican waiter manning the counter.

So he found a nickel-a-hand poker slot machine, took a stool and fed three dollars into it. To his amazement, the three dollars lasted several hours, and along the way he ordered a few gin and tonics from a middle-aged cocktail waitress with a business smile. The flashing cards and ringing of occasional wins distracted him, but did not diminish his loneliness for Zippy.

At daylight, he eyed the Rebbe walking across the casino floor and into the parking lot, and he figured to cash out before all the others woke. So he loaded a small silver tub half full with nickels, but as he stood in the cashier's line, the Rebbe passed back through the casino again carrying a book of Talmud from his car.

"Hello, Rebbe," said Southie, sheepishly.

"I see you did pretty well," said the Rebbe, peering into the tub of nickels.

Southie reached the cashier and changed the nickels into forty-three dollars and fifteen cents.

"Not bad for a three dollar investment," he said, pocketing the money. "Have you ever gambled, Rebbe?"

"My bet is with God."

"I understand that wager, but a little side action. Like this forty-three dollars, I just won?"

"Southie, the real risk is being of good character and soul."

Southie mulled over the Rebbe's words and the vision in the desert came back to him.

"Tell me, Rebbe, you produced a Golem for that football game. How are spirits seen through the eyes of Judaism?"

The Rebbe lifted an eyebrow. "Angels and demons come for specific purposes and with specific powers, but they lack the one thing we have. Free will. That God gave only to mankind."

Their conversation was interrupted by David, who came rushing towards them.

"Isaac's back," he said. "We're all going to meet in his room for the Sabbath."

CHAPTER 32

When Southie arrived at Isaac's room several hours later, every dresser and desktop was filled with platters of corned beef, chicken dishes, noodle and potato dishes, vegetable dishes, pastries and several thermoses filled with hot tea and coffee. Two large silver Sabbath candlestick holders with unlit candles were placed near the dresser mirror reflecting its simple beauty. As there was still an hour before the sun went down and the Sabbath was to begin, everyone crowded around Isaac, begging him to explain his travels to Las Vegas.

"Well, when I first hit town," Isaac said. " I stopped at a Wal-Mart and one of the employees steered me to the Klondike. It's this safe, cheap casino just off the strip.

"The strip?" said David.

Sarah gave her son a strange look.

"Yeah, the main drag with expensive casinos One replicates the Eiffel Tower, another is a giant black Pyramid. One has lions enclosed in glass cages, and all of them have large television rooms with every sports game imaginable on them and pretty waitresses serving free drinks."

"Okay, we get the picture," said Aaron. "But did you visit any of the synagogues?"

"Yes. There's a large Jewish population in a town called Henderson just outside Las Vegas, and several orthodox synagogues. That's where I got all this kosher food from," he said, nodding to the platters of food.

"The schools!" asked Sarah. "My David should start college soon."

"They have great schools," exclaimed Isaac. "UNLV is the college.""

"But did you look into the cost of living and housing for seniors?" asked Myrtle.

"Yes. The rents are very reasonable and I wrote the name down of three or four senior complexes for you and your husband."

"But the people. What was your feel for them?" asked the Rebbe.

"The entire city is filled with people just like us. People starting over! There's big stores like Wal-Mart, but also little shops, delis, bagel joints and shoe stores. Southie was right. Las Vegas has everything."

Through the open curtains and across the balcony, the sun set in the western sky and Sarah lit the candles and the Sabbath prayer was said.

> Come my beloved to greet the bride
> The Sabbath presence, let us welcome!
> For it is the source of blessing!
> From the beginning from antiquity she was
> honored
> Last in deed, but first in thought.
> Come my beloved to greet the bride
> The Sabbath presence, let us welcome!

That night, Southie, heavy with food, tossed and turned until he finally fell into a troubled sleep. He dreamt of coming to his house in Port Decker on a spring day and seeing Zippy, holding hands with Coree and Billy on the front lawn. They were spinning in circles and singing:

> Brown girl in the ring
> Tra la la la la
> Brown Girl In the ring
> Tra la la la la la
> Brown Girl in the ring
> Tra la la la la
> And she look like a sugar in the plum

Suddenly he was walking with Zippy amongst a field of tall reeds outside his high school, and they came to a clearing and saw Coree kissing

AJ from East St. Lewis. The air was thick with rap beats. Coree looked up and she was begging at the side of the interstate. Southie reached into his wallet and Zippy stopped him.

"She's got to learn to make it on her own," she said.

Then the Rebbe appeared in the field and he whispered, "Remember the first commandment and use your *seychel*."

Southie was now spinning alone in the wind, rolling like bramble along the hard Texas ground, until at last he was spat out onto a white sandy beach. He stood up and was face to face with the spirit from the desert.

"You can go backward. You can move forward," it said, "but I'll tell you one thing. You don't need what the others are after. They seek the Promised Land and it's not where they think it is."

The spirit then stuck its finger hard against Southie chest jolting him awake. He looked at the clock to see that it was five in the morning. For awhile he watched two old situation comedies on TV before deciding to go downstairs for a coffee as the morning light crept through his window. So he quickly dressed and went to the restaurant in the back of the casino, where the pot-bellied Mexican waiter was still on duty. However, Isaac sat at the end of the counter reading the Las Vegas newspaper, so he grabbed a stool next to him.

"You couldn't sleep either," said Southie, after the waiter filled Southie's coffee cup and vanished down the counter.

"Just checking out the lay of the land," said Isaac. "You ready for the final leg?"

Southie stirred a little milk into his coffee and then took a gulp. "What would you say if I told you I'm not going to Las Vegas."

"Not going? But why?"

"Nevada just doesn't appeal to me. Casinos open around the clock. Night becomes day. Day becomes night. It's not my scene."

"You're something else," said Isaac.

"In fact, Isaac. I was wondering if you could do me a favor."

"A favor? What kind of favor?"

"I was wondering if you could tell everybody good-by for me. I figured while it's still the Sabbath, I could check out before anyone wakes."

Isaac put the newspaper down on the counter and took a gulp from his own coffee. "That's one thing I won't do," he said. "All your life you've been running and if that's what you choose to do, fine, but it's quite another to just disappear like a thief in the night. Remember, Southie, this whole trip was your idea. So if you want to give everybody a send off, you have to do it yourself."

Southie finished his coffee and put three dollars on the counter. "I'll tell everyone in the parking lot early Sunday morning when they're getting ready to enter Las Vegas."

CHAPTER 33

On Sunday morning, as everyone was packing their cars for the final trip into Las Vegas, Southie checked out of the casino, and met everyone in the parking lot.

"Come round everybody," Isaac said. "Southie has something to say."

"Everybody gathered around Southie's reliable old rust bucket.

"I won't be going with you into Las Vegas," he said, sheepishly.

"What *Mushugina* is this," said Sol. "Your whole family is crazy?"

"I know," replied Southie with a shrug.

Sol's face softened. "What can I say, Southie? You're a *mench*," he said, giving Southie a pinch on the cheek and the two men embraced.

David came up to Southie fighting back tears.

"But why aren't you coming?"

"People do what people have to do," said Southie, embracing David, and then firmly shaking his hand. "Take care of your mother and you Sarah – you're going to have to beat the girls off your son with a stick."

Sarah smiled warmly at Southie. "My David does alright," she said.

Aaron shook hands with Southie and thanked him, and Faygie told him if he should ever come to Las Vegas to make sure to come to them for the Sabbath.

Southie promised he would, and then went over to the Rebbe, who was standing next to his car.

"Southie, you know what you are doing?"

"Not exactly Rebbe, but can you do me a favor?"

"What kind of favor?"

"Can you give Zipporah and our children a blessing?"

The Rebbe straitened up and looked toward the heavens.

"Praise the almighty and may *Ashem* forever watch over Southie's family and let them know your name in their hearts. May you give them the strength of kindness and good will..." the Rebbe stopped and looked at Southie.

"Oh, and if it's not too much to ask," he said, continuing, "may *Ashem* also stay with Samuel here. This is a good man, who led us. May you keep his soul strong and listen to his own prayers as I know him as a man who praises you and knows that the Almighty spirit lives in the hearts of the world – from every leaf on a tree to the wind that blows it – Amen."

Isaac then came forward and pulled out what was left of the money that the fellow Jews collected for them in St. Louis – a little more than twelve-hundred dollars.

"If it's all the same to everybody, I want to give this to Southie," he said.

"No. I can't take the money," said Southie.

"Those who gave it to us did so on the condition it be used if any problems arose while on our journey. We are about to finish our travels, but you Southie are still on the road."

Everybody nodded, so Southie pocketed the money with a nod and a "Thank you." Then he addressed the congregation for the last time,

"Although I am a member of this tribe, I am not going among you. Keep the words of God with all your soul and might. For I know now that it is only the most faithful who keep the laws of the one God, almighty. Remember, too, as Jews, that we're part of a larger people. A people called human beings. Therefore, keep this fellowship towards all humanity in deeds of kindness, compassion and humbleness. To survive, we must stay strong, but we must also be understanding and compassionate to those around us."

The congregation nodded and then got into their cars. Southie watched as the drove from the casino parking area, and disappeared behind a winding mountain pass towards Las Vegas.

Then he climbed back into the rust bucket and backtracked past the Hoover Dam and down the mountain pass toward Kingman. He was halfway across the flat, hot desert to Flagstaff when he realized he didn't even know where he was going. At the next exit he turned off the road and onto a two-lane highway that climbed for some time. At last he came to Humphreys Peak, where there was a gas station and restaurant.

Inside, he used the bathroom and then ordered a coffee from a small, shapely Mexican woman with thick, long hair and shiny dark bedroom eyes.

"If you don't mind me saying — a woman pretty as you must have been dropped from heaven," he said.

"Here's your coffee," she said, returning a white and toothy smile.

Outside in the parking lot, the thin, cool air made Southie lightheaded. He walked past his car and onto a rock overlooking the valley thousands of feet below him. He began to think about America and leadership. How it is thrust upon some, and self-made by others. Then there was his own birth and childhood in Chicago. His innocence seemingly disappearing somewhere in the Illinois cornfields just as Zippy's was taken forcefully from her own father. Then he thought of Coree, a victim of fate and her own actions.

He took a large gulp of coffee and looked down upon the great American valley. A land still filled with great promise, despite its mistakes and worldly success. Perhaps he would head south to Phoenix, he thought or west to see his mother in California. Or maybe back to Chicago to find the loose threads of his life. Or to the comfort of Zippy's arms and their son, Billy on the Navaho nation. His existence now didn't really seem a question of why or who, but rather of what. As in what would be his next move? He drained the last of his coffee and crumpled the cardboard cup in his hand into a small compact ball.

There was still so much left to do.

The LowHearted

A series of tragic coincidences creates an unexpected bond between two strangers from two different worlds who share a dark secret.

֍

The Street Singer

A New York City subway musician learns that which is timeless and that which is finite, following a string of good fortune.

www.ingramcontent.com/pod-product-compliance
Lightning Source LLC
Chambersburg PA
CBHW070104260626
47160CB00004B/1306